10ᵀᴴ ANNIVERSARY

Special thanks to our well-wishers, who have contributed their congratulations and support.

"The best historicals, the best romances. Simply the best!"
—Dallas Schulze

"Bronwyn Williams was born and raised at Harlequin Historicals. We couldn't have asked for a better home or a more supportive family."
—Dixie Browning and Mary Williams,
w/a Bronwyn Williams

"I can't believe it's been ten years since *Private Treaty*, my first historical novel, helped launch the Harlequin Historicals line. What a thrill that was! And the beat goes on...with timeless stories about men and women in love."
—Kathleen Eagle

"Nothing satisfies me as much as writing or reading a Harlequin Historical novel. For me, Harlequin Historicals are the ultimate escape from the problems of everyday life."
—Ruth Ryan Langan

"As a writer and reader, I feel that the Harlequin Historicals line always celebrates a perfect blend of history and romance, adventure and passion, humor and sheer magic."
—Theresa Michaels

"Thank you, Harlequin Historicals, for opening up a 'window into the past' for so many happy readers."

—Suzanne Barclay

"As a one-time 'slush pile' foundling at Harlequin Historicals, I'll be forever grateful for having been rescued and published as one of the first 'March Madness' authors. Harlequin Historicals has always been *the* place for special stories, ones that blend the magic of the past with the rare miracle of love for books that readers never forget."

—Miranda Jarrett

"A rainy evening. A cup of hot chocolate. A stack of Harlequin Historicals. Absolute bliss! Happy 10th Anniversary and continued success."

—Cheryl Reavis

"Happy birthday, Harlequin Historicals! I'm proud to have been a part of your ten years of exciting historical romance."

—Elaine Barbieri

"Harlequin Historical novels are charming or disarming with dashes and clashes. These past times are fast times, the gems of romances!"

—Karen Harper

Ruth Langan

The Courtship of Izzy McCree

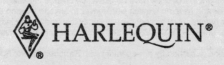

HARLEQUIN®

TORONTO • NEW YORK • LONDON
AMSTERDAM • PARIS • SYDNEY • HAMBURG
STOCKHOLM • ATHENS • TOKYO • MILAN • MADRID
PRAGUE • WARSAW • BUDAPEST • AUCKLAND

For Isabella Mary Shrader
And her proud parents, Mary and Dennis
Her sisters Caitlin Bea, Ally and Taylor
And big brother Bret

And for Tom
For a lifetime of courtship.

ISBN 0-373-29025-X

THE COURTSHIP OF IZZY McCREE

Copyright © 1998 by Ruth Ryan Langan

Matt dragged her closer.

"I can't give you pretty things, Isabella."

All she could feel was his breath, hot against her temple. And the wild stutter of her heartbeat as those big, work-worn fingers kneaded her arms, her shoulders, then began trailing fire along her spine.

"I don't need things, Matthew." *This is what I need. The feel of strong arms surrounding me, soothing me. Protecting me. Arousing me.*

She'd never known such a rush of feelings. Intense, seething emotions. Fire. Ice. Need. All rushing through her system, leaving her stunned and breathless.

He lowered his head until his lips were pressed to a tangle of hair at her temple. "I'm no good with pretty words either, Isabella."

She shivered. "I don't…need the words."

As he continued to torment her by keeping his mouth just inches from hers, she said softly, "This is what I want. Just this." She couldn't bear to wait another moment. Standing on tiptoe, she brought her mouth to his.

"Matthew. Kiss me. Please kiss me."

Chapter One

The California-Nevada border, 1880

"How soon, driver?" Izzy poked her head out the window of the stage and shouted above the pounding hooves and creaking harness. The rushing wind tugged at her hat and would have whipped it loose if she hadn't clamped a hand to it.

"I told ye. The name's Boone. And ye're already on Prescott land, ma'am."

"I am?"

"Yes'm. Been on it for the last couple of miles. Should see the ranch house just over this next rise."

Izzy dropped back to the hard seat and stared out the side window. Who would have thought? All this land belonged to Matthew Prescott. Though the countryside looked forbidding, with rocky fields climbing upward to high, snow-covered peaks, Izzy couldn't help but be impressed. Her husband-to-be owned all this. She clasped her hands to her cheeks, which had suddenly become flushed.

Working quickly, she opened her satchel and removed a pair of shoes. They'd been too fine to wear, so she'd carried them all the way from Pennsylvania. Over three thousand miles she'd carried them. On the train. On a succession of stagecoaches. Handling them like a treasure. Though her traveling gown was soiled and coated with a layer of dust, and her hair beneath the fussy bonnet was windblown and tangled, her shoes were polished to a high shine.

She removed her scuffed boots and stuffed them into the satchel, then slipped her feet into the shoes and carefully laced them. And all the while she rehearsed the lines she'd been preparing.

Isabella McCree. Member of the First Pennsylvania Congregation. So pleased to make your acquaintance.

When she glanced up, she had her first view of the ranch house.

Her heart sank. It looked to be no more than a rough cabin surrounded by several equally rough outbuildings. The structures were dwarfed by the forested peaks of the Sierra Nevada rising up directly behind them.

The horses strained against the harness until they crested the hill. The ground leveled off, and they sped across a high meadow until they came to a shuddering halt at the cabin.

"Here you are, ma'am." The grizzled driver leapt to the ground and yanked open the door to the stage.

Izzy handed him her satchel before stepping down. The new shoes were stiff and uncomfortable, but to her delight, her gait was sure and even. Money well spent, it would seem.

"I don't see anyone, Boone." She glanced uncertainly toward the door of the cabin. "Could Mr. Prescott have gone somewhere?"

The driver grinned, showing teeth stained brown with tobacco. "He's out in the fields, I expect." He handed her a packet of mail. "Haven't been out this way in more'n six months. He'll be happy to get this. Oh, and to see you of course, ma'am."

He heaved himself up to the driver's seat and caught the reins. With a crack of the whip, the horses lurched forward, hauling the stage in a wide turn. Within minutes the team and driver had disappeared below the tree line.

Izzy glanced uncertainly at the closed door. Though her journey had left her weary beyond belief, she didn't think it would be right to let herself into a stranger's cabin. And so she stood, hand lifted to shield her eyes from the thin autumn sun, staring at the distant hilltops.

Within minutes she spotted a figure on horseback coming at a brisk pace from the nearby woods. Running alongside was a baying hound. From the opposite direction came another horse and rider, racing through a stream. Several more hounds ran alongside. In the sunlight the water splashed out in a rainbow of color, making a dazzling display. But before she could admire the beauty of it, she heard barking directly behind her and a child's voice.

"Well, I'll be. Del, look. It's a...lady."

Izzy whirled to find herself facing three scruffy

children. All were dressed in tattered britches and faded shirts with the sleeves rolled to their elbows. All had straggly hair cut in identical fashion, chopped just below the ears, falling in bangs that covered their eyebrows. The youngest had fine blond hair; the middle one had red gold; the tallest had coarse dark hair. Except for the similar haircuts and shabby clothes, they looked nothing alike. These couldn't be Matthew's children.

Circling her were a handful of hounds, sniffing at her ankles, yapping so loudly she knew it would be impossible to make her voice heard.

Still, she was determined to try. "Hello. I'm..."

Before she could continue, the two horsemen reined in their mounts and dropped to the ground, keeping their rifles trained on her. The younger of the two wore his pale yellow hair exactly like these three. The other one was taller by a head. It was difficult to tell what he looked like. Thick black hair hung below the collar of his shirt, and his cheeks and chin were covered by a bushy dark beard, masking his features.

The newly arrived dogs joined in the chorus of barking until their master gave a curt command. At once all the animals dropped to their bellies.

In the silence the older man's voice seemed even more commanding. "My name's Matt Prescott."

"Yes. I know." With a warm smile Izzy handed him the packet of mail. "The stage driver left these for you." She then offered her hand. "I'm Izzy..." She nearly groaned aloud. All these miles and all these hours to prepare, and still the old hated name had almost slipped out without warning. "Isabella McCree."

Instead of accepting her handshake, he pocketed the mail while keeping his rifle pointed at her. "I thought that was the stage I spotted in the distance. Why did Boone drop you here in the middle of my land?"

Her smile faded. "Maybe you didn't hear me. I said my name is—"

"I heard you, Mrs. McCree. What I'd like to know is what you're doing on my land, handing me my mail."

"What I'm...?" She felt the heat rise to her cheeks. "It is Miss McCree. And I am here at your invitation, Matthew."

At her use of his given name, he shot her a frigid look that had her taking a step back.

"Now, what's that supposed to mean, woman?"

"I came in answer to your letter." She could tell by the look on his face that none of this was making any sense to him. She sucked in a breath as the realization dawned. "Sweet salvation. You never got my reply to your letter?"

"Miss McCree, not only did I not get your reply, but I don't have any idea what letter you're talking about."

"The letter you wrote seeking a wife."

"A wife?" His voice thundered, and several of the hounds began to whimper.

She fumbled in her satchel. When she finally located the paper she'd been seeking, she waved it in front of his nose. "This letter addressed to the First

Pennsylvania Congregation, seeking a good woman with the courage to make the journey to your home and assume the care of your family.''

He barely glanced at the words on the paper. ''If this is some sort of joke, I fail to find the humor in it.'' He lowered his rifle and turned away. Over his shoulder he called, ''Children, get back to your chores. There's still an hour or so of daylight.''

''But, Pa...'' Aaron, the oldest boy, who stood nearly six feet, seemed torn between obeying his father and dealing with their visitor. ''What about the lady?''

''She can go back where she came from.'' Matt pulled himself into the saddle.

Izzy felt faint. For a moment she trembled and feared that she might sink to her knees. Instead, she gathered her courage and found her voice. ''That is impossible.''

Matt stared down at her from the back of his mount. ''Why?''

''Because I spent everything I had to get here.''

He gave a savage oath, then caught himself when he saw his children watching in silence. He slid from the saddle and handed the reins to one of the boys. ''Take our horses to the barn and unsaddle them, Benjamin.''

''Yes, sir.'' The boy grabbed the reins and hurried away.

To the others Matt said sternly, ''Take the lady's things inside.''

While the two older ones carried her satchel between them, the youngest one raced ahead to open the cabin door.

Matt turned the full power of his glare on her. "Come along, Miss McCree. Let's see if we can get to the bottom of this."

Without waiting for her reply, he strode to the cabin, leaving her to follow behind. She entered the cabin, then paused just inside the door to stare around in dismay.

The floor was littered with assorted clothing, guns, dog bones and even chickens, hopping and strutting about, leaving a mess in their wake. The windows were layered with so much dust and grime the sunlight could barely filter through. The room smelled of animals, dung and rotted food.

"Del," Matt snarled at his youngest. "You let the damned chickens in again. How many times have I told you about this?"

"But, Pa, if I don't lock them up, the coyotes will get them while we're off doing our chores."

"Then lock them in the barn where they belong. You heard what I said. Not in the house." He picked up a broom and sent the chickens squawking and leaping out the doorway. Then, with a sweep of his hand, he cleared the table of all the clutter.

"Aaron, Clement, as long as we can't get any more work done, you may as well start supper."

"Yes, sir." The two boys began bustling around the cabin.

"Sit, Miss McCree."

Izzy crossed the room, picking her way through the debris, and ran a hand over the rough wood of the chair before sitting. She watched in fascination while the oldest son removed a hunting knife from his belt, wiped it on his pants and began carving slices from a side of beef that had been roasting on a spit. Blood from the meat sizzled into the fire as he sliced, sending a cloud of steam toward the roof. His brother ladled liquid from a blackened pot hanging over the fire. And the youngest poured glasses of thick, clotted milk, handing one to her.

"Ah. Buttermilk." Izzy took a long, grateful swallow. "I must confess I'm parched from my travels."

But it wasn't buttermilk. She nearly gagged as she realized that what she had swallowed was warm, curdled milk. For the space of a few seconds she feared that she would embarrass herself. But after several attempts, she finally managed to get it down, then prayed it would stay down.

When his fourth child returned from the barn, Matt called them all to the table.

Izzy stood. "Would you mind if I washed up first?"

They all looked at her in surprise. Without a word Matt poured water from a pitcher into a bowl and finally located a clean square of linen in a cupboard. Knowing they were all watching made Izzy awkward and clumsy. Her fingers fumbled as she removed her hat and set it aside. With quick, nervous movements she washed her hands, her arms and her face and patted them dry. That done, she made her way to the table and took a seat.

As they began reaching for the food, Izzy bowed

her head and closed her eyes, then whispered a blessing.

"What's she doing, Pa?" the youngest asked.

"Praying." Matt paused a moment and waited until she opened her eyes before passing her a platter of beef.

"Why? Is she scared?"

"Little Bit, some people pray even when they aren't scared," the oldest boy said with authority.

"You're lying, Aaron." The youngest turned to Matt. "He's lying, isn't he, Pa?"

"No, Del. Some people pray even when they aren't afraid. Toss me a biscuit."

Izzy stared in surprise as the youngster tossed a biscuit across the table. Matt caught it and popped it into his mouth. "Hard as rocks," he said after a couple of bites. "Clement, that's the last time you make the biscuits."

"Yes, sir." Following his father's lead, the boy ducked his head and continued to shovel food into his mouth.

While Matt and his children ate, the hounds circled the table, snapping up scraps tossed to them. Occasionally two or three of the dogs would get into a fight over a morsel, until Matt called out a warning. Then the animals would crouch and wait for the next scrap of meat. And the next fight.

The children behaved no better. They tossed biscuits among themselves. They stole meat from one another's plates. Benjamin waited until Clement had his fork to his mouth, then nudged him roughly, causing Clement to miss his mouth entirely and spill his food down the front of his shirt. That brought a roar of laughter from the others.

Matt glanced at Izzy, who had pushed aside her plate. "Had enough, Miss McCree?"

"More than enough, I'm afraid." She swallowed hot, bitter coffee in the hopes of washing away the foul taste of sour milk and meat that was barely cooked. Her plate was swimming with beef blood. The sight sickened her almost as much as the smell of the cabin and the complete lack of civilized behavior exhibited by its inhabitants.

"Good." Matt leaned back, sipping his coffee, watching her over the rim of his cup. "Then I guess we can get to this other business. Where's your home?"

"It was in Pennsylvania."

Was. The word grated. "As I understand it, you came here thinking I needed a wife."

"And your children needed a mother. That's what your letter said."

He clenched his teeth. "Let's get one thing straight. I never wrote any damned letter."

She folded her hands in her lap. "I don't hold with swearing, Matthew."

"Damn it." He stood, nearly upending his chair. "Don't call me Matthew."

"Pa..." his oldest son began.

"Not now, Aaron." Matt swung back to Izzy. "And don't say I wrote a letter when I didn't, woman."

"Pa...."

Matt turned on him. "Didn't I tell you not now?"

"Yes, sir." The boy's cheeks were suffused with color. He glanced at his father, then away. "But there's something you ought to know." He stared at a spot on the table and waited several beats before saying softly, "I wrote that letter."

Everyone stared at him in complete silence.

Matt rounded the table to stand over him. "Say that again."

"I...wrote the letter. But it was more'n a year ago, Pa. I figured, since I never heard, that it had been lost or something. Then I..." He shrugged. "I just forgot about it."

Izzy's eyes were wide with shock. Sweet salvation. She had made this long, hazardous trip at the whim of a boy.

Matt's tone was low with fury. "Why the hell would you do such a thing, boy?"

Aaron pointed to the others around the table. "Look at us, Pa. With Ma gone, we don't live much better'n the hogs. In fact, I think they live better'n us. Last time we went to town, folks were staring at us 'cause our clothes were torn and dirty."

"There's nothing wrong with a little dirt. We're ranchers, not fancy bankers."

"It's not just the dirt. Look at Little Bit here. She doesn't even have any idea how to be a female."

At that, Izzy had to stifle a gasp. The youngest was a girl? With her hair chopped off and in her brothers' cast-off clothes, Izzy had just assumed...

"I figured if we had a woman around the place, we'd all be better off, Pa."

Matt's anger was growing with every word. "And

what about me? Didn't you think to talk this over with me before you did such a fool thing? Didn't you think I'd mind?''

"I..." The boy looked away from his father's accusing eyes. "I figured it didn't much matter. You never smile anyway. You're never happy anymore since Ma..." He swallowed, seeing the look of pain and rage that crossed Matt's face. "But it's not fair to the rest of us. It's not our fault. We can't do anything about Ma. But at least we can give Del a chance."

Matt's hands balled into fists at his sides. "When we're through here, you go to the barn and prepare for a good tanning, you hear me?"

"Yes, sir."

Choking back his anger, Matt strode to the fireplace and rolled a cigarette, then held a flaming stick to the tip and inhaled deeply. Those few precious minutes gave him time to compose himself. He turned, determined to remain calm and logical. "I'm sorry about this, Miss McCree. But as you can see, you've come here for nothing. Since the nearest town, Sutton's Station, is almost twenty miles from here, I'm afraid you'll have to spend the night. In the morning I'll take you to town and you can catch the stage back home."

"Back home? But I can't..." The sour milk was forgotten. As was the fatigue she'd suffered only a short time ago. Now there was only panic. She pushed back her chair and faced him. "That is impossible. You see, I have no home to return to. I...sold all my worldly goods to get here. And the journey took all the money I had."

He took a long, deep drag on his cigarette while he mentally uttered every rich, ripe oath he could think of. His mind reeled at the seriousness of the situation facing him. He had some money saved. But he'd hoped to buy Amos Truesdale's bull. And there was the addition he'd planned for the cabin. And the seed he would need in the spring.

"Maybe she could just stay on, Pa..." Aaron began.

Matt rounded on his son. "We may live poor, but we aren't trash. We have our honor. An unmarried lady doesn't stay under my roof."

"Then why can't you just marry her?" he demanded.

"Because it isn't right. She came here thinking we all wanted her. And the only one who did is you."

"I don't mind if you marry her, Pa." Benjamin, closest in age to Aaron, stuck up, as always, for his older brother.

"Me, either," Clement chimed in.

The youngest, Del, looked from one brother to the other, clearly influenced by everything they said and did. "If Aaron and Benjamin and Clement don't mind, then I don't, either. But she can't turn me into no lady."

"Well, I have something to say about all this, and I do mind." Matt tossed his cigarette into the fire, then stomped out of the room, returning minutes later with a blanket over his arm. "I'll sleep in the barn tonight, Miss McCree. You can have my bed. In the morning I'll drive you to Sutton's Station. I'll give you what money I have. If that isn't enough—'' he shrugged ''—you'll have to take a job in town and earn the rest until you have enough to get back home.''

He turned to his oldest son. ''I'll see you in the barn, Aaron. As soon as you've checked out the herd.''

''Yes, sir.''

''The rest of you get on up to bed. Since I'll have to miss a day's chores to take Miss McCree to town tomorrow, you'll have to take on mine as well as your own.''

''Yes, sir.'' Seeing the fire in their father's eyes, the children scurried to a crude ladder and escaped to a loft.

Matt yanked open the door and the hounds milled about, eager to follow their master. Aaron trailed behind.

When the door closed behind them, the cabin grew strangely silent. Izzy stood in the middle of the room, staring about with a dazed look. Apparently, though it was barely dusk, the children would do their father's bidding and retire for the night. Perhaps it was just as well. At least now she could try to sort through what had just happened.

She thought about the letter that had arrived in their small town in Pennsylvania. It had been the object of ridicule, not only because of the crudely printed words, but also because folks agreed that no woman in her right mind would ever accept the invitation to live in such a wilderness. But the words had touched her. Had stayed with her through the long, cold winter. She had secretly memorized the address and had finally mustered up the courage to accept the challenge.

She sank down on a chair, biting back raw, bitter tears. Oh, the dreams she had spun. The plans she had made. She had seen herself greeted by a courtly gentleman, surrounded by his loving children. She had pictured herself presiding over a genteel household, cooking fine meals, sewing fancy clothes. She would rescue this lonely, helpless family, and they would forever bless her name.

She raised one foot and was horrified to see what was stuck to the brand-new sole. Oh, those hateful chickens. She got to her feet, frantically scraping her shoe against a rung of the chair. Was this why she had traveled three thousand miles? To live worse than hogs? To be tricked, humiliated and ultimately rejected?

Rejected. She brought her hands to her cheeks. That was the worst of all. The cold, cruel rejection by that hateful man.

Tears stung her eyes and she forced herself into action. Unless she plunged herself into some work right away, she would find herself wallowing in self-pity. And once she allowed that, there would be no stopping the flood.

Work had always been her refuge from the rejections she had suffered through the years. And there had been enough to last a lifetime. She blinked furiously, then decided to tackle the dishes. She would think about sleep later.

her mind, she had the vague impression that she... (faded text at top)

Chapter Two

"**O**h, my. Where to begin."

Izzy rolled up her sleeves and set to work. While she waited for the water to heat over the fire, she located a cache of lye soap. She was surprised at such a find, since the cabin smelled as though it hadn't seen disinfectant in a year. She stacked the dishes alongside the basin, then scrubbed the kitchen table and chairs until the rough wood gleamed. While she worked, strands of her hair slipped from the knot atop her head and began to fall in sticky tendrils around her face. She swiped at them with damp hands before resuming her work.

When the water was hot enough, she tackled the dishes. As she washed and dried the first plate, she held it up to the firelight. It was a pretty thing, pale and translucent, with one perfect pink rosebud on the rim. She washed a cup and held it up admiringly. It bore the same small rosebud design. As she continued washing, she thought how lovely that here in this rough wilderness, so far from civilization, she had discovered a complete set of matched china. In her life she'd never seen such a thing before. To Izzy, it was an amazing treasure.

Matthew's wife must have been a lovely lady. As lovely as her china. No wonder he got so angry at his son. How could anyone be expected to take the place of such a fine woman?

Matthew. He wasn't at all what she'd been anticipating. Well, maybe somewhat. He did look like a rough mountain man. The kind of man who would settle in a primitive place, determined to tame it. But from his letter she had expected him to have a tender side. A kind nature. Instead he had already shown himself to be a harsh, unyielding man. One who would order his son to the barn for a thrashing.

Izzy shuddered. Poor Aaron. Her heart went out to him. She knew only too well what he would have to endure. And now that she knew that he had been the author of the letter, she felt even more sympathy. It was Aaron who had been the kind, sweet, gentle soul revealed in his words. He had probably inherited that sweet nature from his mother.

She opened a cupboard and carefully stored the precious dishes away, then tackled the pots and pans and utensils, crusted with burned food. These required a great deal more effort, and she immersed them in boiling water and scrubbed until her knuckles were bloody. But at least, for the moment, she had managed to put aside her troubles.

In the barn Matt crouched beside the lantern, sifting through the packet of mail. Only one held any interest for him. The familiar handwriting had the blood throbbing at his temples as he tore open the envelope. Inside was a single sheet of paper. He read it quickly, absorbing first shock, then pain, and then slow, simmering fury. Then, like a man possessed, he read it again, and yet again, until every single word was committed to memory. By the time he'd read it more than a dozen times, he felt the anger beginning to drain away. In its place was a sort of numb acceptance.

He wondered if old Webster Sutton had felt this way when he'd lost his hand.

Like Webster, a vital part of him had been torn away, and he'd mourned and suffered and tried to function without it. But he had tempted himself, again and again, with the idea that somehow that vital part would grow back. Now, finally, he had to face the fact that it was lost to him forever. He would never get that part of his life back.

He should be relieved. He should welcome the numbness, after the pain he'd suffered. But for a few minutes more, he actually found himself wishing he could embrace the pain. Maybe it would be better than what he was feeling now.

He leaned forward, pressing his forehead to the rough, cold wood of the stall. What was he feeling? He couldn't put a name to it. But maybe the closest thing would be...relief.

Impossible. He couldn't be relieved by such cruel news. Still...that was exactly what he was experiencing. It was finally, irrevocably over. No more sleepless nights, wondering, waiting. Now, like it or not, he knew. And though the things he knew were painful, at least, hopefully, he could begin to heal. He could find a way to get on with his life.

At last he returned the letter to the envelope and shoved it into his pocket.

His glance fell on another envelope and he opened it more slowly. The handwriting was neat, precise, almost childlike. The words were simple but meaningful. He read this letter with a sort of detached fascination.

Dear Matthew,
Your words touched me deeply. I can already see your sweet, motherless children and your lovely, sprawling ranch snuggled in the bosom of the Sierra Nevada. I realize we will be strangers to each other, and that we will have much to learn. But I cannot resist the lure of your family. As soon as I can put my affairs in order, I will begin the journey to our new life together.

Sincerely,
Isabella McCree

The barn door was abruptly yanked open.

"All right, Pa. The herd's fine."

A gust of cold air fluttered the paper in Matt's hand.

Aaron closed the door and turned to face his father. "You can whale away on me if you'd like. I guess I deserve it."

Matt took his time folding the letter and lifting the lantern to a post above the stall. Then he studied his son, whose eyes were downcast. At nearly fifteen,

Aaron was more man than boy. The years of hard ranch chores had layered muscle on his six-foot frame. If Aaron wanted, Matt knew, he could give his father a hell of a fight. But that thought wouldn't even occur to Aaron. As firstborn, the boy was diligent, disciplined and devoted, not only to his father but to his younger brothers and sister, as well. In fact, he had always been like their second father. And mother.

"I'm not going to hit you, Aaron." The thought was absurd. It had been years since he'd even had to reprimand this boy. "But tell me, son. What in the world made you write that letter?"

Aaron shrugged. "It was Christmastime. The younger ones were missing Ma. I got to thinking if they could get a new ma, maybe things wouldn't seem so…bad around here."

Matt absorbed the pain. Would it ever end? Would he ever be able to hear them speak of her without feeling this terrible emptiness?

"Why Pennsylvania?"

"I read about it in that paper you brought from Sutton's Station. It said the minister of the First Pennsylvania Congregation led a prayer for the soldiers heading to California. So I just wrote the letter, and the next time we went to town I left it with Boone."

"You couldn't bring yourself to tell me?"

Aaron looked away. "No, sir."

"I know I've been pretty tough to live with. I guess…" Matt hesitated, then plunged into uncharted territory. "I guess we haven't talked much about men and women."

Aaron flushed clear to the tips of his ears. "I've seen the farm animals. I know enough."

"Then you ought to know that men and women like to know each other, and feel some…sweetening toward each other, before they get married."

"Sweetening?"

"Something that'll attract them, like bees to honey."

"I know that." The boy's Adam's apple rose and fell as he swallowed hard. "But how're you ever going to meet a lady out here and feel any…sweetening?"

It was his father's turn to flush. "So you thought the solution would be to send for a stranger?"

"Pa, do you remember the time the mother duck got killed by a coyote? We gave the ducklings to one of our hens, and she raised them like her own."

Matt's eyes narrowed. "Are you saying any mother's better than none?"

"I guess that's what I'm saying."

"Then I'll remind you what a poor substitute that hen was. She stood squawking on the banks of the river every time those ducklings started swimming. And when they joined a flock of geese and flew off in the fall, she took to her nest in mourning."

The boy nodded. "But you have to admit, she took good care of those babies until they could take care of themselves, Pa."

Matt nodded reluctantly. "Yes, she did."

"They'd have died without her mothering."

The two fell silent for long minutes. Finally Matt

cleared his throat. "We're not talking about ducks and chicks now, Aaron."

"No, sir. But Miss McCree seems nice enough."

"I guess she is. But she's a city woman. What does she know about surviving a winter in the wilderness?"

Aaron shrugged again. "Not much, I'd wager. But we'd be here to help her."

When his father said nothing more, he looked up, studying him carefully. For the first time he felt a flicker of hope. "You thinking of asking her to stay?"

"I might be." Matt's eyes were hidden in shadow. But the lingering pain was still in his voice. "After all, I was outvoted. And there's the money. It's going to cost more than I have to send her home. It doesn't seem fair to ask her to work in town until she's saved enough." At least those were the arguments he was willing to admit to. But the truth was, that damnable letter had changed everything. It wasn't that he wanted a wife, he told himself. But Aaron was right. They needed a woman around the place. And Del needed a mother. And now, right this minute, his back was to the wall.

He indicated the blanket he'd tossed on the straw. "You go ahead and get some sleep. I'll be back in a while."

"Yes, Pa. And, Pa?"

Matt opened the door, then turned.

Across the barn, his son looked suddenly young and scared, with the blanket draped around his shoulders, his eyes wide in the lantern light. "You might want to try asking Miss McCree, instead of making it sound like a command. You know, like honey instead of a stick.''

Matt nodded. "Thanks, son. I'll keep that in mind."

Izzy looked around the bedroom, which was as filthy as the rest of the cabin. Some of Matthew's clothes hung on pegs along one wall. A couple of shirts. Some pants. The rest had been dropped on the floor. A parka made of some kind of animal fur. Boots, one near the door, the other clear across the room. As though he'd tossed them, or more than likely kicked them, in a fit of temper.

There was a dust-covered dresser, with drawers that had fancy knobs. Above the dresser was an oval mirror, cracked down the middle. She turned away, not wanting to look at herself.

She thought about tidying up the room, but the truth was, she was exhausted. And she still had to wash her clothes in preparation for the difficult journey ahead, since these were the only clothes she owned.

She pulled a very small, very sharp knife from its sheath beneath her sash and hid it under her pillow. Then she sat down tentatively on the edge of the bed. The mattress was rough and scratchy. And lumpy. She wasn't surprised. It suited this place. With slow, tired movements she untied her new shoes and set them carefully aside. At once her feet began to throb and she had to wiggle her toes for long minutes before she could stand. Then she stripped off her gown and petticoats and peeled off her heavy cotton stockings.

Finally she slipped out of her chemise and stood shivering until she was able to pull on her night shift.

Carrying all her clothes to the other room, she dropped them into the basin and filled it with hot water. Quickly, efficiently, she scrubbed her clothes, then draped them over the rough kitchen chairs to dry. That done, she added another log to the fire and made her way to the bedroom.

The bed looked sturdy enough, having been carved from rough logs. And at least, she thought, the chickens hadn't invaded this space.

She blew out the lantern, then climbed into bed.

She wished she'd been able to do more work before giving up, but the truth was, she was utterly exhausted. And she was facing a long, arduous journey in the morning.

Hugging the blanket to her chin, she huddled into a little ball and fell asleep.

Matt let himself into the still, silent cabin, then breathed deeply. It smelled different. It smelled... clean. Surprised, he stared around. Though it was by no means spotless, it was cleaner than he'd seen it in a year. Much of the rubble had been swept up, and the rest lay in piles along one wall. The indignities left by the chickens had been cleaned up, as well.

By the light of the fire, the filmy, feminine clothes draped over the chairs looked like ghostly specters, mocking him. He walked closer and touched a hand to the delicate chemise. It was as soft as a cobweb and he found himself remembering things better left forgotten.

With a thoughtful frown he walked to the fireplace and, reaching into his pocket, withdrew an envelope and tossed it into the fire. He watched as the blaze licked along the paper, curling it, then bursting it into flame. In an instant the envelope, and the letter inside, had burned to ash.

Odd, he thought. He ought to feel something. Instead, he felt nothing. No pain. No sorrow at his loss. Nothing. Only a sort of numbness where the ache had been for so long.

He struck a match and lifted it to the lantern's wick. Holding the lantern aloft, he walked into the bedroom.

He felt a momentary shock when he saw the woman lying in his bed. It jolted his already overcharged system to see the spill of plain brown hair curling softly on the pillow. The blanket had slipped, revealing a creamy neck and shoulder and, beneath the modest neckline of a nightgown, the darkened cleft between her breasts.

He walked closer, lifting the lantern for a better look.

That's when she sat up with a cry of alarm.

"Who...? What...? Sweet salvation. What are you doing here?"

The blanket dipped lower, showing an expanse of flesh that had him sweating.

"Sorry. I didn't want to... I came here to..." He stopped, swallowed, then tried again. "Seeing as how my children do need a ma, and a woman could be a help around here, I thought I'd give you a choice."

"Choice?" She was more awake now, though still confused. Behind her, her hand went automatically to the knife beneath her pillow, closed around it. "I don't understand. Aren't you going to take me to Sutton's Station in the morning?"

"Yes. Of course." He nodded for emphasis. He was handling this badly. But he was determined to bluff his way through, now that he'd started. "But what we do there will be up to you. You can take what little money I have saved, and see how far it will get you. Or—" he swallowed and forced himself to finish before he lost his nerve "—we can find a minister and have a proper wedding, so you can live here as my wife."

"Your…" She couldn't bring herself to say the word. Maybe she was still asleep and dreaming.

No. It wasn't a dream. It was real. Matthew Prescott was standing here, leaving the choice to her. She could go back to the life she'd always known, or risk it all for a life with this harsh, unyielding man.

"I won't push for your answer now." He abruptly lowered the lantern and turned on his heel. He had to get out of here. Now. While he still had some of his senses. The sight of those soft female curves had his heart racing and his temples throbbing. "Sleep on it. You can tell me what you'd like in the morning." At the door he paused, his look dark and unfathomable. "I'll understand if you can't find it in your heart to stay."

"Matthew…"

"Good night." He strode quickly from the room.

She heard the door shut, heard the crunch of his footsteps receding as he made his way to the barn.

She released her hold on the knife and lay in the darkness, wondering what to make of their conversation. Had he really had a change of heart? Or was there something else going on here? Something she ought to be wary of?

She hugged the blanket to her chin, grateful for the brief sleep she'd had before he had intruded. It would probably be all the sleep she would get the rest of the night.

Chapter Three

The sky was still awash with stars, but Izzy knew there was no point in staying in bed. She had replayed in her mind every detail of her arrival in this strange place. She had repeated every cutting word, every stinging remark that had been uttered by Matthew Prescott. What could she possibly hope to gain by marrying him and staying here? From all she had witnessed, most men didn't improve with age. If anything, they got worse. Could she possibly embrace the harshness of the life that loomed before her?

Still, the plight of his children tugged at her. It was obvious that they needed help. Aaron had said it all. The hogs lived better than they did. She'd seen that for herself.

And there was one other thing. She couldn't think of a better option. She could marry Matthew Prescott or return to the life she'd left behind. And she would rather die than go back.

She only hoped that, in time, death wouldn't prove to have been the wiser choice.

She wrapped herself in the blanket and made her

way to the other room in search of her clothes. Instead of the still, silent cabin, she found a blazing fire and Matthew, seated at the table, drinking coffee.

She came to an abrupt halt. "I thought…you'd still be sleeping."

"Long day ahead." No sense telling her he'd been up all night, fretting. "Thought I'd get an early start."

"Yes. I…thought the same." She circled the table, collecting her clothes. When she picked up her chemise, she saw the way his gaze fastened on it, and her cheeks flamed.

As she started toward the bedroom, his words stopped her in her tracks.

"You're limping, Miss McCree. Did you hurt yourself?"

"No. Yes." She swallowed and tried again, keeping her head averted. "Nothing serious. I…stubbed my toe."

"Oh. Sorry." He scraped back his chair. Before she could escape he was touching her, his hand on her arm, his voice full of concern. "I'll get a lantern."

"There's no need." But she couldn't flee. Couldn't move. The touch of him caused a flare of heat that caught her by surprise.

"I guess, because I'm so familiar with this old cabin, I forget the need for more lanterns." Up close she had a clean soap-and-water smell that was appealing. Even her hair smelled fresh, like a windswept meadow after a rain.

"It's just me." She swallowed, hating the nerves that had her quivering. But he was too close. Overpowering. She needed to step back. But the touch of his hand had her frozen. "I've always been clumsy."

"I find that hard to believe, Miss McCree." Very carefully he lifted his hand. But the heat of her body stayed with him.

"I'll just—" she turned away, feeling confused and breathless "—get dressed now."

In her haste to flee, her limp was even more pronounced. When she reached the bedroom, she closed the door, then leaned against it, breathing hard.

Sweet salvation. What had she been thinking of, going out there barefoot? The last thing she had expected was to find him already in the house.

Taking a deep breath, she made her way to the bed, where she deposited her clothes. Then, dropping the blanket, she dressed hurriedly. When she had smoothed down her skirts and carefully brushed and tamed her hair, she slipped on her new shoes and tied them.

She took a few more minutes to make up the bed and tidy the room. Then she walked slowly, evenly, to the door.

As she'd feared, Matthew was still seated at the table. To make matters worse, the children had drifted down from their sleeping loft and were busy making breakfast. Aaron, still picking straw from his hair, ambled in from the barn, carrying a bucket of fresh milk. The hounds bounded in on his heels and began sniffing around the table.

"There's coffee on the fire," Matt said as he lifted his cup.

"Thank you. Would you like me to help with breakfast?"

"There's no need. The children will take care of it."

That's what she'd feared. Already Aaron was slicing the bloody beef, and Clement was heating last night's biscuits over the fire.

"I could fetch some eggs," she volunteered.

"That's Del's job." Aaron wiped his knife on his pants and set a platter of beef on the table.

The little girl entered the cabin carrying a basket of eggs.

"How many did you get?" her brother asked.

"I could only find seven that weren't broken. The hens laid some of them right in the straw where the cows walked. There were smashed eggs everywhere, Pa."

Matt winced. "That's all right. As long as the cows didn't step on your hens, they'll lay more tomorrow. Go ahead and fry up what you found."

Del broke the eggs into a skillet, picking out eggshells as she worked. Then she set the pan over the fire. A few minutes later she carried a platter of congealed eggs to the table and everybody began spooning some onto their plates.

"Pass some to Miss McCree," Matt commanded.

"No, thank you." Izzy handed the platter to Benjamin and nibbled on a biscuit. She had softened it by dipping it into her coffee.

"That's all you're having?" Matt studied her. If anything, she looked even more pale and delicate than when she'd arrived yesterday. And far too skinny.

"I'm really not hungry." She wondered how anyone could work up an appetite for such fare.

"I'll have a couple of those eggs, Del." Matt took the platter and slid a blob onto his plate.

Izzy watched in silence while the children and their father shoveled food into their mouths and ate mechanically, washing it down with gulps of milk. Whenever they bit into something hard or distasteful, they merely spit it into their hands and opened up their fingers behind their backs. One of the hounds would snap it up.

"You're awfully quiet this morning, Miss Mc-Cree." Aaron stopped eating for a moment to study her carefully.

"I hadn't thought about it, but I guess—" Izzy nodded "—I guess I am."

"Because you're leaving?" Del asked.

"No. Just because today is a...special day."

"What's special about today?" Matt asked.

She turned to him and felt the heat rise to her cheeks. "Unless you've changed your mind, Matthew, it's our wedding day." There. She'd said it aloud.

The children stared first at her, then at their father.

Aaron let out a whoop. "You mean it, Miss McCree? You're going to marry Pa?"

She nodded. "As long as he agrees."

Matt had been busy swallowing his fourth biscuit. Now it stuck like a stone in his throat, and he had to gulp a cup of scalding coffee to get it down. He glanced at his four children, then at the woman who was watching his face with such intensity. "I believe

I said my piece last night, Miss McCree. All I needed was your answer.''

"Now you have it.''

With absolutely no expression he studied her, as though searching for something in her eyes. Abruptly he pushed away from the table. "I'll hitch up the team. We have a long ride ahead of us.''

"What about the children?'' she called to his retreating back.

He turned. "What about them?''

"I think it would be nice if they came along.''

He could see the pleading in the children's eyes and tried to ignore it. "They're needed here. To do the chores.''

"Maybe if we all pitched in,'' she suggested, "we could do at least the necessary chores and leave the rest until we returned.''

"I'll do double duty tomorrow, Pa,'' Aaron promised.

"Me, too,'' Benjamin put in quickly.

It was on the tip of Matt's tongue to refuse. Instead he turned away, calling over his shoulder, "One hour. But we'll have to catch up when we get home.''

He didn't stay around long enough to see the excitement in the children's eyes. But Izzy saw it and was warmed by it. Maybe what she was about to do wouldn't seem so bad, as long as she knew they would benefit.

Wasn't that why she had suggested they come along? She'd like to think so. But the truth was, she hadn't wanted to be alone with her husband-to-be.

The horses and wagon had been heading downward for hours. When they had started out in the mountains, the air had been crisp and cold. But now there was only bright, clear sunshine and a breeze so fresh and clean it almost hurt to breathe it in.

Izzy was crowded onto the seat beside Matt, with Aaron next to her. In the back Benjamin, Clement and Del were laughing and teasing, clearly overjoyed at the thought of escaping their daily chores for a rare visit to civilization.

The horses crossed a long, flat stretch of meadow before splashing through a stream. Izzy held tightly to the seat of the wagon as the horses fought their way up the bank.

"Careful." Matt caught her when she swayed. Like the first time he'd touched her, the flare of heat was instantaneous, and she had to fight the urge to push away.

"I'm fine." She lowered her shawl and lifted her face to the sun. "Why did you build your home so high in the mountains, when the weather seems so much gentler here?"

"Look around you." He pointed to several ranch houses in the distance. "That's the way most folks think. They want to settle where it's easy. Where they'll have friends and neighbors. And pretty soon someone else will be making the rules for them. They won't be able to move without stepping on someone else's property. Then they'll find themselves fighting someone else's battles and even breathing someone else's air."

Izzy breathed deeply, hoping to diffuse the anger

simmering in his tone. "It smells fresh and clean to me."

"Give it time, Miss McCree. With enough people, they'll find a way to foul even the air."

She shot him a quick, sideways glance. "I take it you don't have much use for people."

"I can take them or leave them. Long as they don't cross me or mine."

He flicked the reins and the team moved smartly. After crossing another meadow, they looked down on a pretty valley. Clustered in the middle were several houses, as well as a saloon and a general store.

"That's Sutton's Station. Old man Sutton was the first to settle here. He runs the boardinghouse and stagecoach stop."

As they drew closer, Izzy saw that one of the houses was a dispensary, and another bore a wooden sign proclaiming it a house of worship.

When Matt turned the team toward the general store, Izzy pointed toward the church. "Shouldn't we be looking for the preacher?"

He nodded. "That's what I'm doing. But he won't be there. He's only there on Sunday. The rest of the week he can be found at the saloon."

He pulled up in front of the store and climbed down to secure the team. Then, leaving Izzy and the children in the wagon, he made his way to the saloon.

Izzy watched his smooth, easy stride until her glance was caught by movement in the upper window of the saloon. A woman wearing what appeared to be nothing more than a chemise and petticoat stood in full view, watching her. Then she abruptly lowered the curtain and disappeared.

Izzy sat very straight and tall, wondering if the children had noticed the brazen display. But they were busy watching a group of children who had abandoned their game of hide-and-seek to walk closer and look over the newcomers.

"You here to trade goods?" a little boy called.

Aaron, Clement and Benjamin remained silent, refusing to even look at the boy.

"Uh-uh." When her brothers refused to respond, Del chose to answer for all of them. "Our pa's getting married today."

"Why?" a little girl asked.

"So's we'll have a ma." Del stood up in the back of the wagon and proudly tapped a hand on Izzy's shoulder. "This is Miss McCree. She's going to be our new ma."

"Why would you want to take on that mangy litter of pups?" a bigger boy taunted.

His friends laughed.

"We aren't pups," Del shouted back. "These are my brothers. And I'm their little sister."

That had the whole group of children laughing and pointing. "A girl? Liar. You ain't no girl."

"Am, too."

"Well, if you are—" the bigger boy glanced at his friends for support "—you're the ugliest girl I've ever seen."

In a flash Aaron leapt from the wagon and grabbed the boy by the front of his shirt, lifting him off his feet. "You take that back, right now, or you'll never be able to say another word."

"Won't," the boy managed to say before Aaron turned him around and wrapped his arm around his throat. Without a word he began to squeeze.

"Aaron, stop," Izzy shouted, but he ignored her and continued to shut off the boy's air.

When the rest of the children moved in closer, Benjamin and Clement jumped down from the wagon and held them at bay, leaving the bigger boy alone to defend himself against this young giant.

"I...take it back," the boy finally managed to croak.

"Say you're sorry." Aaron's gaze was fixed on his little sister, whose eyes were filled with tears of shame.

"I'm...sorry."

Aaron gave the boy a shove that sent him sprawling in the dirt. "Don't you ever call my little sister names again. Or you'll answer to me. Understand?"

The boy nodded, too frightened to speak.

When Aaron and his brothers returned to the wagon, the boy struggled to his feet and raced away to join his friends.

It had all happened in the space of a few seconds. And yet, Izzy realized, it had widened the chasm between Matthew's children and these children here in town. Her heart turned over at the hunger she could read in the eyes of Benjamin, Clement and Del. As for Aaron, he looked as stiff, as unyielding as his father.

"Would you like me to talk to them?" she asked. "Maybe if I did, they would ask you to play."

"No, ma'am." Benjamin spoke for all of them. "We're not welcome here. They call us trash."

"But why?"

"'Cause our ma…"

Aaron shot him a look and he turned away with a shrug. "Just because."

In the distance Izzy could make out the shouts and laughter of the children. And the cruel taunts aimed at the strangers in the wagon.

Some things, she thought with a rush of remembered pain, never changed.

She glanced at Del, whose tears trickled down her cheeks, making dirty streaks. In an effort to soothe, she drew her close. "Shh. Don't cry, Del. They don't mean anything by it. A lot of folks just don't know how to treat strangers. So they say things that are hurtful." She wiped the little girl's tears with the hem of her skirt. "You're so lucky to have big brothers to look out for you."

Del sniffled. "Do you have a big brother, Miss McCree?"

Izzy shook her head. "No. But there were times when I surely wished I did."

Aaron touched a hand to her sleeve. "You won't tell Pa what I just did, will you?"

"But why not, Aaron? I should think he'd be proud that you stood up for Del."

"No, ma'am. Pa doesn't hold with fighting."

"But…" She thought about the war that had divided this country and sent so many of its fine men to their graves. Could it be that Matthew Prescott had refused to fight? Or had he run away, as so many had, when faced with the horror of it all?

She nodded. "I don't see any reason to mention what you did, Aaron."

He gave a sigh of relief. "Thank you, Miss Mc-Cree."

She glanced at the open door of the store and saw an old man with his hands tucked beneath a dirty apron, studying her with grave interest.

A tiny trickle of sweat made its way between her shoulder blades and down her back. What was taking Matthew so long?

She heard strangers' voices. A woman's, then a man's. Both raised in anger. Glancing at the swinging doors of the saloon, she saw the woman from the upstairs window now standing beside a bewhiskered man who seemed to be pulling on his clothes. As Izzy watched, he tucked his shirt into the waistband of his pants, then slipped his suspenders over his shoulders. Matt helped him into his jacket and handed him a hat. He accompanied Matt outside, while the woman remained at the door, looking visibly annoyed.

As the two approached, the stranger stumbled and would have fallen if Matt hadn't caught him and held him upright. With his hand beneath the man's elbow, Matt paused beside the wagon.

"Aaron, help Miss McCree down."

As she climbed down, the stranger, in a courtly gesture, doffed his hat and made a slight bow. "Miss McCree, I understand you've come to marry this fine gentleman. This is indeed an honor. I am the Reverend Jonathon Carstairs. At your service.''

She took a step back, evading the stench of his breath. The reverend was as drunk as a skunk. And as aromatic.

She glanced at Matt, "I think…''

"You're right. Come along, children.'' He caught her hand and dragged her along, all the while holding up the preacher, while the rest of the children scrambled out of the wagon and trailed behind. "The lady thinks we should get this over quickly.''

"My thoughts exactly,'' Carstairs said as he coughed, hacked, then spat in the dirt. "The night looms ahead and I still have a great many…'' He glanced at Izzy and the children before finishing lamely, "Hymns to sing.''

He climbed the steps and pushed open the door to the meeting hall. After fumbling through a drawer, he came up with a dog-eared book. Then a thought occurred. "You'll need a witness.''

"What about the children?'' Izzy asked.

"How old are you, boy?'' the preacher asked Aaron.

"Almost fifteen,'' he replied.

"To make it legal, we need an adult,'' Reverend Carstairs announced.

Matt headed for the door. "I'll be right back.''

Within minutes he returned with the man Izzy had seen in the general store. "Miss McCree, this is Webster Sutton. Web, this is Isabella McCree, my… intended.''

Now Izzy understood why Sutton had kept his

hands hidden beneath his apron. His left hand was missing, and his shirtsleeve hung limply over a bony wrist.

Webster offered his right hand to Izzy, looking her up and down as he did. "Ma'am. Like I said, Matt, I can't spare much time. The wife's ailing. How do, Aaron, Benjamin, Clement, Del."

Before the children could acknowledge his greeting, the preacher said abruptly, "Time's a-wasting. Let's get started." He was leaning heavily on a wooden stand that held a hymnal, and he probably would have toppled forward without its support. "Did you two come here of your own free will?"

Izzy and Matt avoided each other's eyes as they nodded.

"Will you, Matt…" He squinted. "What's your given name?"

"Matthew Jamison Prescott."

"Will you, Matthew Jamison Prescott, take this woman for better or worse, for richer or poorer, in sickness and in health, forsaking all others, until death do you part?"

Matt's tone was hoarse. "I will."

"And will you, Isabella McCree, take this man for better or worse, for richer or poorer, in sickness and in health, forsaking all others, until death do you part?"

Izzy chewed her lip. "I will."

The preacher glanced at Matt. "Did you bring a ring?"

Izzy felt the heat of embarrassment color her

cheeks. But to her amazement, Matt reached into his pocket and withdrew a small gold band.

"You may place the ring on her finger, Matt."

Matt did as he was told.

"Now repeat after me. With this ring I thee wed."

Matt's voice was low and deep, more nearly resembling a growl as he repeated the words.

"I pronounce you husband and wife. You may kiss your bride."

At the same moment that Matt bent forward, Izzy stepped back. The thought of kissing him for the first time in front of his wide-eyed children, a drunken preacher and an impatient shopkeeper had her face flaming.

To cover the awkward moment, Matt shook hands with Webster Sutton and Jonathon Carstairs, slipping the preacher a dollar as he accepted a signed document. Then he caught Izzy's hand and led her and the children outside.

"Well." He shoved his hands into his pockets to keep from touching her. "I thought I'd pick up some supplies before we leave. Do you need anything?"

She shook her head and walked along, struggling to keep up with his impatient strides. "I'll go inside with you, though."

"We can't spare much time." He waited for her to precede him through the open doorway.

Inside he gave Webster Sutton a list of supplies, then he and the children helped load them into the back of the wagon. There were sacks of flour and sugar, a pouch of bullets, another pouch of tobacco and a packet of coffee beans.

Matt came up behind Izzy, who was standing at the counter staring at the jar of candy sticks. "Would you like one?"

"Oh, no." She glanced away. "I was just thinking about the children."

"Wouldn't want to spoil them," he muttered.

"No. Of course not." She swallowed her disappointment and turned away, heading toward the wagon, where the children had already settled.

A few minutes later Matt shook Webster's hand before walking out. He climbed up to the wagon seat and flicked the reins. The team started up with a jolt. And within minutes, the town of Sutton's Station was left in their dust.

When they were once again climbing toward their mountain cabin, Matt reached casually into his pocket and withdrew a handful of candy sticks.

The children's eyes went wide with surprise and pleasure.

"Miss Mc—" He cleared his throat and started over. "Isabella wanted you to have something to celebrate our wedding," he said as he passed the candy around.

Izzy experienced a jolt of pleasure so unexpected she had to stare hard at her hands to keep from clapping them together in delight. She had wanted so desperately to erase the jeers and insults the children had endured. And now, at least for a few minutes, they would know only sheer joy.

"Ooh." There were long sighs and exclamations as the children accepted the special treats and popped them into their mouths.

Matt handed one to Izzy. ''I thought you might like one, too.''

''Thank you.'' She took a long, slow taste. ''Peppermint. It's my favorite. How did you know?''

He seemed suddenly pleased with himself. ''I didn't know. I had to guess. I just liked the color.''

''Did you get one for yourself?''

He shook his head. ''But if you don't mind, I'll have a smoke.''

He lifted the cigar from his pocket, studying it a moment. Back at the store, he had debated the expense of such luxuries. Now, when he saw the happiness in his children's eyes, not to mention his new bride's, it seemed the perfect touch.

He scratched the end of a match, holding the flame to the tip. Breathing deeply, he emitted a stream of smoke that curled around his head before dissipating into the air.

''Miss McCree, now that you're married to Pa, what should we call you?'' Del asked from the back of the wagon.

''How about my given name, Isabella?''

''Isabella.'' Del managed the word around the sticky candy, since she couldn't bear to take it out even for a moment. ''It sounds...musical.''

''If you'd rather not...''

''Oh, no. It's pretty. I like it,'' the little girl assured her. ''It's just so fancy. But it sure does suit a fancy lady like you.''

As the team ate up the miles, Izzy was left to ponder what she had just done. Was it wrong to pretend to be something she wasn't? Was that the same as lying?

She chanced a quick sideways glance at the rugged profile of the man beside her. If he learned the truth, would he have the right to declare their marriage a lie, as well, and order her back to Pennsylvania?

And what of the children? What would they think if they ever learned the truth about her?

To calm her racing heart she reminded herself that she was thousands of miles away from anyone who had ever known her. Her past was dead and buried. She was now Mrs. Matthew Jamison Prescott. From now on, her life was whatever she chose to make it.

Chapter Four

"We'd better rustle up some supper, Pa." Aaron had long ago finished his candy and licked his fingers until there was no trace of the sticky sweetness left.

"I was just thinking the same thing." Matt stubbed out his cigar after smoking only half, saving the other half for later. "We'll stop over by that stream and see what we can find."

He slowed the team to a walk and finally brought them to a halt in a clearing. "Get your rifle, Aaron," he called as he climbed down.

Matt started to turn away, then, remembering his manners, extended a hand to help Izzy down.

The moment their hands touched, she felt a tingling along her spine that had her jumping. It wasn't Matthew, she told herself as she struggled to calm her racing pulse. It was just the excitement of the day. She glanced at his face, to see if he had felt the jolt. But all she could see was his familiar frown. And those dark, penetrating eyes looking back at her.

"You and the children can gather wood and twigs

for a fire. As soon as Aaron and I finish hunting, we'll start supper."

"Here?"

"You're in the wilderness, Isabella. One place is as good as another."

"Yes. Of course." She turned away, eager to put some distance between them.

When he and his oldest son melted into the woods, Izzy and the others began searching for firewood. Before long they had enough for a bonfire.

"I wish Matthew had left us some matches," Izzy muttered, drawing her shawl around her shoulders.

"We don't need matches." Benjamin took a flint from his pocket and huddled over the wood, which he'd layered with a patch of dried grass. In no time he had a tiny flame, which he soon coaxed into a blaze.

"Oh, Benjamin." Izzy knelt in the grass and held her hands to the warmth. "That's so clever of you."

The boy beamed with pride. "It's easy, once you know how."

"I've never lived in the mountains before." Izzy glanced at the three children, sprawled comfortably around the fire. "There's so much I'll need to learn."

"We could teach you," Del offered. The little girl glanced uncertainly at her brothers. "Couldn't we?"

Clement nodded, intrigued by the thought of teaching an adult what he took for granted. "Pa says the only ones who can't survive in the wilderness are fools who never learned to use their heads."

Izzy gave a shaky laugh. "Then I certainly hope I learn to use mine before I lose it." She glanced at the wagon. "All those sacks of supplies, and no way to cook them. I wish I could make some biscuits and coffee, but I don't have anything to make them in."

Benjamin grinned. "We don't have any kettles. But we do keep an old pot in the wagon for emergencies. It's under the flour sack. And I'll bet if I look around I can find something for you to cook the biscuits on."

Izzy walked to the wagon, returning with a handful of coffee beans and a battered old pot, which she filled with water from the stream. Soon the wonderful fragrance of coffee filled the evening air.

When Benjamin handed her a flat, round stone, she was puzzled, until he said, "This ought to work as well as any pan. Give it a try."

Mixing flour and sugar with a little water, she pressed the batter around the flat stone and set it on the fire.

A short time later Matt and Aaron returned from the forest, balancing on their shoulders a young sapling on which was tied a deer. The weight of it would stagger most men, yet they handled it with ease.

"You're going to cook the whole thing?" Izzy blanched, thinking about the half-cooked side of beef back at the cabin. She was ravenous. But she didn't think it would be possible to choke down another bloody meal.

To her relief, Matt shook his head. "We'll take it with us. But we can cut off enough to cook for a quick supper."

He and Aaron unsheathed their knives and set to work, skinning the animal and slicing a portion for their use. Izzy and Del cut the meat into chunks and threaded them onto sticks, which they set over the flames to cook. Soon they all gathered around the fire.

After his first bite Matt looked up. "Benjamin, these are the best biscuits you've ever made."

"I didn't make them, Pa. Isabella did."

He turned to her. "What did you do to them?"

At his probing look, Izzy flushed clear to her toes. "Nothing special. I just used what I had. Sugar and flour and water. They would be better with a little lard. But it was Benjamin who found the stone to bake them on. Without that, we'd have been eating raw dough."

"That was good thinking, Benjamin." Matt's praise added to the boy's pleasure. Then he muttered, "We've made do with much worse than raw dough."

He broke off another portion of biscuit, before passing it to the others. With a sigh he ate more slowly, savoring each bite. Finally he leaned back and sipped strong, hot coffee.

Turning to his daughter, he said, "You'll have to pay attention to how Isabella makes her biscuits, Del."

"Why, Pa?"

"So you'll know how to make them when she lea—" He gulped coffee, hoping to hide his slip of the tongue. But he saw Izzy glance at him across the fire and knew she'd heard.

So. He expected her to leave. Her nervousness must be even more obvious than she'd thought. But if he believed that, why had he married her? She stared down at her hands. Maybe he had begun to realize that she was the only woman foolish enough, or desperate enough, to take a chance on a ready-made family and a man who barely eked out an existence in this wilderness.

To cover the sudden silence she turned her attention to the children. "Why don't you tell me a little about yourselves? Aaron? I remember hearing you tell the preacher you're almost fifteen."

"Yes'm." At a look from his brothers he added, "Well, I will be in a couple of months."

She tried to hide her surprise. "You seem much older."

He ducked his head. "Pa says there wasn't much time for being a baby out here in the mountains."

"I suppose that's so." She turned to Benjamin. "And you are...?"

"Twelve," he said proudly. "And Clement's ten and Del's eight."

Izzy glanced at Del. "I've been meaning to ask you. Is Del short for Delphine?"

"No, ma'am." The little girl glanced at her father before saying, "Delphinium." She made a face to show her disgust.

"Why, that's a lovely name. Did you know it's the name of a flower?"

Del seemed intrigued. "A flower? What kind?"

"It's like a buttercup. I believe it's also called a larkspur. It has lovely ruffled flowers as yellow as your hair."

At her words the little girl was positively glowing. "Maybe my name's not so bad. But I'd still rather be called Del. Or Little Bit." She glanced adoringly at her oldest brother.

"Little Bit?" Izzy glanced from one to the other.

Aaron tousled his sister's hair before glancing at Izzy. "That's just a name I've always called her. What about you, Isabella? How old are you?"

She felt a ripple of unease. She didn't want to talk about herself. "I'm twenty-three."

"Why'd you wait so long to get married?" Benjamin asked.

"I guess..." She felt the first stirrings of panic. "I guess I just never met the right man."

"Until Pa," Del said innocently.

"Yes. Until now."

The little girl was still obviously pleased with her new knowledge about her name. "Were you ever called anything besides Isabella?"

Izzy thought about the taunts she'd endured for a lifetime. Names so cruel, even now, just thinking about them caused her pain.

"No." She reached for the coffee, averting her gaze. "Just plain Isabella."

Beside her Matt watched, wondering what had caused her abrupt mood change. One moment she'd been relaxed, animated. The next she seemed nervous, wounded. He watched as she poured coffee, then topped off his cup, before placing the blackened pot back on the coals. Her hands, he noted, were rough and work-worn, the nails torn and ragged. Not the hands of a refined, elegant lady. And he'd noticed something else. Though her gown was spotless, the hem and cuffs were frayed and the fabric was nearly threadbare.

She'd arrived with nothing more than the clothes

on her back and a small valise. Where was the accumulation of a lifetime? Clothes, linens, dishes, treasured mementos? Years ago, when he and his family had set off from home across the country, Grace had insisted on bringing every single one of her treasures. In fact Grace had...

Annoyed at the direction of his thoughts, he stood. ''Time to get moving.''

Aaron got to his feet and helped his father load the buck into the back of the wagon. The others, as if by some unspoken command, set to work dousing the fire and packing up whatever food remained. In no time their campsite was nearly as clean as when they'd arrived.

The children climbed into the back of the wagon and settled themselves comfortably among the sacks of supplies. Matt climbed up to the driver's seat and offered a hand to Izzy. With a flick of the reins they started off.

As they climbed higher into the mountains the air grew sharper, clearer. Izzy drew her shawl tightly around her shoulders and looked up at the big golden moon, the stars glittering in a velvet sky.

''Cold?''

Matt's voice beside her had her jumping. ''No. I'm fine.''

''There are some blankets in the back of the wagon.''

She shook her head. ''Leave them for the children. I expect they'll be asleep soon.''

He nodded. ''It's been a full day for them. And for you.''

When she remained silent he said, "I'm sorry about the preacher."

"You couldn't help that he was drunk."

"No. But we…caught him at a particularly bad time."

She turned to glance at him. "Is there a good time?"

Matt shrugged. "I don't see him much. But I expect he stays sober on Sundays, at least until his service is over."

After a long moment of silence he said, "I was afraid he'd keel over before he could finish the ceremony."

The warmth of unspoken laughter in his deep voice had Izzy smiling. "He would have, if it hadn't been for that music stand. I'm sure it was the only thing holding him up."

Laugh lines crinkled Matt's eyes. "Did you notice that he had his pants on backward?"

"No. Really?" Izzy's hand flew to her mouth, but she couldn't smother the laughter that bubbled. "That explains why he kept tugging at his suspenders. I thought he seemed to be dressing when you first went to fetch him."

"I found him upstairs over the saloon with Lil. Interrupted him before…" A deep chuckle turned into a roar of laughter. "I don't know who was madder. The preacher or Lil. But I told him I'd give him a dollar if he could be dressed and downstairs by the count of ten. He made it with seconds to spare. And I'm sure by now Lil has that dollar tucked into her bodice."

Izzy knew that she ought to be shocked by what she was hearing. But she couldn't help herself. The silly mood and the rumble of laughter were contagious.

As the horses and wagon climbed ever higher, she and Matt continued laughing about the preacher and his unholy ways, until she heard a sound that had her blood freezing.

"What was that?"

"A wolf, calling to his mate."

"A...wolf." Fingers of ice pressed along her spine. "I didn't realize there were wolves in these mountains. Will they attack?"

"If they're hungry enough. Or cornered. But don't worry. Mostly they attack livestock. They would only attack humans as a last resort."

"How—" she touched a hand to her throat "—comforting."

When the darkened outlines of the cabin and outbuildings came into view, Izzy turned to glance at the children. "They're all asleep," she said in hushed tones.

"They'll be glad to climb into their beds," Matt muttered. "And so will we."

We. Whatever remained of Izzy's light mood vanished. She had known, of course, that he would want to sleep in his own bed tonight. With her. But she hadn't allowed herself to think of it. Until now. Sweet salvation. What was she going to do?

She shivered.

"You're cold."

"No. Just..."

Ignoring her protest, he removed his cowhide jacket and draped it around her shoulders. That caused her to shiver more violently. She could feel the heat of his body, and the dark, musky scent of him that lingered in the folds.

As they neared the cabin the hounds leapt out of the darkness, setting up a chorus of barking that had the children sitting up, rubbing their eyes. Even before the wagon came to a stop the dogs had jumped into the back, tails thumping, tongues licking as they greeted their family.

"You can all get out here," Matt called, "except for Aaron. He and I will get this carcass into the barn and gut it before we go to sleep."

"Yes, sir." Though the boy had been sound asleep just minutes before, he helped Izzy down, then climbed up and took the space beside his father.

Izzy watched the silhouette of man and boy as the wagon rolled toward the barn. When it disappeared inside, she turned and followed the others into the cabin.

Benjamin, half-asleep, was busy getting a fire started. Clement struck a match to the wick of a lantern and set it on the table. Del raced around collecting her precious chickens and shooing them out to the barn. When their chores were completed, the three children climbed the ladder to their sleeping loft.

"Good night, Isabella," they called.

"Good night." Izzy stepped gingerly around the chicken droppings and made her way to the fire, where she stood shivering. It wasn't the chill of the cabin that had put this ice in her veins, she realized. It was knowing what was to come.

She'd known, of course. When she'd answered the letter. When she'd pulled up stakes and headed across the country. When she'd set foot on this mountain. She wasn't addled. She knew what a man expected of a wife. And she was fairly certain she could comply. It's just that it was so…unappealing to her. No, that wasn't the word. It was frightening. Terrifying. Sickening. Loathsome. But she would find a way to get through it, as she had found a way to get through so many other disgusting and painful things in her life.

She picked up the lantern and a basin of warm water and made her way to the bedroom, taking care to close the door. She set the basin on a small table and took no notice of the litter as she sank down on the edge of the bed and began to undress. As she had the previous night, she placed the knife under the pillow, then removed her gown and petticoats, her shoes and stockings and chemise. One by one she washed them in the basin and hung them on pegs to dry. Then she proceeded to wash herself.

She was shivering by the time she slipped the simple ivory night shift over her head. She carefully fastened the row of buttons that ran from throat to waist. In the bottom of her valise she found the hairbrush with the worn handle. Unpinning her hair, she began to brush until the tangles were smoothed. She set the brush on the dresser top, refusing to glance at her reflection in the cracked oval mirror. It wasn't necessary. She knew what she looked like.

She'd been plain all her life. Plain and...invisible. At least for the most part. Of course, there were times when men had noticed her. But she had always dreaded those times even more. Because then she'd had to fight to hold on to the only thing no man had ever been able to take from her—her honor.

And now she was about to relinquish it willingly. Not for love. But for some feeble attempt to belong. She closed her eyes a moment, struggling against the tears that threatened. Then she straightened as she heard the cabin door open and close; heard muted voices as father and son bade good-night; heard the creak of the ladder as Aaron climbed to the loft. She felt the hair at the back of her neck rise as the bedroom door opened and closed.

She turned to face Matt and felt a jolt to the midsection. His clothes, his hands, his arms to the elbows were covered with blood. It streaked his beard and was smeared down the front of his shirt.

"Sorry." Seeing the way she was staring at him, he began to unbutton his shirt. "Gets pretty messy gutting a deer. I usually clean up in the barn, but there wasn't any water in the bucket, and it was so late and so cold, I figured I'd just do it in here."

"Yes. Of course." She forced herself into action. "There's a basin here. When you've finished washing, I'll soak your clothes overnight. I should be able to get most of that blood out."

He sat on the edge of the bed and nudged off his boots, then peeled away the bloody shirt. Crossing to the basin, he began to scrub the blood from his hands and arms, his torso, his face.

While he washed, Izzy stood to one side watching. She couldn't seem to look away. Never had she seen such a man. His skin was tanned and bronzed from his years in the sun. His body was lean and hard and muscled. With each movement the muscles of his back and shoulders bunched and tightened. At the sight of it, she gave an involuntary shiver.

He was so big. So strong. A man like that could be rough. Or cruel. She shivered again.

When he was finished washing, he lathered his face, picked up a straight razor and began to remove his beard.

Izzy watched in fascination, wondering what he would look like. With each stroke his features became more visible. Now the lower half of his face matched the thoughtful forehead, the dark, penetrating eyes. He had handsome, sculptured cheekbones. Wide, firm lips. A cleft in his chin. He looked so much younger. No more than perhaps thirty-five, she calculated. When she caught him watching her in the mirror, she blushed and turned away, busying herself with his discarded clothes.

Matt continued watching her while he finished shaving. He couldn't quite figure Isabella out. There was an earthiness about her. In the way she'd laughed when they discussed the preacher. Some ladies might have been outraged by the display of drunkenness. But though she'd been shocked, she hadn't seemed offended. And there was an innocence in her, as well. In her eyes, when she thought no one was looking. In the way she seemed to devour everything in sight, as though trying to take it all in at once.

She was a bit small for his taste. Too fragile looking. But she had beautiful eyes. It was the first thing he'd noticed about her. Eyes more green than blue. Unless she was angry. And then they took on an amber hue that was fascinating. Like storm clouds rolling over a summer sky.

Her hair defied description. He'd thought it to be brown, until the sunlight had touched it today. Then he had discovered rich red strands, and some the shade of honey. He liked her hair like that, long and loose and curling around that small, fair face.

He felt a purely male reaction to her, enjoying the contrast between the pristine gown buttoned clear to her throat and the spill of lush hair inviting him to touch. Maybe this wouldn't be such a bad arrangement after all.

He rinsed off the lather and dried his face. When he turned, Izzy was just picking up the last of his clothes. As she carried them to the basin, he noticed her foot.

"You're limping again. You've hurt yourself."

"No." Shocked, she stopped and turned to face him.

"You have. Give me those." He crossed to her and tried to take the soiled clothes from her hands.

She hugged them to her like a shield. "That isn't necessary."

"It is. You'll get blood all over your clean gown." He yanked them free and dropped them into the basin of water.

When he turned, she was still standing where she'd

been, holding her arms across her chest, looking like a bird about to fly.

"What's wrong, Isabella?"

"Nothing." She backed away. The movement only served to emphasize her limp.

"You have hurt yourself." He stared down at her bare toes peeking from beneath the hem of her gown. "Don't be afraid to tell me."

"It's…nothing. A little pain from the stubbed toe. It comes and goes." She limped to the door. "I'll get some lye soap to soak the blood out."

In quick strides he crossed the room. Reaching over her head, he pressed a hand to the closed door. "Leave it. The clothes will keep until morning."

She couldn't bring herself to face him. With her back to him she said, "I could make some coffee."

"No coffee. It's too late. Let's just go to bed." He dropped a hand to her shoulder and she flinched as though he'd struck her.

She flinched? Sweet heaven, was she afraid of him?

At once he lifted his hand away. But in that one instant he'd determined that she was shivering. Violently.

"I realize I'm not like the men you probably knew in Pennsylvania." His voice was low, the tone intentionally soothing. "Out here, so far from civilization, we sometimes forget about the things we once took for granted."

When she didn't move, he grew bolder and touched a hand to her hair. It was as soft as it looked. Thick and lush and inviting. He leaned close, breathing in the clean woman scent of her as his fingers closed around a silky strand.

Though she was standing very still, she couldn't hide her reaction. Tremors ripped through her, leaving her quaking.

He withdrew his hand, curling it into a fist at his side. "Get into bed." His tone was rougher than he'd intended.

"What?" She looked up, confused by his abrupt command.

"I said go to bed. You're freezing."

"No, I..."

"Now, Isabella."

Seeing the look in his eyes, she limped across the room and climbed under the blankets.

He waited until she had carefully tucked the blankets around her, leaving only her face exposed. A face that seemed as pale as the bed linens. And eyes big and round with fear, watching him warily.

What was going on here? She was more than afraid. She was terrified. Of him. Or of...

It struck him like a bolt of lightning. Of course. She was afraid of what they were about to share.

He swallowed back his disappointment. He had been so long without a woman, and he'd thought, hoped, that the drought would end tonight. But he could wait another night.

She was bound to be exhausted from all her travels. And the truth was, he was weary, as well.

He crossed to the dresser and blew out the lantern. In the darkness he made his way to the bed and climbed in beside her.

Izzy lay, stiff and frozen, steeling herself against his touch. He'd seemed so angry. She would probably have to get used to his many moods. When he was angry like this, would he be cruel? After such a long time without a woman, would he use her like a brute?

After long, agonizing minutes, she chanced a glance at the figure next to her. He was lying on his side, facing away from her. His breathing was slow and deep.

As she listened, she realized that he was asleep.

It was her wedding night, and her new husband was asleep beside her.

She nearly wept with relief. She had escaped, at least for one more night, the thing she most feared. And if she had to deal with it tomorrow night, well, that was for tomorrow.

For several minutes she watched the man beside her. Watched his chest rise and fall with each measured breath. Studied the broad shoulders, corded with muscles.

Now that she had a moment to think, she had to admit that his touch had been unexpectedly gentle. She was truly ashamed of her reaction. But she'd been expecting something vastly different. By the time it had registered in her brain, it was too late. The damage had been done. She'd stood there, quaking like a leaf.

Oh, what must he think of her? There was no way she could possibly explain. The thought of speaking about something so intimate was too shocking to imagine.

She studied the dark hair that reached almost to his

back. She even lifted a hand to touch it as he had touched hers. But she couldn't bring herself to do it. Instead she lowered her hand and closed her eyes. And, like the man beside her, fell into an exhausted sleep.

Chapter Five

"Sweet salvation."

Izzy awoke with a start. She sat up, rubbing her eyes, then glanced quickly toward the other side of the bed. It was empty. She'd been so sound asleep she hadn't even heard Matthew moving around the room.

His bloody clothes were still soaking in the basin. But his boots and jacket were missing from the floor.

Without bothering to wash, she pulled on her clothes and shoes and hurried out of the bedroom.

The cabin was empty. There was a fire burning, and dirty dishes littered the table.

She draped a shawl around her shoulders and went in search of the others. The sound of voices led her some distance behind the barn.

The first thing she spotted was Del, staring up a tree. Benjamin, high above her, was inching his way slowly along a branch, holding a smoking torch in his hand. Just above him was a beehive. Swarming around his head were dozens of bees.

"Benjamin." Izzy's voice was choked with fear. "Look out. You're going to get stung."

"I guess he's been stung a hundred times or more." Del's voice rang with pride. "But it's the only way he knows to get their honey."

As Izzy watched in amazement, the boy held the torch near the hive. After a few minutes the activity around it seemed to slow down, as the bees were overcome by the smoke. In one quick motion Benjamin reached into the hive. When he withdrew his arm, it was black with bees. He merely brushed them off as he shinnied down the tree. Once on the ground he held out his prize, which he broke into pieces to share with the others.

"Here, Del." He gave the biggest piece to his little sister.

"This is for you, Isabella."

She accepted the sweet treat and smiled as she licked the honey from the comb. "If you find more, I'll be happy to use them for a special dessert."

"There's plenty more." Benjamin pointed to the trees that towered over them. "I know of a dozen or more hives right around here."

"He brings me honey whenever I get hungry," Del said proudly.

Izzy studied the boy with new respect.

Then, feeling she owed the children an apology, she said, "I'm sorry I slept so late. My journey must have left me more weary than I realized."

"It's all right." Del gave her a smile that was sweeter than the honey that dripped from her lips. "Pa said to let you sleep as long as you wanted."

Izzy glanced around. "Where is your father?"

Benjamin nodded in the direction of the mountain. "Pa and Aaron went up into the hills to track a herd of mustangs."

"What for?"

"That's how Pa earns his living. By taming wild horses to saddle for the army."

"I thought he was a rancher."

Benjamin mopped his brow with his sleeve. "That's what Pa wants to be. But right now, until our herd is big enough, he has to do something else to pay the bills."

"Isn't it dangerous, chasing after wild horses?"

Brother and sister shared a knowing smile.

"It isn't the chasing that's dangerous," Benjamin said. "It's breaking them to saddle. Pa's been thrown off a horse so many times, it's a wonder he can still walk."

Izzy felt her heart lurch at the image. "Will he and Aaron be back for supper?"

The boy shrugged and returned his attention to the honeycomb. "We never know. Sometimes they're home in a day. Sometimes, when they find the tracks of mustangs, they follow them for days or weeks."

"Weeks?" Perhaps she had won a reprieve. It could be weeks before she would have to deal with her private fears. Suddenly another thought intruded. "But what about you children? Do you mean you're left alone for weeks at a time? "

"Yes'm." Benjamin seemed surprised by the question. "It doesn't matter. We just go about our chores, the same as always."

"But what if you should have a need of your father or older brother?"

"What for?" the boy asked innocently.

Izzy's mind raced. "I don't know. An accident, for instance."

"One of us would head up into the hills for Pa. And the other would go to town for the doc." Benjamin pointed to the rifle resting against the trunk of a nearby tree. "Pa taught us how to handle a gun as soon as we were old enough to hold it. And he taught us a signal to use in case of any kind of trouble. Three shots, one after the other, would bring him and Aaron running."

"Well, that's certainly comforting. If he's close enough to hear." She felt sick at heart thinking about these children, who were apparently raising themselves.

Just then she glanced up to see Clement emerging from the woods. Over his shoulder he carried a fistful of pelts. "Have you been trapping, Clement?"

He shrugged. Unlike Benjamin, with his coarse dark hair and wide smile, this golden-haired boy seemed more comfortable with the hounds and horses than with people. "Yes'm. I don't much like killing critters. I'll only trap those that give us trouble. Like this one." He held up a sleek white-and-bronze pelt. "This mountain cat was ready to pounce on Del's pony a few days ago. I had to shoot it. Then I skinned it and hung the pelt to dry on some tree branches."

"What will you do with it?"

"Make a parka for Del. And maybe some leggings." He reached into his shirtfront and held out a small, twitching bundle of fur. "Found this in the woods, too. What was left of its ma was nearby. Probably killed by a coyote."

"Ooh. Can I keep it, Clement?" Del eagerly accepted the bunny and pressed it to her cheek.

"I guess so. But you'll have to hide it from the hounds."

"Maybe we could build a cage," Izzy offered.

The boy nodded. "I guess we could."

"Clement's always had a way with critters." Del cuddled the bunny like a rag doll. "The first time he came home with a family of rabbits that had lost their ma, Pa raised holy…" She stopped, realizing what she'd almost said. "And even after they were big enough to be turned loose, they kept coming back to the cabin, looking for Clement."

"Pa had a hard time getting us to eat rabbit stew after that," Benjamin said with a laugh.

"Oh, my." Izzy was aghast. "I guess I'd have a hard time, too. After all, they were your pets."

The boy gave a shy shrug. "They aren't really pets, except to Del. They're food. Just like the geese and ducks and deer. Without them we'd starve. Game gets pretty scarce here in winter. Especially if we have a blizzard. And nothing's wasted. Pa taught me how to tan the hides for mittens and boots."

Izzy knew what it was to go hungry. Still, she admired the boy's ability to handle these creatures in such a forthright manner. It was a trait he'd obviously inherited from his father.

"Here, Clement." Benjamin handed his brother the last of his honeycomb. "I saved this for you."

"Mmm. Thanks." The boy dropped his pelts and began to lick the honey, enjoying every drop.

Izzy sighed. "I guess I'd better get back to the cabin and start something for a midday meal."

"No need." Clement gave her a smile. "Pa had us pack up some biscuits and venison before we left the cabin this morning."

"It looks like your father thought of everything." She turned away. "I'll expect you at suppertime, then."

She left them and made her way back to the cabin. Along the way she mulled over all she'd seen and heard. These children had learned to take good care of one another. They were willing to share unselfishly. It was plain that they'd had a good teacher.

Matthew Prescott, it would seem, was a man who took nothing for granted. And she would try not to think too harshly of him. After all, circumstances had thrust him into this situation. Without a mother to be there for his children, he'd been forced to teach them that there was no room for sentimentality. Instead they needed to be self-sufficient, industrious, independent. And loyal to one another.

She intended to prove that she would be no less.

Not wanting to ruin her only gown, Izzy slipped one of Matt's shirts over her clothes. It hung below her knees.

She knew that it would take superhuman effort to clean the cabin in a single day. But she could at least make a dent in the debris.

She began by hauling buckets of water from a

nearby creek and heating them over the fire. Into these she poured a generous amount of lye soap before filling them with all the clothes that were lying around the floor. Soon a length of rope strung between two trees bloomed with britches and shirts and assorted stockings. Next she hauled all the bedding outdoors and hung it out to air, as well as the animal hides that served as beds for the children in their loft. Then she climbed to the loft and swept it clean before descending the ladder and sweeping the debris out the door. That done, she emptied the buckets of hot water and soap onto the cabin floor and the floor of the loft and scrubbed until the wood gleamed.

While the floors dried she walked around the cabin, washing the windows. That led to the discovery of a root cellar, dug beneath the cabin. Descending wooden stairs, she found several shelves filled with assorted fruits, most of which were dried and shriveled. There were apples, cherries, berries and nuts. Packed into the cool earth and covered with a layer of sand to keep them fresh was a variety of vegetables—potatoes and carrots, beets and rutabagas. To Izzy, it was a treasure trove. She chose carefully, wrapping her selection in the tail of Matt's shirt.

In the barn she located the venison, cut into portions and wrapped in the hide. She selected a choice cut, then carried it to the cabin and placed it in a huge kettle, along with the vegetables. She then kneaded dough and set it aside to rise, before returning to her chores.

The sun was beginning to set by the time she hauled the clothes and bedding inside and began sorting and folding. She climbed the ladder to the loft several more times before all the beds were made up. On pegs along one wall she hung the children's clean clothes.

Downstairs she carefully hung Matt's clothes on pegs in the bedroom and made up the bed with fresh linen.

Knowing it would soon be time for supper, she removed the old shirt rolled her sleeves, and washed carefully. Then she brushed her hair and tied it back with a comb. That done, she carried the basin to the other room, filled it with fresh water from a bucket, and placed it on a small stand beside the door, with a clean linen towel and a portion of lye soap beside it.

For a moment she stood back, admiring her handiwork. She was exhausted. But it was a good exhaustion. She had been doing what she had always dreamed of—cleaning her own home.

Oh, the very thought of that word filled her with a quiet joy.

She was just setting the table with the pretty china plates and cups when she heard the sound of hoofbeats. She opened the door in time to see Matthew and Aaron striding from the barn, with Benjamin, Clement and Del alongside.

At their feet were the hounds, wet and bedraggled from the stream they'd just forded.

Before she could say a word, the dogs pushed past her and bounded inside, shaking themselves furiously, spraying muddy water in all directions before circling the table, sniffing the air.

"Oh!" Izzy stared in horror, then stood with her hands on her hips. "Shoo. Get out of here. Go on."

They ignored her cries. Even when she applied her hands to their rumps and tried shoving them away, they didn't budge. In fact, thinking it was a display of affection, they decided to return the favor by wiggling and licking her until she managed to get free of them.

When she turned, she caught sight of the trail of muddy footprints left by Matt and the children, who were busy tossing aside their jackets and prying off their mud-caked boots, which they left in a heap.

"Something smells good." Aaron turned to her with a big smile. Then he caught sight of the look on her face. "What's wrong, Isabella?"

"What's wrong? After all my work, the dogs just...and all of you just..."

"The dogs are hungry, and so are we," Matt said with a frown. "We've put in a long day."

"Have you now? And what about me?" Glaring, she faced him while the dogs milled about their feet.

"The last time I saw you," he said through gritted teeth, "you were sleeping like a baby."

In frustration she turned away before she said more than she ought. After all, she reminded herself, this wasn't really her house. She had only been fooling herself. This was Matthew's house. It belonged to Matthew and his children. It even belonged more to his dogs than it did to her. "I—" she indicated the basin of water "—expect you to wash up before supper."

Matt glowered at her stiff spine, her hands fisted at

her sides. What the hell did she have to be angry at? He'd left her alone last night, hadn't he? And he'd allowed her to sleep in while he and the children went off to their chores. And now she was insisting that he wash before she would feed him. Well, if it was a fight she wanted, he'd be happy to oblige.

Still... something did smell wonderful. And he was starving after a day on the trail.

They'd settle this later.

Without a word he rolled his sleeves and began to wash. When he'd finished his hands and arms, he splashed water over his face and hair, then dried himself.

"Will you look at this, Pa?" Aaron lifted the lid on the kettle, inhaling the wonderful fragrance that spiraled upward. He reached for the knife at his waist, intending to slice off a piece of meat.

"Wait," Izzy cried. "I think... you should wash up first."

Aaron glanced at his father. Without a word, a signal passed from father to son. The boy reluctantly moved to the basin and washed.

"Benjamin, Clement, Del," Izzy said, "I'd be grateful if you would do the same."

"What for?" Benjamin spoke for all of them. "We'll just get dirty again when we do our chores tomorrow."

"Yes, you will. But at least you'll be clean when you gather around the table."

The three turned to their father. "Do we have to, Pa?"

"I think," Matt said, "if you want to sample Isabella's cooking, you'd better do as she asks."

"Yes, sir." Benjamin went first, dipping his hands into the water as though he expected to be burned. When he picked up the linen towel, Izzy shook her head.

"Use the soap, Benjamin. And wash all the way to your elbows, and then your face, neck and ears, as well."

The boy looked as unhappy as a condemned man, but he did as he was told. His younger brother and sister followed suit. When they were finished, they took their places around the table.

Izzy turned from the fire with a platter of venison surrounded by potatoes and carrots and a bowl of rich brown gravy. On another plate she arranged a dozen perfectly browned biscuits. Before she could even take her seat, Matt and the children filled their plates and began stuffing the food in their mouths.

"Mmm, this is just about the best I've ever tasted," Del said over a mouthful. "It's even better'n yours, Benjamin."

"I was just thinking the same thing," Aaron muttered.

"Toss me a biscuit," Matt called, and Benjamin tossed one across the table. Matt caught it, popped it into his mouth, then, surprised, began to chew more slowly.

By the time Izzy got to the table, the others had already eaten their fill and were busy tossing scraps to the dogs.

"I don't know how you got the gravy so smooth," Benjamin said, draining his second glass of milk.

"And the biscuits," Clement added. "How'd you get them so soft?"

"The next time I bake them, I'll show you," Izzy said.

She bowed her head and whispered a prayer. Ordinarily she would ask a blessing on the food. But this night she prayed for patience. In ample supply to keep from killing the entire Prescott family.

The others watched in silence.

"What do you say, Isabella, when you pray?" Del asked innocently.

"If you'd like, I'll teach you the words."

Seeing the looks on her brothers' faces, the little girl shook her head. "That's all right. I guess I don't need to know."

Aaron reached for another helping. "Isabella, Pa and I have cooked lots of venison. But it's never been this tender."

"That's because it had time to cook. If I were going to cook a whole side of beef, as you did the other day, I'd leave it over the fire for a day and a night."

"A whole day and a night?" Aaron looked doubtful.

Benjamin wiped the milk from his mouth and asked, "Did you make this dinner special because it was your first, Isabella? Or is it always going to taste like this?"

Despite her disgust at their lack of manners, she had to smile. "I guess that will depend on what your father provides. As long as the venison and vegetables hold out, you won't have to worry."

As the children began to drift away from the table she said, "You may want to stay around for a while."

"What for?" Del asked.

"I made a special dessert."

"Dessert? Where is it?" They dashed back to the table.

"I'll get it as soon as I've finished eating." She deliberately took small bites, chewing slowly, making them wait impatiently.

She felt the heat stain her cheeks as they sat watching her.

Finally she crossed to the fire, where she removed a pan that had been warming. Into bowls she spooned a mixture of honeyed apple slices, topped by biscuit dough and cinnamon.

"This is Apple Betty," she said as she placed one in front of each of them. "It's even better if you pour a little sweet cream over the top."

As she sipped her coffee, she watched with satisfaction while Matt and the children devoured the treat.

At last Matt leaned back, sipping strong, hot coffee. He nodded toward the dessert. "Aren't you having any?"

She shook her head. "I've had enough to eat. I thought I'd leave the rest for seconds, if the children would like some more."

Seeing their eager smiles, she refilled their bowls and watched as the second serving disappeared as quickly as the first.

"That sure was good," Aaron said as he licked his spoon clean.

"Thank you, Aaron."

Not wanting to be outdone, the other three agreed.

"It was the best ever." Benjamin licked not only his spoon, but his bowl, as well.

"We have you to thank," she said with a grin. "It was your honeycomb that sweetened the apples."

The boy blushed with pleasure.

"I think I could eat a whole tub of Apple Betty." Clement pushed away from the table.

"Me, too," his little sister echoed.

Izzy couldn't stop smiling at their compliments. "If you did, you'd soon be as round as tubs."

They chuckled at her joke as they left the table and gathered around the fire. They were surrounded at once by their wriggling dogs.

Matt drained his cup. "That was a fine meal, Isabella."

"Thank you." His words warmed her more than the food or the fire. "Would you like some more coffee?"

Before she could get up, he retrieved the coffeepot and carried it to the table, filling both their cups.

He glanced around. "I can see you did a lot of work today."

"I just…cleaned." She felt uneasy sitting there with him, but she felt obligated to drink the coffee now that he'd poured it.

Sensing her discomfort, Matt bit back the smile that threatened. For some strange reason, he liked making her uncomfortable. "It smells different in here. Clean."

"I hope you don't mind that I used the soap I found in a cupboard."

"That's what it's there for. We just haven't had time to use it ourselves."

"Yes. I can see that. I mean, you and the children work very hard." She swallowed a sip of hot coffee, gathering her courage. "I have a question."

"Ask it. Then I'll have a few for you." He leaned back, feeling replete. Content. There was nothing like a good meal and a hot fire to soothe a man after a day of hard work. Of course, it didn't hurt to have a woman all primed to spar with, either.

"Why doesn't Del want to keep her chickens in the barn?"

"Because dozens of eggs have been trampled. But she can't leave them outside. She's already lost several to the coyotes."

"Then why don't you build a coop?"

"I'd like to." He gave a sigh of impatience. "It's one of those things I always say I'll do when I find the time. But for now she'll just have to get used to them in the barn." A grin tugged at his lips. "Unless you'd like to keep them in here with you."

She knew he was teasing. But the way he was staring at her had the heat rising to her cheeks. She gulped down her coffee, eager to escape. "I'll wash the dishes now."

"Not just yet." His tone was easy enough, but she sensed a hint of steel beneath. "I've got a couple of questions of my own now."

She glanced beyond him to where his children were sitting. "Why don't we wait until later, when we're alone."

He shrugged. "Suit yourself. I've got some harness to mend." He picked up a length of leather harness, which he'd tossed over a peg near the door, and walked to the fireplace. As he settled into a chair and rolled a cigarette, Izzy stood a moment, watching.

This was a scene she had pictured in her mind for a lifetime. A snug cabin. A handsome, rugged man, children and dogs at his feet.

Yet, for all its beauty, she wasn't really a part of it. She didn't belong.

The yearning of her heart was so raw, so real she had to turn away to hide the tears that sprang to her eyes.

Needing to be busy, she filled a basin with hot water from the kettle on the stove and began to wash the dishes. She blinked in surprise when Aaron picked up a square of linen and began to dry.

Since he was at least a head taller, she had to look up when she talked to him. "Aaron, there's no need. I'm sure you've done your share of hard work today."

He took the pretty cup from her hands and dried it, then placed it carefully in the cupboard. "Yes'm. And so have you." He gave a nod behind him. "I haven't seen our place this clean in years."

"It was awfully dirty. Of course, the chickens and dogs didn't help."

They shared a laugh.

He dried a platter and placed it under a stack of

plates. "I'm sorry about the mud. I saw what our boots and the dogs did to your clean floor."

"It's your clean floor, too, Aaron."

"Yes'm." He dried in silence for a couple of minutes, digesting her words. "We didn't mean to make such a mess. But with Ma gone, it's just…" He shrugged. "It's been a long time since we could think about anything except just getting by." He glanced at her. "Do you understand?"

Under the water she gripped the fragile china plate tightly in both hands. "Yes, Aaron. Of course I do."

He accepted the plate, drying it carefully. "But we'll get better about things if you'll just give us some time."

Time. He was so sweet. And wise beyond his years. She waited until he dried the last dish, then took the linen cloth from his hands. "I have all the time in the world, Aaron. Now, why don't you join your sister and brothers by the fire."

"Yes'm."

"And, Aaron?"

He turned.

"Thank you."

He gave her a smile so like his father's, she felt her heart melting.

When he walked away she continued cleaning, wiping the table, the chairs, even the floor, erasing all the muddy spots and footprints she could find. She knew she was filling time, avoiding the moment when there would be nothing more to do.

Matt glanced up from the harness. "Are you going to join us?"

"In a minute." She walked into the bedroom, then returned with a basket filled with clothes.

"What's that?" Benjamin asked.

"Things that need mending." She took a seat by the fire and began to thread a needle.

"Clement," Matt called. "Set that lantern beside Isabella."

The boy did as he was told and she gave him a smile before bending to her task. She picked up a torn shirt and began to make fine, even stitches.

When she was done, she dropped it and picked up another. Del, who had been watching, caught up the shirt and examined the neat seam. "How'd you do that?"

Izzy motioned her close. "I'll show you if you'd like."

The little girl sat beside her and watched as she gathered a small section of fabric and stitched it with needle and thread.

"Want to try?"

Del shrugged.

Izzy handed over the shirt, along with the needle and thread, and watched as Del's little fingers fumbled with the task. Though she managed to stitch a small section, the fabric was bunched and puckered, the seam jagged.

"I hope that isn't one of my shirts," Benjamin said teasingly.

"If it's mine," Clement said with a laugh, "I'm never going to wear it again."

Embarrassed, Del tossed aside the shirt. "I didn't want to learn anyway."

Izzy caught her hand. "It takes practice to master anything. I'll bet the first time you tried to walk, you fell right on your little bottom. But in no time you were able to keep up with your brothers." She turned to the boys. "Now, since you're having so much fun teasing your sister, why don't we challenge you to do it better?"

"Not me." Benjamin shook his head. "That's girl stuff."

"Yeah," Clement chimed in. "Who needs to sew, anyway?"

"That's probably what your father said. But it would have been nice if he could have mended some of these clothes that were piling up."

Matt winked at his sons. "Isabella has you there. Why don't you give it a try?"

"There's nothing to it." Benjamin picked up the shirt and wasted no time sewing a seam. When he was finished he held it up. The seam was so crooked, the shirt hung at a lopsided angle. The whole family burst into laughter.

"All right, Clement," he said, passing the shirt to his brother. "Let's see you do better."

Clement took a great deal more time. But when he was finished, the shirt looked no better.

Their laughter grew.

"You see," Isabella said gently. "It isn't as easy as it looks. But I think you all show great promise. With a little practice, you could soon be mending your own things."

Aaron, seated closest to the fire, stifled a yawn.

He'd been up since dawn and in the saddle for most of the day, doing the work of a man.

"I think I'll turn in, Pa." He stood and the dogs, as if on command, headed for the door. Aaron let them out, then started up the ladder to the loft.

"Good night, Isabella," he called.

"Good night, Aaron."

One by one the others followed him, calling out their good-nights as they did.

Izzy picked up another shirt and bent to her work, glad for the excuse to avoid looking at Matt.

"I haven't heard them laugh like that in a long time," he remarked.

"They're good children, Matthew."

"Yes, they are. I know it hasn't been easy for them." He worked in silence, occasionally glancing over at her.

He liked the way she looked, with the lantern light spilling over her. Head bent. Eyes downcast. Fingers moving in a graceful dance.

He stood and draped the harness over a peg, then crossed the room and banked the fire.

"I think it's time we turned in."

Izzy's heart started pounding. It was the time she had been dreading. Once again, it was time to face her fears.

Very deliberately she set aside her mending and picked up the lantern, then led the way to the bedroom.

Chapter Six

Matt followed Izzy into the bedroom, then closed the door and leaned against it. Even before he looked around, he knew it was different. It smelled clean. Fresh. As clean and fresh as she looked.

He tore his gaze from the woman long enough to glance around. "Are you sure this is the right room? I don't recall ever seeing it look like this."

Though her heartbeat was erratic, she managed a smile. "I wasn't certain you'd notice." She set the lantern atop the dresser.

"I notice a lot of things." He took a step closer and saw the wary look that came into her eyes. "For instance, the way your hair looks by lantern light."

No one had ever said such a thing to her before. Confused, she took a step back and felt the press of the cold wall against her back.

He drew closer. "And the way your eyes widen when you're troubled."

"I'm not..." She brought a hand to her throat.

Before she could finish, he caught her palm and

pressed it between both of his. "Don't lie to me, Isabella. And don't lie to yourself."

Her cheeks flamed.

His eyes narrowed. "That's what I thought. Now it's time for some truth. What are you really doing here?"

"I told you. I came in answer to the letter…"

"And this?" From his waist he pulled out her knife and held it up.

In her haste this morning, after discovering she'd overslept, she had forgotten about her knife. In fact, she'd been so busy all day, she hadn't even missed it. The razor-sharp blade glinted in the light of the lantern.

"How did this happen to find its way under your pillow?"

"I…put it there."

"So you could kill me while I slept?"

"Of course not. It's just a habit."

"You mean a fine, upstanding lady from the First Pennsylvania Congregation always sleeps with a knife under her pillow?"

"Yes. No." She gave an exasperated sigh.

"Which is it, Isabella? Yes? Or no?"

She hated lying. But each one led to the need for another, and then another. "I was warned that there would be many dangers in the wilderness. Like—" her mind raced "—those wolves we heard last night. My friends advised me to carry a weapon. And since I don't know how to shoot a pistol…" Her voice trailed off as she looked up into his dark, watchful eyes.

"Is that the truth now?"

She swallowed, crossed her fingers. "Yes."

"Why were you afraid to tell me?"

"Because I thought you would consider me foolish. After all, this is your home. The things I fear probably seem quite harmless to you." She glanced away. "Now, do you have any more questions?"

"No questions. But maybe it's time to admit some truth of my own."

Before she could pull free he dragged her into his arms. With his lips mere inches from hers he muttered, "The truth is, I've been wanting to kiss you since I first walked in that door tonight."

She turned her face away at the last moment, and instead of her mouth, all he managed to kiss was a tangle of hair at her temple.

The heat that flared between them was instantaneous. And shocking.

This wasn't what she expected. This...strange curling sensation deep inside. This dizziness, as though she'd spun like a top. This weakness in her limbs, causing her to clutch the front of his shirt for support.

Moonlight spilled through the clean window, bathing her in its golden rays. He reached up, lowering the wick until the light of the lantern was extinguished.

"What are you doing?" she demanded.

"It can't compete with the moon." He brushed his lips across her cheek, knowing she would welcome the darkness. "You look even lovelier in moonlight."

Her lashes fluttered, then closed as his lips made a slow, lazy exploration of her face. Against her will she sighed. Until his hands moved up her back, igniting little fires of their own. Then she stiffened, tried to push away.

"Don't be afraid. I don't bite." His voice was low, seductive. "How about you, Isabella? Do you bite?"

She knew he was trying to put her at ease. She attempted a smile. "I haven't been known to."

"Good. We're both safe, then. Let's get undressed."

Nerves skittered along her spine.

He felt the tremors. "Would you like some help, Isabella?"

"No. I..." She took a deep breath, fought to control the tension she knew he would detect. "I can do it myself."

Before she could lift a hand to the buttons of her gown, he stripped off his shirt and sank down on the bed to nudge off his boots.

"What's wrong?" He sat very still, watching her.

"Nothing." The sight of him, half-dressed, had her heart pumping overtime.

She could do this, she told herself. Maybe she couldn't work up as much enthusiasm as Matthew, but she would get through it.

With nervous, fumbling fingers she undid the first button, then the second. And all the while he was watching. Even when embarrassment had her looking away, she could feel his dark gaze burning into her as she finished unbuttoning her gown to the waist. But she couldn't remove it. Instead she drew the fabric together to hide the delicate chemise that couldn't quite cover the display of flesh beneath.

"Come here." He patted the bed beside him.

Slowly, as though being led to her execution, she crossed the room and sat down.

When she bent to untie her shoes, he dropped to his knees in front of her.

"Let me help."

She should have been moved by his thoughtfulness. Instead she was distressed by the touch of his hands as he unlaced her shoes. He removed first one shoe, then the other, holding them in his palms for a moment as though weighing them. He gave her a curious look before setting them aside. Then, before she could stop him, he reached up beneath her skirt and began to unroll her stockings. The feel of his strong, callused fingers against the softness of her inner thighs had her stifling a gasp.

She stared down at his bent head, wondering if he knew what this invasion of her privacy was doing to her. Could he feel the trembling in her limbs? Could he detect the strange collision of fire and ice that occurred with each touch of his fingers against her flesh?

"You have strong legs." He set aside the stockings, then glanced up at her. "You must have spent a great deal of your time walking."

"I... Yes." She knew her cheeks were flaming.

"I'll help you off with your dress."

"No."

Ignoring her protest, he caught her hands and drew her up. But instead of letting go, he linked his fingers with hers and dragged her close. "Your modesty is admirable, Isabella. But it certainly isn't necessary now that we're properly wed."

He slid his hands along her upper arms, across her shoulders, kneading with his thumbs the knots of tension in her neck. She closed her eyes a moment, allowing a sigh of pure pleasure. With her eyes still closed she moved her head from side to side like a cat, unable to resist the lure of his seductive touch. Oh, she could stay this way all night, lulled by his tender ministrations.

''That's better.''

At the sound of his deep voice her lids snapped open. She found herself staring into dark, fathomless eyes that glittered with a strange light. His face was so close their lips were almost touching. She could feel the warmth of his breath as it feathered the hair at her temple, could feel the way his breath hitched slightly as their gazes locked, held.

His hands, those wonderful, clever hands, had lowered slightly, until they were now stroking the pulse at the base of her throat.

She swallowed, and the sound seemed overly loud in her ears.

He moved his hands lower, to the front of her gown, sliding it open, then easing it over her shoulders. In the shaft of moonlight, her lacy chemise revealed more of her breasts than it covered.

Feeling suddenly naked and vulnerable, she crossed her arms over her chest and took a step back.

''Isabella, don't...''

The moment he reached a hand to her shoulder she reacted as though she'd been burned. Flinching, she shrank back, evading his touch.

His eyes, which just moments earlier had burned

with desire, were now narrowed with anger. "What the hell is wrong with you, woman? Am I so repulsive to you?"

"Of course you're not...repulsive."

"Then what is it? Am I asking too much of you?"

She was too overcome with fear and embarrassment to speak.

Frustration made his words harsher than he intended. "Dammit, woman. This life might be different from the one you left behind. You may think of me as primitive and unworthy. But I'm just a normal man, with a normal man's appetite. I haven't abused you. In fact, I think I've been more than patient. Now..." He reached for her again and she flinched.

Flinched.

Her reaction cut him to the quick. He muttered a string of fierce, coarse oaths.

"In my whole life, I've never had to force a woman. And I'll be damned if I'll start now."

Stung, she seized on the only defense she could think of. Forcing the words from between chattering teeth, she said, "I've told you before, Matthew. I will not tolerate swearing in my presence."

"You won't tolerate...?" For the space of a heartbeat he was shocked into silence. Suddenly he snatched up his shirt and boots. "Then you needn't worry. You won't have to tolerate my presence any longer. I'd rather sleep in the barn."

With that, he spun on his heel and stormed from the room.

The slamming of the door reverberated through the cabin.

Izzy lay in the big bed, staring at the shifting patterns of moonlight along the walls. Her thoughts were too troubled to allow for sleep.

What had she done? What if Matthew decided to send her back? He would have every right. After all, their marriage had not been consummated. It was, in fact, a fraud. A lie. She had tricked him. Cheated him. And all in the guise of charity.

She had thought, once they were wed, that she would be able to put aside her fears. But they were too deeply rooted. Perhaps, she thought with an edge of panic, it was too late for her to ever live a normal life like other women. Maybe each time he came near her she would freeze up and shut him out.

How long would he tolerate such behavior in a wife? And why should he? Indeed, why should any man?

I'm a normal man, with a normal man's appetite.

His words mocked her.

"I'm the one who isn't normal," she whispered. "And no amount of pretending will ever change that."

Oh, she'd tried. She had really convinced herself that this new life, so far from all she'd ever known, would be the beginning of a new Izzy, as well. She would be Isabella Prescott. Mrs. Matthew Jamison Prescott. Mother of his four children. A respected pillar of the community.

She felt tears spring to her eyes. It had all been a silly, useless dream. There was no community. Matthew's four independent, resourceful children had no need of her. In fact, they could manage very well without her. And she would never be a wife to Matthew. Not in the way he wanted.

She wiped away the tears and rolled to her side, squeezing her eyes tightly shut. She would do what she had always done when sleep evaded her and trouble threatened. She would spin the wonderful, familiar dream. Of a fine big house. A brave, handsome husband. And loving children, twined around her like flowers on a vine.

She struggled to hold on to the dream. But she could feel it slipping, fading, growing dim.

Matt leaned his back against a stall and drew smoke into his lungs. Damned lying female had him tied up in knots.

What the hell was she after? He fingered the hilt of her knife, which he'd tucked into his waistband. Her story made sense. Maybe. After all, a city woman would have reason to be afraid of what she'd find in the wilderness. Still, she could have told him. He would have allayed her fears.

And why did she keep it under her pillow?

Unless she thought her greatest danger was in bed.

That was what was really driving him around the bend.

All right, he thought, watching a smoke ring dissipate into the night air. So she'd been hurt in the past. That was pretty obvious. He'd sensed her fears. In fact, he'd taken great pains to show her he wasn't some kind of brute. Still, she flinched whenever he touched her. Flinched. As if she expected him to hurt her.

If she was so afraid of being with a man, why in hell had she married him? His eyes narrowed in sudden thought. Maybe she was in trouble. Maybe she was from a good, decent family and running from their criticism. Could she be carrying another man's child? Hoping for some poor fool to shoulder the blame and the responsibility?

His nostrils flared. He crushed the cigarette under the heel of his boot.

Too annoyed to think about sleep, he picked up an ax and headed toward the woodpile. He might as well burn off this anger on something useful.

As he began to chop wood he was forced to see the folly of this latest argument. If Isabella had been looking for a father for another man's child, she would have seduced him the first night, to make certain he was trapped.

That would have been simple enough to accomplish. She was easy to look at, with those big eyes and shy smile, and a body that curved and sloped in all the right places. And the truth was, he was a man who'd been alone too long now and dying of starvation. If she'd given him any encouragement at all, he'd have devoured her like a feast.

Hell, if she'd wanted to ensnare him, he'd have been a pushover.

In the past he hadn't always been the world's best judge of character. But if he was a betting man, he'd lay odds that Isabella McCree was just plain running scared. Whatever her reasons for wanting a husband, they didn't include love.

Well, he'd lived without love for a long time now.

And had learned to fill his life with other things. Like children. And work. Hard, demanding work.

No reason to change now.

Isabella awoke to the sound of the hounds baying. Dawn light barely threaded the horizon, but the others were already up and moving. Annoyed that she had once again overslept, she dressed quickly, then hurried from the bedroom.

Benjamin, Clement and Del stood clustered in the doorway, peering into the darkness. Aaron looked up from tossing the rest of last night's biscuits into a saddlebag.

"Good morning," he called. "I thought we'd be gone before you got up."

"Gone?"

He nodded. "Me and Pa are heading up into the hills."

She walked to the doorway just in time to see Matt pulling himself into the saddle. He wore a cowhide jacket and wide-brimmed hat to ward off the chill.

Over his shoulder he called, "Let's get a move on, Aaron. I want to catch those mustangs before they get too far."

"Yes, sir." The boy brushed past Izzy and the children and tossed his saddlebag over his horse's back.

"You children stay close to the—" Matt glanced over and caught sight of Isabella in the doorway. She was wearing the same faded gown she'd worn the night before. Her hair was neatly tied back with a ribbon. She held her hands in front of her, nervously twisting the folds of her skirt.

"Good morning, Matthew."

So. She intended to be civil, did she? Well, he could be just as civil. "Good morning."

"You're leaving?"

He nodded.

"How long do you expect to be gone?"

"As long as it takes to bring home the herd we've been tracking. If we're lucky, we'll be back in a couple of days. But there's no telling how long it'll take."

He forced his attention back to the children. "Stay close to home. Remember our signal."

"Yes, Pa."

He touched a hand to the brim of his hat, then nudged his horse into a trot.

Aaron did the same, turning in the saddle to shout, "So long, Little Bit. Benjamin, Clement. You watch out for Isabella."

"We will," they called.

The hounds set up a howl, eager for the hunt. At Matt's command, three of them stayed behind, retreating into the cabin, while the others started off at a run.

Though Aaron had turned in the saddle to wave, Matt continued staring straight ahead.

A few minutes later the two horses dipped below a rise and were gone from view.

Isabella turned away, a mixture of relief and regret flooding through her. Though she was fearful of being alone so far from civilization, she knew she had the children and dogs for company. And, she reminded herself, for a few days, or perhaps even a week, she could relax and let down her guard. There would be no pressure to be a wife.

She would use the time wisely. To familiarize herself with the routine. And to get acquainted with these children, who were so self-reliant.

After all, at least part of her dream had already come true. Though she might not be much of a wife to Matthew, she was determined to learn how to be a mother to his children.

Chapter Seven

"Here's their trail. I knew we'd pick it up on this side of the creek." Matt looked up at the sun, just beginning to set on the western horizon. He wiped the bandanna across his face, then pulled himself onto the back of his horse. "We'll follow them until it's too dark to see. Then we'll pick up their trail again in the morning." That was, he realized, the most he'd spoken all day.

He turned to glance at his son, who was slumped in the saddle. "Coming?"

"Yes, sir."

He pulled ahead, leaving Aaron to follow. As they entered a stretch of dense forest, father and son were forced to bend down to avoid low-hanging branches. Occasionally Matt or Aaron would pause to snatch up a handful of horse hair snagged on the bark of a tree. Assured it was from the roan stallion they'd been trailing, they moved on.

Matt knew his son was weary. Except for a meager breakfast of cold meat and biscuits, they hadn't taken time to stop all day. He'd pushed them both to the limit. But he'd needed this time on the trail, away from the constant distraction of ranch chores and children's needs. Needed to clear his mind and think things through.

He was a man of few words. And when he had something on his mind, he preferred to keep his own counsel.

Always play your cards close to your vest, son. He could hear his father's voice even now. *No sense letting others know what you're holding.*

Hell, just what kind of hand was he holding now?

A full house, he figured. A very full house. But not the winning kind.

He'd jumped into this without taking time to think it through. But the truth was, Aaron's remarks about Del had been the deciding factor. Del hadn't had a single break in her young life. Her mother gone. Only her rough, rowdy brothers for friends. A father who was definitely not equipped to raise her to be a young woman. He figured a fine upstanding church lady like Isabella had been heaven-sent.

But he hadn't counted on the fact that she might not want to be a wife in the bargain. He'd been without a wife for a long time now and thought he'd adjusted to doing without. But it was one thing to be alone; it was quite another to have a woman, a living, breathing, flesh-and-blood woman, in his bed and still have to sleep alone. He was going to have to do some heavy thinking and decide if she was worth keeping.

On the one hand, Isabella was a hard worker. He liked that in a woman. She'd jumped right in, washing, sweeping, scrubbing. In no time she'd have that old cabin shining. And she was a damned good cook. He hadn't eaten food that fine in a long time. And she was clean. Another thing in her favor.

But she didn't know a wolf from a grizzly. Couldn't handle a gun. Would probably run like a rabbit at the first sign of trouble. And she was a city woman, who might not adjust well to being so far from civilization.

And she's scared to let me touch her.

There. He'd admitted it. That was the thing that stuck in his craw. If there were a million good things about her, they couldn't weigh in against that.

What the hell good was a wife who held all her affection inside like a miser? Who jumped out of her skin every time he touched her?

"...see anything, Pa. What do you think?"

His head came up sharply. His son had been calling him, but he'd been so engrossed in his thoughts, he'd completely missed the words. "What?"

"I said it's too dark to see anything, Pa. We have to stop and make camp for the night."

"Yes. Of course." He glanced ahead to a stand of trees along the bank of the creek. "That looks like a good spot."

They reined in their mounts, tethering them nearby, and set about making a fire. Soon the tang of roasted meat and the aroma of coffee filled the air.

Father and son lay in their bedrolls, their saddles beneath their heads, eating in silence, sipping hot coffee.

Several times Aaron tried to engage his father in

conversation, but Matt continued to slip into his own thoughts.

Now Aaron cleared his throat. "I noticed something this morning, Pa."

Matt looked over at him.

"You slept in the barn last night. In the stall with old Blue."

Matt took a sip of coffee and held his silence.

"And when we left, you didn't kiss Isabella goodbye."

"I didn't kiss Benjamin or Clement or Del, either."

"No, sir. But...Isabella's different. I mean, she's your bride."

"I'm aware of that. What're you getting at, son?"

Aaron shrugged. "I just think..." He swallowed, weighing his words carefully. He knew his father wouldn't be happy to hear what he had to say. Still, he felt responsible for bringing Isabella into their lives. "You said a man and woman aren't the same as farm animals. You said they need to feel a... sweetener to one another before they get married."

Matt clenched his jaw. He didn't know who was more embarrassed by this conversation—he or Aaron. "I know what I said. Now say your piece."

"I was thinking that since you and Isabella got married so fast, neither of you had time for that sweetener."

"What would you have us do now?" Matt's voice was as tight as his clenched teeth. "Get unmarried?"

"No, sir. But I thought..."

"Get it out, Aaron." Matt tossed the last of his

coffee into the fire, watching the flames hiss and spit before flaring up again. "I'd like to get some peace and quiet soon."

"Yes, sir." Aaron started talking faster. "I thought maybe you ought to court Isabella. With little gifts and nice words. So she'd…fall in love with you. And stay with us." He knew his face was flaming. And from the look on his father's face, he'd said way too much. Lifting his blanket, he hunkered down and wrapped it around himself. "That's all I've got to say. 'Night, Pa."

"'Night." Matt reached into his shirtfront and withdrew the little pouch of tobacco from around his neck. He shook some into a paper and rolled it, then held a match to the tip. For a moment the light flared in the darkness. Then he drew smoke into his lungs and thought about what his son had just said.

Damned fool kid. Thought love could be bought with a couple of trinkets and a few sweet words. If that was the case, the whole world would be courting.

That was all he needed in his already miserable life. A silly ritual called courtship.

With an angry toss of the blankets he slipped out of his bedroll to check on the horses. Then he paced around their campsite, occasionally pausing to draw in smoke and stare up at the darkened sky.

He had no time for such foolishness. And even if he did, he wouldn't be any good at it. Hell, he had a ranch to run. Horses to break. And a family to be taken care of. How much more should a man have to do?

He took a last drag and tossed the stub into the fire.

Then he crawled into his bedroll and drew his hat low over his face.

Damned if he'd waste another minute thinking about Aaron's half-witted suggestion. He wasn't about to try anything as stupid as courtship. Especially with his own wife.

"Aaron, keep them close. Don't let them scatter." In the fading daylight Matt watched as his son wheeled his mount and rounded up a mare that had broken from the herd of mustangs. The boy wielded his rope like a seasoned cowboy, easily snagging the black-and-white beauty and bringing her back into line.

Matt whistled to the hounds and they snapped at the heels of the stragglers, urging them to keep up with his steady pace. He rode in front, keeping a firm grasp on the rope around the roan stallion's neck. As long as he kept their leader moving, the others would follow.

He rolled his shoulders and touched a hand to the scratchy beard. It had been a long week. The stallion had led them on quite a chase. But it had been worth it. The herd numbered more than fifty. And at five dollars apiece, or ten if broken to saddle, he was about to earn a very tidy profit. He'd be able to start the addition to the cabin in the spring. And maybe have enough left over to build a second barn.

As the familiar outline of his cabin came into view, he let out a sigh of pleasure. Smoke curled from the chimney. Soft lantern light glowed in the windows.

He was building something good here. Something

lasting for his children. They could be free here. Free to learn, to grow, to take pride in their accomplishments. Here, far from civilization, the madness of the war that had divided the nation seemed almost forgotten. Here the shame and pain of the past could be put to rest.

Matt's horse, sensing food and shelter at the end of a long journey, broke into a run. The stallion raced alongside. When they reached the corral, Matt swung the gate wide and turned the stallion loose. It reared, pawing the air as the rest of the herd followed suit.

As soon as the last mare was safely inside, Matt closed the gate and secured it. Inside the enclosure, the herd milled about in confusion.

The cabin door was thrown open and the dogs rushed out, barking their welcome. Behind them streamed Benjamin, Clement and Del, and behind the children, Isabella.

"You got them, Pa." The two boys clapped their father on the back.

"We sure did."

"Aaron." Del threw herself into her big brother's arms and he swung her around and around before setting her down. "I missed you."

"I missed you, too, Little Bit." He tousled her hair before releasing her.

The children climbed the rails for a better look at the mustangs.

"Oh, my." Izzy brought her hands to her mouth and gaped at the herd. "I didn't realize they'd be so...beautiful."

Matt didn't know why he felt such pleasure at her

words. "I guess they are beautiful. Sometimes I forget to think about that and just see them as a means to pay the bills."

"That old roan sure is smart, but Pa's smarter." Aaron's voice rang with pride. "He led us on some kind of chase before we caught him."

"Were you in any danger?" Izzy looked fearful.

"Nah. We've chased wild mustangs before." Aaron couldn't help boasting just a little.

"If they're wild," Izzy asked, "how do you get so many of them at one time?"

"Long as Pa had their leader, they'd follow him anywhere." Aaron indicated the roan, who was still rearing up in a gesture of defiance. "I expect those mares would even go through fire for that stallion."

"So you caught their leader. That was very wise of you, Matthew." Izzy moved closer for a better look, and her shoulder brushed Matt's arm.

He absorbed the heat of her touch. Pleasure curled through him, softening his words. "Just lucky. Here, Benjamin." He handed over the reins of his horse to his son. "See that Blue gets an extra portion of oats tonight. And a good rubdown."

His son shot him a look of surprise. "Yes, sir."

Clement took the reins from Aaron's hands and got the same instructions.

Just then Matt's gaze was caught by an extension in the wall of the barn.

"What in the hell is that?"

Izzy winced as the children replied, "Our new chicken coop. Come on, Pa. We'll show you."

"A chicken coop?" Matt strolled closer, and the others followed.

"Isabella said we were losing too many eggs in the barn," Del explained happily. "So we all worked together to lash some logs together to make a lean-to against the side of the barn." The little girl pulled the latch, lifting the small door that allowed the chickens to enter and exit. "See, Pa. We even built a perch, so the hens could roost up there."

"I built the perch myself," Clement said proudly.

"I see." Matt was staring at his children, seeing the pleasure and pride.

"Isabella said I could probably sell some of my eggs at Sutton's Station, Pa. She said my chickens could help pay our bills. Isn't that right, Isabella?"

Izzy nodded. "I don't see why not. After all, everyone has a taste for eggs. And not everyone has a fine big coop for raising chickens. Maybe you could even sell some chicks in town to anyone wanting to start their own flock."

She felt the heat of Matt's gaze focused on her with such intensity she was forced to look away when Benjamin said, "Isabella thinks I could sell my honey in town, too. She said everybody gets a sweet tooth now and then."

"Did she?"

"Yes, sir."

"And Isabella says I could probably sell my pelts, Pa." Clement was fairly twitching with excitement. "She said folks in town would probably pay a lot of money for the chance to make a parka out of mountain cat pelts, or any of the warmer hides that would get them through our cold winters.''

Matt's eyes were narrowed on her. One eyebrow was quirked as he studied her.

''Well.'' Izzy drew the word out, playing for time. She wasn't certain just what that look on Matt's face meant, but she figured she had probably overstepped her bounds. There was something primitive about him. And more than a little dangerous. He looked the way he had when she'd first arrived. Like a wild mountain man, heavily bearded, bundled into a cowhide jacket, his eyes shadowed beneath the brim of his hat. There was no way to tell if he was angry or glad. But the way he was watching her made her more than a little nervous.

She turned toward the cabin to avoid meeting his eyes. ''Benjamin, Clement, do as your father said and see to the horses now. Matthew, Aaron, I'm sure you two will be wanting some supper.''

''Now, that's the best thing I've heard in days, Isabella.'' Aaron dropped an arm around his little sister, and the two followed Izzy to the cabin.

Matt remained at the barn a few minutes longer, staring at the lopsided coop. But it wasn't the sagging building he was seeing. Or the hope and enthusiasm Isabella had planted in his children's minds, though that had clearly impressed him.

It was the sway of her hips as she'd walked away.

Damnation, maybe he'd been on the trail too long. Maybe he was allowing himself to imagine that somehow things had magically changed. That she would emerge from that shell of fear and suddenly open her arms wide to make him welcome. But he hadn't imagined that touch. Or the admiration in her tone.

Or the pains she'd taken to impress him.

Maybe after supper he'd take a long, leisurely bath. And shave off his beard. And sleep in his own bed. With his wife.

He started toward the cabin, whistling a little tune.

"I've been thinking about these biscuits a long time." Aaron mopped up the gravy on his plate, then reached for yet another biscuit. "Haven't you, Pa?"

Matt nodded and ate in silence.

While they ate, Benjamin, Clement and Del sat at the table, listening to Aaron's account of the past week.

"I guess we traveled fifteen, maybe twenty miles a day." Aaron paused, chewed, swallowed.

"Where'd you sleep?" Clement asked.

"Near a creek one night. On a rock ledge another. We seemed to be heading higher every day. I think our old stallion Red wanted to get his mares high up in the mountains where they'd be safe till spring."

"I bet you were cold," Del said.

"Nah." Aaron took his role as hero to his little sister seriously. He wouldn't admit to being cold if his feet froze off. "We had our bedrolls. And we slept close to the fire."

"Don't you ever get lost?" Izzy stood at the fireplace, turning potatoes in a blackened skillet, stirring dumplings in a pot of stew.

"Not with Pa along. He knows these mountains better'n anyone. Don't you, Pa?"

Matt barely nodded as he continued eating. It was taking all his willpower to keep from staring at his wife's hips as she moved around the fire.

Izzy turned. "Do you have room for seconds?"

"Yes'm." Aaron held out his plate and she ladled more food.

"Matthew?"

He held out his plate.

After emptying the kettle, she wrapped a towel around the handle of the battered coffeepot and lifted it from the fire. Matt breathed in the soft woman scent of her while she paused beside him to fill his cup.

Across the table Aaron sipped his milk. "How'd you get this so cold?"

Benjamin spoke up. "Isabella lowered a crock of milk down in the well. She said that keeps it from curdling."

"That's really smart, isn't it, Pa?" Aaron wiped his upper lip. "I wonder why we didn't think of that."

"It's nothing." Izzy lifted the crock and poured another glass for him. "Folks in Pennsylvania have been doing that during the heat of summer for years."

"I still think it's real smart of you, Isabella. Isn't it, Pa?"

Matt gave a sigh of impatience. The boy was as transparent as that window, which was cleaner than he'd ever seen before. It was obvious that Aaron was trying his darnedest to get his father to mouth some silly words of praise.

Ignoring the pointed question, he shoved back his chair and got to his feet. "That was a fine meal, Isabella.'' He saw her flush with pleasure. "Now, if you don't mind, I'll check on the mustangs. Then I'd like a bath before I turn in." He shot a meaningful glance at his children. "It's been a long week. Aaron and I need our rest."

Before he had time to pull on his jacket and hat, Aaron was herding his brothers and sister up the ladder to the loft.

Izzy deposited the dishes in a pan of hot water and proceeded to wash and dry them. Then she filled the kettle with water and placed it on the fire.

By the time Matt returned from the barn, a tub of warm water had been set in front of the fire. On a chair beside it was a glob of lye soap and several thick towels, as well as his straight razor.

A slow smile began to spread across his face as he glanced at the closed door of the bedroom, then at the tub of water. Isabella was certainly making every effort to accommodate him.

He stripped off his shirt and lathered his face, then shaved away the heavy growth of beard. Then he nudged off his boots, peeled away the rest of his clothes and sank gratefully into the tub.

He wanted to wash slowly, to take his time and enjoy this rare luxury. But the thought of what was awaiting him in the other room had him hurrying. He soaped himself, then worked his hair into a lather and ducked beneath the water. When he came up for air, he stood, the water sheeting off him as he reached for a towel. Minutes later he had the towel tied around his waist and was striding purposefully toward the bedroom.

Izzy lay in the bed, her heart thumping, her palms sweating. She'd had an entire week to prepare for this moment. If sheer determination was enough, she was bound to succeed.

She had taken the time to wash herself and even to apply a drop of the precious rose water she had brought from Pennsylvania. Her night shift had been freshly washed, her hair brushed until it crackled.

She had coaxed stories from the children, learning all she could about Matthew Prescott. And though they couldn't or wouldn't offer much in the way of family history, she had heard the love and respect in their voices when they spoke of their father. It was Benjamin who had told of the time Matthew had once turned back to town when he was better than halfway home, because he'd discovered that Webster Sutton had given him back too much money after paying for his supplies.

"But why didn't he just wait and return the money the next time he went to town?" she asked.

"Because," Benjamin said solemnly, "Pa knew that Mr. Sutton doesn't have much. And that money might leave him unable to pay his bills when he needed more supplies."

It was Clement who told her of the time that Matt, despite his dislike of towns and people, had once risked his own life to search for a hunting party trapped in an early autumn blizzard atop the mountain.

"Nobody knows these mountains like our pa," Clement said proudly. "But when they tried to pay him, Pa refused. He said kindness doesn't have a price.''

Not only a good and honest man, but a noble one, as well, it would seem.

Izzy fought to still the tremors that snaked along her spine.

She hoped he lived up to his reputation, because tonight she was going to let Matthew Prescott, the good, honest, noble mountain man, have his way with her. If it killed her.

Chapter Eight

Matt stepped into the room and closed the door. For a moment he stood still, allowing his eyes to adjust to the dim light. The lantern had been extinguished, but there was enough moonlight spilling through the window to let him see quite clearly.

The room had been scrubbed to a high shine. It smelled of lye soap and…roses. He could swear he smelled roses.

His clothes were hung in a neat row on pegs along one wall. Instead of the rough, scratchy wood floor, his bare feet encountered the softness of a rug. The worn coverlet on the bed had been patched and mended until it resembled a brand-new spread. And lying under the spread was his wife, watching him with eyes that seemed too big for her face.

"Looks like you were busy while I was gone."

"I hope you don't mind."

"Now, how could I mind this?" He spread his hands. "I've never seen the place so clean."

Izzy should have felt a glow of pride. But she was too busy watching the way the towel at his hips slipped a notch, revealing the flat planes of his stomach, and below, a whorl of dark hair.

"I'm glad you found your mustangs, Matthew."

"So am I." He ran a hand over the stack of clean clothes she had laid out for him for the morning. Sturdy pants, a soft woolen shirt, his spare boots, polished to a bright sheen. "When the army buys them from me, I'll have enough to add on to the cabin. I'm even thinking about building a second barn."

"That's wonderful. How long will it take you to tame the horses, Matthew?"

He chuckled as he sat down on the edge of the bed.

"What's so funny?" She sat up straighter, revealing a prim and proper night shift buttoned clear to her throat. "Is it something I did?"

He shook his head. "It's hearing you call me Matthew. The only other person who ever called me that was my mother."

"I'm sorry."

"No." He reached out a hand to her and felt her stiffen. At once he withdrew his, determined this time to move slowly, to do everything right. "I don't mind. Really. In fact, I like it."

"You do?"

He nodded and busied himself running his finger across the quilt to keep from touching the curl that dipped seductively over her eye. "This bedcover looks as good as new."

"I just patched the holes."

"You work fast." He stilled his movements and waited, hoping she would touch his hand.

"It gave me something to do each evening after

supper.'' He was so still, so watchful it was disconcerting. She was so aware of him. Of his near nakedness. Of the clean, soapy scent of him. Of the wide, muscled shoulders, the hair-roughened chest.

She cleared her throat. "You never told me how long it will take you to tame the mustangs."

"I won't really tame them. I'll just break them to saddle." The rose fragrance was stronger here and he realized it came from her skin. He yearned to lean close and breathe it in. He could imagine it, beside her ear, along her throat, between her breasts. The thought of it was driving him mad.

"Break them?" She shivered. "That sounds so... cruel. As though you would beat them until their spirit is broken."

"It's not that way at all." He spread a hand over a mound in the coverlet, knowing her thigh was just beneath. He saw her eyes widen for a fraction before she caught herself. "But they're wild creatures, Isabella. They need to get accustomed to being around people and carrying them on their backs. I guess it's really a matter of trust, between man and animal."

Trust. How she wished she had a little of that right now.

"You don't—" her eyes were wide with fear "—beat them into submission?"

"Of course not." He fought to keep the impatience from his tone, reminding himself that she was a city woman. And as skittish as a colt. "Maybe you'd like to come out to the corral once in a while and see for yourself."

"I don't know." The fear was still there, but he

could see that she was considering his invitation. "The children told me it's quite dangerous. That you've often been thrown from wild horses."

He smiled, and she noticed the way his eyes crinkled at the corners. "I've been thrown too many times to count. And believe me, every time it happens, it hurts. I have the bruises to prove it."

"Then why do you keep doing it?"

"Because it pays the bills. Selling mustangs to the army allows me to live here and raise my children the way I choose."

At the mention of his children, her eyes softened. "They're fine children, Matthew."

His smile grew. "Yes, they are. And I'm grateful that you were willing to come all this way just to help me raise them. Now—" he shifted, leaning toward her "—I'm starting to get chilled. If you don't mind, I'd like to climb under the covers."

She had expected him to walk around to the other side of the bed. Instead he stood and casually discarded his towel. She knew she had the right to look at him. They were, after all, husband and wife. But she couldn't. She simply couldn't allow herself to look. And so she turned her head, averting her gaze, until the mattress sagged beneath him.

As he settled himself beside her, his foot brushed hers. She was instantly frozen in shock. All these long days and nights hadn't prepared her for this. She had thought she could bury her fears and give him what he craved. But the thought of lying next to a naked man, who expected her to give herself to him for his pleasure, had her trembling.

"Isabella." He rolled to his side and caught her by the shoulder.

Warning herself not to flinch, she lay, stiff, unmoving, waiting for whatever would come next.

As soon as he touched her, Matt could feel the tremors that rocked her. He cautioned himself against rushing her. This time he was determined to break through the wall she had built. This time he would coax her to relax and savor the pleasure they could bring to each other.

"Isabella, I just want to kiss you." He drew her close and brushed her mouth with his. She kept her lips pressed firmly together. Even when his tongue traced the outline of her mouth, then slowly parted her lips, she kept her teeth clamped so tightly it was impossible to break through.

And so he settled for pressing soft, moist kisses over her temple, her cheek, the tip of her nose.

That had her relaxing, and even smiling, until he traced the curve of her ear with his tongue, then darted it inside. A series of shock waves jolted through her system. She pressed her hands to his chest. But before she could push away, he wrapped her in his arms and drew her close while he continued to kiss her jaw, her throat and the sensitive little hollow between her neck and shoulder.

Izzy had been prepared to feel disgust or revulsion. Or, with luck, perhaps nothing at all. But she was completely unprepared for the tiny thread of pleasure that curled along her spine. And the swift, unsettling rush of heat when the hard contours of his body pressed into her softness.

"Can't you kiss me back, Isabella?" His warm breath fanned her face, adding to her discomfort.

"I can't."

"Why?"

"I...don't know how." It shamed her to admit such a thing. She could feel the heat staining her cheeks as she waited for him to mock her. How he must be secretly laughing at her admission.

Instead, he said simply, "Then I'll show you. First, you do this." He touched his mouth to hers in the sweetest of kisses. He felt her go rigid with shock. At once his voice took on a soothing note as he murmured against her lips, "And then you do this." Easing his hands along her sides, he forced her arms upward until they were twined around his neck. "Now," he muttered against her mouth, "you're holding me the same way I'm holding you. How does it feel so far?"

"Fi—fine." The word was barely a whisper. It was all she could manage, because her throat was so constricted. His mouth was actually touching hers. Now that they were facing each other, their bodies touching, she could feel him in every part of her. Her thin night shift was no barrier.

She lay perfectly still, afraid to move, afraid even to breathe.

"Now, Isabella," he said softly, "you touch your lips to mine."

He saw her eyes widen, before she pursed her lips and screwed up her courage. He half smiled as her mouth brushed his and her lashes fluttered, then closed. But his smile fled at the sudden jolt to his system.

He hadn't expected such a reaction. This innocent little kiss of hers was far more potent than anything he'd anticipated.

"Now, this is what we call kissing. It isn't so bad, is it?" Before she could pull back he took the kiss deeper and heard her little moan. Pleasure? Or protest? There was no way to know as he gathered her close and kissed her until they were both breathless. Then, before she knew what was happening, he ran his hands down her sides until they encountered the swell of her breasts. She gasped as his thumbs began to stroke.

"Sweet salvation." It was all she could manage to say over the sudden wave of intense pleasure that nearly swamped her. Her body was behaving in the most unnatural way. Her breasts tingled and seemed to swell with each stroke. Deep inside she felt a fist tighten and then relax into a liquid warmth. Her nerves were coiled as tautly as bowstrings, and she felt that at any moment she might snap.

And still he moved against her, his body brushing hers, adding to her pleasure. And her confusion.

Suddenly she became aware of his arousal. Her gasps turned to a muffled cry. "Oh, stop. You must stop." Gathering all her strength, she pushed away.

Matt ran a hand through his hair in frustration. His own breathing was none too steady. And his heart was racing as though he'd just outrun a rampaging steer. "What's wrong with you, Isabella? You liked it. I could tell."

His words made her flush with shame. It was true. She had liked it. And that was what was so frightening. This mating wasn't supposed to be pleasurable. At least, she didn't think so.

"I suppose…" She avoided his eyes. "I suppose I liked it well enough."

"Then why did you want to stop?"

"Because I can't think when you're…when we're…doing that." How could she possibly defend herself if she let herself get lost in the pleasure? She needed a clear head to think this through. And she couldn't think when he was holding her, touching her, kissing her.

"Why do you need to think? I thought by now you had learned to trust me."

"I do. I trust you." Even her voice was different, the words breathy, halting. She hated the way she sounded. Weak. Silly. Like those women who said one thing but meant another. Oh, she'd watched them, teasing, flirting, pressing their bodies against the men, then pretending to be offended when the men responded.

"This doesn't feel like trust." He touched a hand to her cheek and felt her flinch.

After all this, they were back where they'd started.

His tone hardened. "I'm not going to hurt you, Isabella."

"I know."

"That's funny. You don't act as though you know that." His eyes narrowed. "Who hurt you like this?"

She closed her eyes, wishing he would remove the offending hand, yet praying he wouldn't. There was something about his touch. Something that was different from all the others who had ever touched her. But how could she possibly admit such a thing to him?

He waited for the space of several heartbeats. He tried to keep the edge from his tone. "Are you going to answer me?"

She squeezed her eyes tightly shut, as though to blot out the memories. But they were there, even in the darkest corners of her mind, taunting her, haunting her, hurting her still.

"I…can't."

"Can't?" His words were rough with anger and frustration. "Or won't?"

She refused to open her eyes. She couldn't bear to see the disgust in his.

"I had hoped this time apart would change things." With quick, angry movements he tossed aside the blanket and scrambled out of bed. He wasn't sure what angered him more—her rejection, or the fact that, even knowing how she felt, he was still aroused. And about to be denied once again. "But I see now I was wrong. You didn't really come here to be a wife and mother. You just wanted a place to hide."

He stepped into the clean pants, then yanked on his boots. Without even bothering to button his shirt, he strode across the room. "I suppose the best thing for both of us would be to send Aaron to town in the morning with a message for Webster Sutton."

"A…message?"

"For old Boone. The next time he comes to town,

he can drive his stage out here to pick you up and take you back to wherever you came from. It seems the only fair thing to do."

Thoroughly shaken, Izzy lay stiff, unmoving, unable to say a word in her own defense.

He flicked a glance over her, then away, mistaking her silence for approval. "I guess that's that, then. In the meantime, I'll have to content myself with sleeping in the barn."

With his words ringing in her ears, Izzy heard the door slam. Heard the crunch of his footsteps as he stalked away.

One tiny tear slipped from between her tightly closed lids. She wiped it away and buried her face in the pillow. She had no right to weep. She had brought this on herself. She had risked everything on this journey, thinking she could leave the darkness of her past behind and create a whole new life for herself. But there were simply too many memories. She hadn't escaped them after all. They were locked inside her mind. And every time she tried to forget, they leapt out at her, paralyzing her with fear.

And now, her new husband was feeling cheated. He had every right to such feelings. He'd thought he was taking a wife. But all he'd earned in the bargain was another mouth to feed. Oh, he'd gained a cook and housekeeper, and someone to help with his children. But he was still being denied a wife.

She'd tried to do her wifely duty. God knows she'd tried. And she had really thought she could go through with it. Especially when it felt so good to be held in his arms. And kissed. And touched.

But the fear was stronger, blotting out the pleasure, bringing back all the old memories, until she thought she would suffocate beneath their weight.

And now he was sending her away.

That's what she got for pretending to be something she wasn't. When she took off the mask at day's end, Isabella became just plain Izzy all over again.

Matt stood hunched inside his cowhide jacket, watching the mustangs. After the week he'd put in, he ought to sleep for the next ten hours or more, even if it was in the barn. Instead, he was too keyed up to even go inside and lie down.

How could he have been such a fool? He'd actually convinced himself that Isabella had been flirting with him. He'd fooled himself into believing that he'd read invitation in her eyes.

And all the while, it had been fear.

He rolled a cigarette, held a match to the tip, then leaned on the railing. Damn the fates that had brought her here. Didn't he already have enough to deal with? The last thing he needed was another problem.

He wasn't thrilled about the idea of sending her away. Not just because of the money it would take. Money he could ill afford. But also because of this niggling little guilt that was beginning to eat at him. Was her silence acquiescence? Or had he misread her?

She'd traveled so far, uprooting herself from family and friends to answer a stranger's needs. She'd risked everything safe and familiar to step into the role of wife and mother. And she had told him that there was nothing left to return to.

Still, what was that to him? After all, he hadn't invited her here in the first place. In light of this impasse between them, it would be foolish to try to hold her to her vows. After all, what future could they have together?

Of course, there were the children. If she couldn't be a wife to him, at least she could be a mother to them. He could see that Aaron, Benjamin, Clement and Del had already taken to her. They were easy and comfortable with her, and she with them. If only she could be as comfortable with him. But theirs was a far different problem. One he didn't wish to dwell upon, since it was such a blow to his masculine pride.

The children, though, were another matter. They would be disappointed. They would want to know why he was sending her away. And he'd never be able to explain.

Aaron would know why.

The thought crept unbidden into his mind. Aaron and his uncanny ability to watch, to observe, to see what others couldn't see. Aaron had already noted the tension between them. And had even come up with a solution.

Aaron and his silly notion of courtship. Trinkets and pretty words.

As Matt watched, the stallion began threading its way through the milling throng of mares. When one began sidestepping nervously, the stallion whickered low in his throat. The mare's head came up, and the stallion nuzzled her, as gently as a kiss, until she became perfectly calm.

Matt found himself shivering at the tenderness of the scene. Did all of nature's creatures have this need for tenderness? For trust?

An odd little thought began to take shape in his mind. Could it be that Aaron's notions weren't so silly after all?

What would it take to court a woman like Isabella? Gifts. She needed another dress. The one she had was threadbare. She had to wash it every night, so that it would be clean for the next day. But he didn't feel he had the right to waste needed money on something so frivolous as a woman's dress. He'd suffered enough guilt just buying her candy.

He smiled at the memory of her face, flushed with surprise and pleasure, when he'd handed her the peppermint stick. It had been worth the price.

He fisted a hand at his side. Who was he kidding? Hell, he couldn't afford gifts.

Still, flowers, perhaps. Some still bloomed in the lower meadows, where the cold hadn't yet reached. But he couldn't spare the time it would take to search them out. Not if he intended to break this entire herd to saddle as quickly as possible.

He found himself thinking of other things he might do. Something special to cook? She loved cooking for them. Maybe an elk. But that meant spending time away from home, tracking, stalking, killing and skinning.

His frustration grew. Why was he wasting his energy on such nonsense? He just didn't have time for this. How could he possibly court a woman? He barely had time for his family now. How could he justify anything more?

He took a final drag on his cigarette, then dropped it and ground it out beneath his boot.

No matter what Aaron or the others thought, it would be best if he sent her away now, before she insinuated herself more deeply into their lives.

In the morning he would dispatch Aaron to town with a message for old Boone to swing by the next time he was in the area.

The decision did nothing to satisfy the restlessness she'd stirred in his loins. In fact, the decision brought him no comfort at all. And a great deal more guilt.

Chapter Nine

"Better keep away from Pa today."

Izzy looked up from the fire when she heard Benjamin's whispered command to his brother and sister.

"He's mad as a hornet about something." Benjamin turned to his little sister. "You do something to rile him, Del?"

"Not me. Maybe it was Clement."

The younger boy shook his head in denial. "It wasn't anything I did. Pa's been grouchy since early this morning." Clement pulled on his parka, prepared to start his chores. "I saw him coming out of the barn just about sunup, and he looked mad enough to wrestle a bear. Pa didn't even give Aaron a chance to eat breakfast before sending him to town with a note for Mr. Sutton." He turned to Izzy. "You know anything about that, Isabella?"

Izzy felt her cheeks burn and turned away, avoiding his eyes. "Maybe he needs some supplies."

"Maybe." Benjamin eyed the last biscuit, then decided he'd lost his appetite. His father hadn't even come inside for breakfast, choosing instead to get right to work. Not a very hopeful sign. "Guess I'll go out to the corral and see how Pa's doing with those mustangs."

"I'll come with you." Del reached for her sheep-skin jacket, but her older brother shook his head.

"I think you'd better stay in here with Isabella."

"Why?"

"Pa said it's time you learned how to do lady things. Like cook and clean and stuff."

"I don't want to do lady things. I want to go with you."

"Fine, then." Benjamin slammed out of the cabin, with Del in tow. "But don't blame me if Pa jumps all over you for something."

"It won't be the first time." The little girl's words trailed behind her as she struggled to keep up with her brother's strides. "But I don't know why he's so grumpy now that Isabella's here. I thought Aaron said she was going to make Pa smile again."

Izzy's heart lurched. As she added lye soap to the tub of hot water and began to scrub Matt's dirty clothes on the washboard, she berated herself for the mess she'd made of things. It seemed to be the story of her life. When was she ever going to learn to ac-cept her limitations? Look at her, trying to act as though she belonged. Trying to make herself into a fancy lady.

She tossed the clothes into a bucket of clean hot water and stirred them around until they were thor-oughly rinsed. Then she hauled a basket of clothes outside and began to hang them on the line.

She glanced toward the corral, where the children

were whooping and shouting. Every so often she could see a horse rear up, and see Matt's body jerking and lurching as he stuck in the saddle and held to the reins.

What he was doing looked barbaric. What kind of man lived in the wilderness and rode wild horses?

As she had so often since her arrival, she wondered what had ever possessed her to come to this godforsaken place and pledge herself to a man like that. He might try to pass himself off as a simple farmer, but he was far different from any farmer she'd ever known. There was something wild and dark about Matthew Prescott.

Still, he had been patient with her last night. More patient than she had a right to expect. Maybe, if she worked very hard, and did everything as perfectly as possible, she could make up for it.

When the last of the clothes flapped on the line, she drew her shawl around her shoulders and hurried inside, determined to find a way to make amends.

The fireplace gleamed. Izzy had polished the stones until every trace of soot and smoke had been erased. Now, as late afternoon sunbeams streamed through the windows, they shot little rainbow prisms across the ceiling.

A venison roast simmered in a skillet. Several loaves of freshly baked bread sat cooling on the table. The cabin was sweet with the fragrance of apple slices swimming in brown sugar and cinnamon.

Izzy placed a clean towel over a mound of biscuit

dough she'd set aside to rise. Then she made her way
outside to fetch the dry clothes from the line.

The shouts and hoots of laughter from the corral
snagged her attention. She glanced at the three children seated on the top wrung. There was no sign of
Matt.

Curious, she made her way across the yard and
peered through the rails. Matt was just picking himself up from the dirt. When he saw her, his frown
deepened. He stared at her for the space of several
seconds. Then, limping, he snatched up his hat and
jammed it back on his head before crossing to where
a spotted mustang stood eyeing him.

"Think you've won, don't you?"

At his angry words Izzy pressed her hands to her
throat. Had he directed those words to the horse? Or
to her?

He heaved himself into the saddle, and the horse
reared up, pawing the air.

When that tactic didn't manage to dislodge the
weight on its back, the mare sped around the corral,
bucking and kicking.

From her vantage point Izzy watched in amazement
as Matt's body underwent a series of contortions.
Shoulders hunched, head snapped, back arched. How
could any person take such punishment? Still, he
managed to remain in the saddle. And as the minutes
ticked by and finally stretched into an hour, the
horse's reactions became less violent. Except for an
occasional rebellious toss of the head, the mustang
seemed to accept the stranger on its back, and even
to respond to his directions. Slowly, gradually, horse

and rider began to move around the corral in some semblance of rhythm.

Izzy watched as Matt methodically put the horse through its paces, walking, trotting, running, then coming to a halt before he slid from the saddle.

He ran a hand through the tangled mane and kept his voice low, soothing. "You did just fine. But then I'm not surprised. That was all just bluster and show to cover up how scared you really were. No need to be afraid anymore. You're going to be well taken care of."

He took hold of the bridle. In slow, limping strides he led the mare to the gate. His face, his clothes were streaked with sweat and grime. He looked for all the world as though he'd been through a war. And lost.

"Here, Benjamin. Unsaddle her and rub her down before you turn her into a stall."

"Yes, sir."

"How many does that make today, Pa?" Clement asked.

"Five." He shook his hat against his knee, sending up a cloud of dust. Then he wiped his sleeve across his forehead in a weary gesture. "Ought to be able to break the whole team inside of a couple of weeks."

Izzy shuddered at the thought of how much abuse he would be forced to endure before this was over.

"You through for the day, Pa?" Del climbed down from her perch on the railing and walked along beside him.

"Yep. Don't think I can take much more punishment." He glanced up as he brushed past Izzy. "Hope you got a heap of food ready. I'm one hungry man."

Despite the fact that his tone had been completely impersonal, she felt a little thrill of excitement. It was the first time he'd spoken to her all day. "I'll get it on the table right away."

"Don't rush." He paused beside a watering trough. "I'll need a few minutes to wash up here first."

As she gathered the clothes off the line, she paused to watch him plunge his arms into the trough and splash water over his face. Before long the children had joined in, imitating their father. When he ducked his head underwater, they did the same, laughing as they came up for air.

Izzy hurried over with clean towels. Too late, she realized Matt had removed his shirt and was busy splashing water over his chest. When she handed him a towel, she struggled not to stare.

"Thank you," he said formally.

"You're welcome." She knew her words sounded stiff and stilted, but she couldn't help herself. The wall between them was growing higher and wider by the minute.

"I'll…get supper now." She turned away and hurried to the cabin.

In the bedroom she folded clothes, laying aside clean pants and shirt for Matt. Then she made her way to the kitchen. While she went about setting the table, slicing bread, carving the roast, she agonized over this latest change in Matt's mood. She almost preferred his anger to this polite formality.

The stage might not come this way for months. How could she possibly endure his disdain for so long? In fact, how would she manage to get through an entire meal in Matt's presence?

"Mmm. Something smells good." Del opened the door to the cabin and the dogs raced inside, sniffing at the table, at the skillet.

Out of the corner of her eye, Izzy watched Matt walk into the bedroom. The door closed. Minutes later, wearing clean clothes, he made his way to the table. The children were already seated, their hair slicked back, faces shiny.

They looked up at the sound of hoofbeats.

"Aaron." Del let out a screech and raced outside, the dogs hot on her heels.

"Benjamin," Matt said quietly, "right after supper I want you to rub down old Blue and turn him into his stall. I expect he and Aaron have both put in a hard day."

"Yes, sir." The boy's grin brightened when his older brother strode through the open doorway.

As always, Del was walking in his shadow.

"You made good time, boy."

"Yes, sir. Pushed it a bit. Blue and I were both hungry."

As he took his place at the table, Matt asked, "You delivered my message?"

"Yes, sir." Aaron avoided Izzy's eyes. Though his father hadn't told him what the message was, he figured it had something to do with her. And not something good, since he'd seen his father emerging from the barn before dawn. He didn't have to know much about men and women to figure out that whatever was wrong between them wasn't getting better. "Mr. Sutton said old Boone's out on a long run. But when he gets back in town, he'll do as you asked.''

Izzy closed her eyes a moment against the pain.

"This sure looks good, Isabella." Aaron helped himself to a slab of venison and passed the platter to his father.

"This bread is still warm, Pa." Del slathered on freshly churned butter and took a big bite, then decided to take a second piece before passing the rest to her brothers.

Clement wrinkled his nose at the plate of vegetables. "I don't like turnips."

Aaron took a taste, smiled. "Well, you'll like these. What'd you do to them, Isabella?"

"Just mashed them. With a little butter, onion and potato."

Clement took a tiny taste, then spooned more onto his plate. "Guess I could eat a little."

Izzy sliced the fat off the roast and mixed it with other scraps to entice the dogs away from the table. As she set a pan outside the door they began leaping over one another to get to the food. When they were all outside happily eating, she closed the door, effectively shutting out the commotion.

At the head of the table, Matt ate in silence. Maybe it was just hunger that made everything taste so good. But even after he was full, he managed to eat one more slice of tender venison and one more piece of bread that melted in his mouth. He found himself wondering if the food tasted so good because of that other hunger that was gnawing at him.

"There was an army captain in town, Pa." Aaron

drained a glass of milk, then helped himself to another. "I told him about the mustangs. He said he'd send some soldiers out to fetch them next week."

"Next week? Didn't you tell him how many we had to break?"

"Yes, sir. But he said they're in a big hurry. Got new recruits from the East and need mounts right away."

Matt passed a weary hand over his eyes. "I'd hoped to handle the herd by myself. Looks like you're going to get your chance to break mustangs, Aaron."

"You mean it?" The boy's eyes lit with pleasure.

"How about me, Pa?" Benjamin cried. "I'm only two years younger'n Aaron."

"I know, boy. And your day will come. But I'd just as soon spare you the bruises for a little while yet."

"I don't mind a few bruises, Pa. And I'm nearly as good a horseman as Aaron."

"That you are. But you and Clement and Del are going to have to pick up my chores and Aaron's for the next week. I think you'll have more than enough to handle."

"But..."

Izzy touched a hand to Benjamin's shoulder to silence him. She could see the weariness in his father's eyes. The last thing she needed was to have Matthew and Benjamin engaged in a battle of words. "Benjamin, I made something to fill your sweet tooth. Cinnamon biscuits. And apple slices in cinnamon with sweet cream."

Whatever protest he'd been about to make was forgotten as she served the dessert. The biscuits were so tender they melted in the mouth. And the apple slices warming over the fire were smothered in mounds of whipped, sweetened cream.

Nobody said a word until their bowls were empty.

''Isabella.'' Aaron downed a third glass of milk and wiped his mouth on his sleeve. ''That was the best meal I've ever tasted.''

She blushed as she paused beside Matt and filled his cup with hot coffee. ''That's just hunger talking.''

''No, ma'am. I was just being honest. I've never tasted cooking as good as yours.''

She could feel Matt's gaze, steady and probing. Her movements were awkward as she returned the coffee-pot to the fire.

''Del.'' Matt's tone was stern. ''You'll help Isabella clear the table and wash the dishes.''

''Yes, sir.'' The little girl cast a longing glance at her father and older brother as they made their way across the room and sank down on chairs in front of the fire.

''Benjamin, you'll see to Blue now. And, Clement, give your brother a hand and check the mustangs before you come in.''

''Yes, sir.'' The two boys pulled on their parkas and headed outside. The hounds set up a chorus of yapping as they joined them.

Izzy filled a pan with hot, soapy water and began to wash. Beside her, Del dried. And sulked.

To distract her Izzy said, ''I'm making you a dress, Del. A pink one, out of some old scraps I found in the loft.''

"Don't know why you'd bother. I'd just as soon wear Clement's castoffs."

Izzy shrugged. "I'll go ahead and finish it. In case you ever decide you want to dress like a girl." To change the subject she asked, "Do you know the letters of the alphabet?"

"'Course I do." She recited the letters in a sing-song voice. "See? Pa teached me."

"Your pa taught you."

"Yes'm. That's what I said."

"And he taught you well." Izzy smiled. "Did he teach you to read and write, too?"

"Some. I can do my name." Eager to show off, she began spelling her name, and then Aaron's, Benjamin's and Clement's. "But I'm not very good with words I haven't seen before."

"Then maybe we can work on some new words." Izzy began with simple words like *cabin, table* and *dishes,* and was surprised at how quickly the little girl was able to absorb knowledge. "How about sums, Del?"

The little girl shook her head. "Pa explained about adding and subtracting. But I just don't see the need for all that other stuff."

Benjamin and Clement, who had returned from the barn, hung their parkas by the door and joined in the conversation.

"You mean like the multiplication tables?" Benjamin didn't bother to hide the note of derision in his tone.

"And division?" Clement made a face.

Del nodded.

''Never could figure them out. But it doesn't matter. We'll never need to know those things anyway,'' Benjamin said importantly.

Izzy dried her hands and hung the linen square over the back of a chair. ''You won't? Let's see now.'' She thought a moment, then said, ''What if your herd numbers fifty horses, and the army says they'll pay you a hundred dollars? Does that sound like a fair price?''

The children turned to their father, but Matt was watching and listening with absolutely no expression. They realized they would get no help from him.

They began arguing among themselves.

''A hundred dollars is a lot of money,'' Del said.

''Uh-huh.'' Clement was trying to count on his fingers. ''Pa said mustangs were worth five dollars a head wild, and ten dollars a head when they're saddle-broke.''

''Then a hundred's not enough.'' Benjamin, who had done some figuring of his own, was hopelessly lost.

Izzy nodded. ''You're right. How much more would you ask?''

''I'd want at least...fifty dollars more,'' he said with importance.

''That's still not enough. Let me show you something.'' Izzy plucked a slate from a shelf over the fireplace and knelt on the floor. The children formed a circle around her.

Aaron, caught up in the excitement of the discussion, joined them.

''You have fifty mustangs, worth five dollars a

head.'' She wrote the numbers, then showed them
how to figure. ''That means your herd is worth two
hundred fifty dollars, before you even break them to
saddle. Now, once they're tamed, they're worth even
more. At ten dollars a head, they'll bring you five
hundred dollars.''

''Five hundred.'' Aaron shot his father a look of
amazement. ''Is Isabella right, Pa? Is that what the
army is paying?''

Matt nodded.

The children were clearly impressed with Isabella's
lesson.

''What else can you do with those numbers?'' Benjamin asked.

''Just ask me some questions, and I'll show you
how to find the answers.''

For nearly an hour the children shouted numbers
and watched as Izzy scratched out sums on the slate.
After each one, she would hand over the slate to one
of the children and guide them through the maze until
they were able to arrive at the same conclusion.

Finally she glanced at Del. The little girl had rested
her head on her hands. Her eyes were closed, her
breathing slow and even.

''I think we've done enough for tonight. Tomorrow
is going to be another long day. Especially for you,
Aaron.''

The boy nodded. ''Thanks, Isabella. Good night.''
He tapped his little sister on the shoulder and she
barely stirred. With a grin he lifted her into his arms.
''Looks like I'll have to tuck her in.'' He turned to

his father, who was still sitting by the fire. "'Night, Pa."

"Good night, son."

Aaron led the way up the ladder to the loft, his little sister held gently in his arms. Benjamin and Clement followed.

As soon as the children were gone, Isabella felt the first stirrings of panic. The thought of being alone with Matthew had her heart suddenly racing, her breath coming in short bursts.

She could feel him watching her as she reached up to the shelf to put away the slate. She had a sudden urge to smooth down her skirt, to brush her hair from her eyes. Instead, she kept her arms stiffly at her sides and turned.

"Oh." Finding him standing directly behind her, she jumped back a step before she composed herself and stood perfectly still.

"That was a nice thing you did, Isabella. I don't believe I've ever before seen my children so interested in learning."

"It wasn't anyth—I just—" She hated the fact that she was babbling. But he was so close. And he was staring at her with such intensity she had to look away. She clasped her hands tightly in front of her, determined to clamp down on her emotions. "I enjoyed it, too. They have bright, curious minds."

She was startled when he touched a hand to her chin, forcing her to meet his gaze. The mere touch of him had the blood pounding in her temples.

"I don't know what to make of you, Isabella."

For the space of several seconds he studied her,

and she felt certain he wanted to kiss her. Just the thought of it had her limbs growing weak. And though she tried to deny it, she knew she wanted him to. Wanted desperately to feel his mouth on hers. Wanted to be crushed in his arms and kissed until she was dazed and breathless.

Sweet salvation. Could he read it in her eyes? Could he tell, just by looking at her, that her bones were melting and her skin flushed? She actually swayed toward him. But in that same instant, he took a step back, releasing her.

For a moment she was too stunned to react. Then, fighting a wave of bitter disappointment, she forced herself to move. Very deliberately she lifted a lantern from the shelf. Her hands, she noted, were shaking.

She prayed her legs wouldn't betray her as she headed for the bedroom.

At the door she paused. "Good night, Matthew."

He didn't look at her. It was too painful, stirring something that was better left alone. He kept his tone deliberately bland. "Good night."

When the door closed behind her, he rolled a cigarette and held a match to the tip, inhaling deeply. He stared into the fire, watching the flames dance. But it was Isabella he was seeing. Sitting on the floor, surrounded by his children. Hardly more than a child herself, with her hair mussed, her cheeks flushed, her eyes dancing with some inner light. When she was with his children she forgot to be afraid. The self-consciousness slipped away. In its place was sweetness, goodness, lighthearted laughter.

With no effort at all she had coaxed them to learn.

Had understood their need to know the why and how of things. Had fed that hunger in their souls.

Maybe he had acted in haste. Maybe she deserved another chance. Not for himself, of course. For the sake of his children.

He tossed the last of his cigarette into the fire and strode across the room. The sudden movement reminded him that every bone in his body ached. How he yearned to sleep in his own bed.

His frown returned. Who in hell was he kidding? Whatever damage had been done to her had left deep scars that would take a lifetime to heal over. He had neither the time nor the inclination to add to his burdens.

The sooner she was out of here, the sooner he could get back his life.

He let himself out of the cabin and headed for the barn.

Chapter Ten

The next few days became a blur of endless work as Matt drove himself and those around him to the limit of endurance.

While Matt and Aaron worked the herd of mustangs, Izzy and the younger children doubled up on their chores.

The last of the crops had to be harvested and stored. Hay and wheat filled the rafters of the barn. Potatoes, turnips, apples, pears began to take up every available space in the root cellar.

Some mornings there was a sheen of frost dusting the ground. On such days the clothesline bloomed with frozen pants and shirts, and Izzy's fingers were stiff and sore as she struggled to remove them. Other days the sky was a clear, cloudless blue that made all the work seem easier. But even the gentlest of days now carried a bite in the wind, a harbinger of the winter looming on the horizon.

Izzy and the children hitched old Blue to a cart and hauled logs from the woods. Late at night, after spending hours in the saddle, Matt and Aaron would chop and split the logs, stacking them against the walls of the cabin.

In the evenings Izzy taught the children how to make candles and how to knead dough for bread. In return, they taught her how to coax a fire with a flint and how to load and shoot a rifle. These lessons, interspersed with reading, writing and sums, always seemed to bring on gales of laughter.

"Isabella, this doesn't make any sense." Del stood, with hands on her hips, studying the list of words on her slate. "You said *n-o-w* spells *now*."

"That's right."

"Then how come, when we put an *s* in front of it, it becomes *snow?* Shouldn't it sound like s-now?" she asked, drawing out the word with a nasal twang.

Izzy laughed. "Well, I never thought about it before. You're right, Del. It doesn't make any sense. But that's the way it is."

"And," the little girl went on, "how come we have *no* and *know, write* and *right, see* and *sea?*"

Matt looked up from the saddle he was mending and winked at Izzy. "We did that just to confuse you, Del."

While the others chuckled at his joke, Izzy felt her heart do a series of crazy somersaults. All week, despite the endless, backbreaking chores, she had sensed a change in her relationship with Matthew. Though he drove himself and the others endlessly, in her presence he had become more relaxed, more lighthearted. The more she engaged his children, the less determined he seemed to press for an intimate relationship. What was all the more strange, now that he had stopped pursuing her, she felt drawn to him in a way she never expected to be. It was as though a barrier had fallen away, and she was seeing him in a new light.

What foolishness, she told herself. She was simply imagining things that weren't really there. He was, after all, a man. And all men had the power to hurt women. If they let down their guard to men.

Still, he had made no further attempt to kiss her. And she found herself thinking, late at night, about the way his lips had felt on hers. And the way his body felt, all hard angles and planes, pressing into her softness.

"Bet I can." Del's reply to her brother's challenge brought Izzy out of her reverie. *"Knowledge. N-o-l-e-g."*

As the boys laughed, Izzy said gently, "You sounded that out perfectly, Del. But that's one of those words that has all those extra letters we talked about. The *k* at the beginning is silent. And so is the *w* and the *d* in the middle and the *e* at the end."

The little girl tossed down her slate in frustration. "I'll never learn all these words."

Izzy picked up the slate and patiently handed it back. "Of course you will. It just takes time. I'll bet by tomorrow you'll master it."

Aaron looked up from the harness he was mending. "Did your mother teach you, Isabella? Or did you go to a real school?"

"I...no." Taken by surprise, she couldn't seem to engage her brain. Then, seeing Matt's head come up, knowing she had unwittingly snagged his attention, she felt her cheeks redden. "I didn't go to a real school. I was taught at home."

"You're real good with numbers and letters."

"Yes. I...always enjoyed the challenge of learning. Now, Del, let's work on your sums."

"What was your life like in Pennsylvania?" The little girl ignored the column of numbers Izzy was writing on the slate. "Did you have brothers or sisters, Isabella?"

"No." Her voice was tight, controlled. "There was just me."

"And your ma and pa," Benjamin corrected. "Was your pa a farmer?"

"I had n—" She noticed that Matt and his children had stopped what they were doing to watch and listen.

She'd had plenty of time to anticipate these questions and to plan her answers. And yet, now that the moment had actually come, she felt a wave of guilt and shame.

She was about to dig herself into a hole. One that just might swallow her. Still, what was one more lie, after all she'd told this far? She took a deep breath and thought about the daydreams she had spun.

"I had really nice parents. My pa was a preacher. Tall and handsome, he was, with dark hair just turning silver around the edges." She conjured up the image of the town preacher she'd watched so many times through the window of the church. She had always imagined what her life would be like if he was her father. "And his wife...my mother," she corrected quickly, "was small and pretty. A real lady, with a gentle voice and the sweetest smile." She caught herself before she said too much, and finished lamely, "They were good people."

"How did they die?" Del asked.

"Die?" Izzy blinked.

"You said 'were.' They were good people. Aren't they dead?"

"Yes. Of course. They died...in their carriage. It was awful. All bloody and such."

"They overturned?" Aaron asked.

She nodded. "They were trying to cross a swollen stream. They were carried downstream by the current and drowned."

"If they drowned, how'd they get all bloody?" Benjamin asked.

"They...got snagged on some rocks."

"Wouldn't the water wash away all the blood? And how come you weren't with them?" This from Clement.

Izzy looked around almost frantically. "I...I was back at the church. With friends. I...don't like to talk about it."

The children were staring at her, their eyes big and round, a dozen questions on their lips. Before they could say another word Matt set aside the saddle. "I think that's enough for tonight. We have another full day ahead of us. And if Aaron and I push hard enough, we just might have the entire herd ready by the time the army comes for them tomorrow." He took the slate from his daughter's hands. "Say goodnight to Isabella now. And don't bother her with any more questions."

"Yes, sir. 'Night, Isabella."

"Good night, Del." Izzy's voice was still shaky.

As the little girl climbed the ladder to the loft, the others called out their good-nights and followed suit. When they were alone, Matt placed the slate on the shelf.

For a moment there was an awkward silence. Then, with his back to her, he asked, "Got any of that coffee left?"

"I think so." She walked to the fire and wrapped a square of linen around her hand before lifting the hot pot and pouring. "Just enough for one cup."

When she handed it to him he took a sip, then surprised her by offering it back.

"We'll share."

"Thank you." She was touched by his generosity. And grateful that he'd given her time to compose herself.

"Let's sit by the fire a minute." With his hand beneath her elbow he led her across the room, where they sat in companionable silence and drank their coffee.

She waited, anticipating more questions about her past. She was ready now. Cool and composed.

Instead he surprised her by stretching out his feet toward the fire and giving a long, slow sigh of comfort. "I always like this time of night best."

"Why?"

"The children are safely in their beds. The chores are done. The horses are secure. There's a kind of peace that settles over the land after sundown." He shrugged. "My father used to say, 'God's in His heaven. All's right with the world.' I guess that says it all.''

"Tell me about your father."

Matt stared into the flames. "He was a hard man. A military man. Educated at West Point. Expected his only son to follow in his footsteps."

"Did you?"

"For a while. But it wasn't my dream." His tone deepened. "I wanted something else."

She studied his handsome, rugged profile. "Do you have it?"

"Some of it." He swung his gaze to her and she felt the most purely sexual jolt she'd ever known. "I suppose nobody ever gets everything they want in life."

"No. I guess not." She drained the coffee and, to avoid looking at him, studied the delicate rose pattern on the cup. "Your wife's dishes are so pretty."

His eyes narrowed. "Grace had a habit of collecting pretty things."

"Tell me about Grace. That's a lovely name—"

He moved so quickly she had no time to react. One moment he was out of the chair. The next he was hauling her to her feet, dragging her roughly into his arms.

"I don't want to talk about Grace."

The cup slipped from her fingers, shattered at their feet.

"I…" She could feel the tension humming through him. Could actually see the effort it took to control the range of emotions that were struggling to be free. "All right, Matthew. We won't talk about…"

He dragged her closer. "I can't give you pretty things, Isabella."

His hands were rough, almost bruising. She didn't care. All she could feel was his breath, hot against her temple. And the wild stutter of her heartbeat as those big, work-worn fingers kneaded her arms, her shoulders, then began trailing fire along her spine.

"I don't need things, Matthew." *This is what I need.* The thought startled her as her blood began to flow like lava through her veins. *The feel of strong arms surrounding me, soothing me. Protecting me. Arousing me.*

Sweet salvation. She'd never known such a rush of feelings. Intense, seething emotions. Fire. Ice. Need. All rushing through her system, leaving her stunned and breathless.

He lowered his head until his lips were pressed to a tangle of hair at her temple. "I'm no good with pretty words, either, Isabella."

She shivered. "I don't...need the words."

"What, then?" His lips traced the curve of her brow, the softness of her cheek, the slope of her jaw. And still he avoided her lips until she thought she would go mad from wanting. Waiting. Needing.

"I don't know." Then, as he continued to torment her by keeping his mouth just inches from hers, she said softly, "This is what I want. Just this." She couldn't bear to wait another moment. Standing on tiptoe, she brought her mouth to his. "Matthew. Kiss me. Please kiss me."

For the space of a heartbeat he went very still, as though unable to believe what he'd just heard. He framed her face with his hands and stared down into her eyes.

His face lowered to hers so slowly she thought her heart would surely stop. And then his lips covered hers in a kiss so soft, so gentle it had her breath backing up in her throat.

His eyes were open as he took the kiss deeper, then deeper still. He could actually see her changing. The flush on her cheeks. Enchanting. The flutter of her lashes. Bewitching. The hitch of her breath, the soft sigh that she couldn't stifle. Thoroughly arousing.

She tasted of flour and sugar and cinnamon. Sweeter by far than any confection. She smelled as clean, as fresh as a cool breeze through an evergreen forest. He breathed her in and wanted more. So much more. And from the way she was clinging to him, and returning his kisses, he could sense the same in her. Perhaps they had finally opened a door. A door that had been closed between them for so long.

''I want you, Isabella.'' He lifted his head and took a deep draft of air to clear his head. It took all of his willpower to keep from taking her, here and now. But he wanted to make it right this time. Wanted to be very careful, so that she wouldn't retreat once again behind her wall of fear. ''Is it the same for you?''

She took a deep breath, struggling to find the words. How could she tell him? How could she explain that everything was so new, so frightening? She wasn't supposed to feel this way. She must be a very wicked woman to think what she was thinking.

He stared down at her, wanting, needing to hear the words.

When she remained silent his fingers dug into her shoulders, holding her a little away so he could see her eyes.

"Answer me, Isabella. Do you want this? Do you want me?"

"I..." Afraid, confused, she brought a hand to his cheek. "I don't know what I want."

He caught her hand and pressed it to his lips. A thrill shot along her arm, igniting a fire in her blood.

"I need to know," he whispered against her palm. "I need to hear it from your own lips."

She pulled back, her eyes wide.

Passion? he wondered. Or the same old fear?

"Have mercy on me, Isabella." The words were torn from his throat. "I can't stand this anymore."

"I don't think..." She swallowed. "I don't want..."

She hung her head, unable to say what he needed to hear.

"Can you tell me you don't want this?" He dragged her close and plundered her lips, kissing her until she was breathless. Then he lowered his mouth, trailing hot kisses along the column of her throat.

Her breath was coming faster now, in short, shallow bursts as she struggled to hold on to her last thread of sanity.

"Tell me, Isabella. Tell me you don't want this, either." He brought his hands to the top button of her gown and tore it in his haste.

Reflexively, she flinched and let out a gasp. "No. Stop. I don't..."

At once he stiffened, then backed up. Need, all consuming, vibrated through him.

God in heaven, what had possessed him? He had almost been on the verge of forcing her. He had actually begun to believe that she had somehow changed. That overnight she had developed some affection for him. That she wanted what he wanted. This hunger was turning him into someone he didn't know. Or like.

She could see the mix of anger and frustration darkening his eyes. "Matthew, I just need time to—"

"Time." He swore, viciously.

"Matthew, it's not what you—"

"Not another word." His voice was a low growl of rage. "You're driving me to the brink of madness, Isabella. And I vowed I'd never go there again. Not for you. Not for any woman."

Before she could explain, he turned on his heel and slammed out of the cabin, leaving her alone and trembling.

The only thing left to her was the chill that enveloped her like a shroud. His words rang in her head as she moved about the cabin in a state of shock. Her mind was numb, her body frozen as she banked the fire, extinguished the lanterns.

Even when she crawled into bed and huddled beneath the blankets, she couldn't dispel the cold that seemed to have seeped into her bones. All she could see was the pain of rejection in Matthew's eyes. A pain she had known intimately all her life.

And all the while, the taste of him was still on her lips.

Chapter Eleven

"Get back in that saddle, boy. We don't have any time left to waste if we're going to have these damned mustangs ready." Matt's temper was simmering just below the boiling point.

"Yes, sir." Aaron picked himself up from the dirt and limped over to where the mare stood, breathing fire. He winced in pain as he pulled himself into the saddle and continued trying to win the horse's trust.

All day his father had driven him unmercifully. They'd started at dawn and had gone until dusk without a break. And even now, though Matt was working with the most defiant member of the herd, the stallion they called Red, there was no doubt the horse would be ready when the army came to call. For above all, Matt was hardest on himself, pushing to the very edge of collapse.

"Del." Matt's voice, angry, gritty, sliced through the silence. "What in hell are you doing sitting there on the corral? Get back to your chores."

"Finished 'em, Pa. It's almost suppertime."

He seemed startled. Where had the day gone?

"Then help Benjamin and Clement with theirs. Or I'll find something useful for you to do. Now get."

One salty tear coursed down her cheek as she climbed from the rail and headed for the cabin. Inside, Izzy looked up from the scraps she'd been piecing together for Del's dress. She searched for some way to soothe over the tensions, though she was still struggling with her own tender emotions.

"Your pa doesn't mean anything by this, Del. He's just worried about having the herd ready in time."

"That's not my fault."

Feeling clumsy and tentative, Izzy dropped an arm around her shoulders. "Of course it isn't. And Matthew knows that. But sometimes folks say things they don't mean when they're feeling upset."

"But why is Pa so upset? This is the worst I've ever seen him." Del pushed away and stared out the window, watching as her adored brother was tossed from the saddle yet again. It pained her to see him struggling so hard to please his father. "Even after Ma, Pa was never this mad."

Izzy was reminded of the words Matt had shouted at her the night before. *Driving me to the brink of madness. And I vowed I'd never go there again for any woman.* She paused beside the little girl to watch as Aaron picked himself up yet again. "Sometimes grown-ups just have too much on their minds. I don't think your father could ever be intentionally cruel." She turned away, not wanting to see the way the father and son were punishing themselves. Every fall, every bruise hurt her heart.

"Come on, Del, you can help me with supper. I've

planned a special one to celebrate the sale of the herd. Once your pa concludes his business, I'm sure he'll be more like his old self.''

At least that was her fervent hope. She couldn't bear another scene like the one last night. She still wasn't certain just what had brought it on. Was it something she had said or done? Oh, she knew so little about men. And this man in particular. He was hot one minute, cold the next. So kind he made her want to weep, then, in the blink of an eye, cold and distant.

If only she had someone to confide in. She felt so alone and helpless. But there was no point in cursing her ignorance. All she could do now was muddle through. At least, she consoled herself, things couldn't get any worse.

She looked up at the chorus of barking from the hounds, followed by the sound of hoofbeats. A group of soldiers was dismounting outside the corral.

Del ran to the door. ''The army's here, Isabella. Is it all right if I go outside and watch?''

Izzy nodded, seeing Benjamin and Clement coming in from the fields to join their father and brother. ''I don't see why not. Just keep out of their way.''

''I will.'' The little girl skipped away and Izzy returned to her bread. When it was sliced, she set it aside, then stirred the pot of stew. Perhaps, she thought, the soldiers would stay for supper. She would invite them, as soon as she brought in the clean clothes. She picked up a basket and headed for the clothesline.

Maybe, she prayed, once the herd was sold and

Matthew had all that money in his pocket, his attitude toward his children would soften, at least a little. And then, she added fervently, maybe he would soften toward her, as well. After all, with winter coming, he ought to be able to slow down a bit. Perhaps this temper of his was just a result of too much work.

The breeze had picked up, whipping her skirts around her ankles. She paid no attention as she reached for the first shirt on the line. From across the clearing she could hear every word spoken by the men.

"Mr. Prescott. I'm Lieutenant Gideon Trowbridge."

The young officer looked hardly old enough to shave. Matt was certain it was his first assignment. "'Evening, Lieutenant. Was your father Gabriel Trowbridge?"

"No, sir. My uncle. How did you…?"

"We served together at Chancellorsville."

"Chancellorsville, huh?" A big, burly soldier slid from the saddle and turned to glare at Matt. "Which side did you serve on. Union? Or Reb?" He had rolled the sleeves of his uniform to reveal the bulging muscles of his forearms. He wore the long, thin scar on his cheek and his broken nose like a badge of honor.

"This is Sergeant Harlan Cutler," the young lieutenant said. "And Private Luther Davis."

"Private." Matt nodded toward the thin youth who looked to be no older than Aaron, then turned his back on Cutler, not bothering to hide his disdain. "I've met the sergeant."

"I bought a bunch of Prescott's mustangs in June." Cutler glowered at him. "You didn't answer my question. That must mean you're a Reb." He spat a stream of tobacco between his teeth, aiming it toward Matt's boot, and turned to Aaron. "These all saddle-broke, boy?"

"Yes, sir."

"How 'bout that one?" Cutler nodded toward the stallion, still saddled and edging away from the men.

Matt ignored him and spoke instead to the lieutenant. "There are fifty-four, total. All broke to saddle. That'll be five hundred forty dollars."

Gideon Trowbridge reached into his jacket, withdrew a leather pouch. "It's all here, Mr. Prescott. Would you care to count it?"

As he started to hand over the money, Cutler stepped between the two men. "Before you pay up, maybe you'd better let me do my job. The captain sent me along to make sure the army was getting its money's worth."

"Mr. Prescott has assured…"

"Yeah. Well, I'll just check and make sure." He turned to Aaron. "Climb up in the saddle and put that stallion through his paces, boy."

Before Aaron could comply, Matt touched a hand to his sleeve. "Leave it, son." He turned to the lieutenant. "If the sergeant wants to check any horse in this herd, that's his business. As for us, our job here is done."

"We'll see about that." With a string of curses Cutler crossed to the stallion and pulled himself into the saddle. He gave a vicious tug on the reins that tore at the horse's mouth and was rewarded with a cry from the little girl perched on the rail. He glanced over, pleased to see both Matt Prescott and his sons clenching their fists. So, they cared about their precious horses, did they? Well, he'd give them a show they wouldn't soon forget.

"Frisky." He gave a cruel sneer. "But I'll soon beat it out of him."

As horse and rider circled, Cutler swore and dug his spurs into the stallion's flesh. At once the horse reared, and his rider brought a whip down with enough force to send the animal into a frenzy of bucking.

"Pa," Del shouted. "He's hurting Red."

"Lieutenant." Matt struggled to keep a lid on the rage that was seething. "If I were you, I'd order Cutler to dismount."

"Sergeant Cutler." The young lieutenant was offended by the brutality. But, being new, he wanted to be careful not to reprimand one of his men in front of civilians. He might never see these ranchers again, but he would have to face Cutler daily. And the sergeant had a reputation as a bully. "That will do."

"I don't think you understand, Lieutenant." Cutler raised the whip again. "Prescott said this animal was saddle-broke. Only he forgot to tell the horse. Now I'm about to teach this mustang who's boss here."

He brought the whip down again, tearing the animal's flesh. In a haze of pain, the stallion bucked and reared in an effort to dislodge its rider.

"Pa. Stop him, Pa."

Hearing Del's cry and the sound of the horse's

frantic whinny, Izzy dropped her basket of clothes and started toward the corral at a run.

"That's enough, Sergeant." The young lieutenant cupped his hands to his mouth in order to be heard above the din. "You will dismount at once and turn over that horse to Private Davis."

Cutler took his time following orders, giving the stallion one last crack of the whip as he handed the reins to the young private. As he strode past Matt, he spat another mouthful of tobacco, making certain this time it landed on Matt's boot.

Just then he caught sight of Izzy, standing to one side, wiping Del's tears with her apron. "Didn't know you had a woman way out here, Prescott."

The way he looked at her had Aaron's protective instincts surfacing. He shouted defiantly, "She's Pa's wife."

"Wife, you say? I'll be damned. It looks like…" Cutler squinted, stared, then let out a howl of laughter. "By God, it is. All the way from Pennsylvania." He stepped closer. "Bet you didn't expect to see anybody who knew you way out here in this godforsaken wilderness, did you?"

Izzy had gone rigid with shock. All she could do was stare at this remnant of her past with a look of horror and revulsion.

"Got shipped out here with the First Pennsylvania. Me and Otis. You remember Otis, don't you?"

His cruel laughter mocked her.

"Still carry that knife for protection?"

His taunts filled her with shame. She lowered her head, refusing to look at him.

Cutler turned to Matt with a knowing smirk. "Better watch your back, Reb. Miss High-and-Mighty Tavern Wench thought she was too good for the men of our town. Carried a knife in her pocket. Cut up one of my friends real good. Otis still carries the scars. Threatened to do the same to anyone else who ever tried to touch her. As if any of us needed to touch the likes of her. She's nothing but a crazy, crippled old maid."

"You shut your mouth." Aaron started toward him, fists raised. "Don't you talk about Isabella like that."

"Isabella?" Cutler gave a shrill laugh. "My, my. Isn't that fancy? Know what we called her back in our town? Izzy the Gimp. That's 'cause she's got a gimpy leg. We used to poke her with sticks when she walked through the tavern. Go ahead, Izzy the Gimp. Do your little dance for us."

"Cutler." Matt's voice was low, controlled. "I see you enjoy inflicting pain." He unfastened his gun belt, tossing it to his son. "It's going to be a pleasure to beat the hell out of you."

Cutler spun around. His evil grin widened. "A fight, Reb? Hell, nothing I like better. The pleasure's all mine."

As the two men began circling each other, Private Davis pulled his gun from his holster. At once Aaron aimed his father's pistol.

"Put those away," the lieutenant ordered. "There's no need for gunplay. Let's just see that it's a fair fight." If he were a betting man, he'd put his money on this rancher. Especially from what he'd heard about him.

"Yes, sir."

Aaron and the private shoved their guns back in their holsters and stood on the sidelines along with the others.

Cutler threw the first punch, grazing Matt's temple. Matt retaliated with a fist in his gut that had him doubled over. With a cry of rage Cutler lowered his head and charged, knocking Matt to the ground.

Though Matt was strong and muscled from his years of ranching, Cutler had the advantage of weight. He used it now, throwing punches that would have shattered most men.

The two rolled around the dirt exchanging blows until Cutler managed to pin Matt.

Matt tasted blood as Cutler's fist exploded against his jaw. Another blow to the temple had him seeing stars. He brought a knee to Cutler's groin and managed to throw him off for the moment. He rolled to one side, shaking his head to clear it.

"Watch out, Pa," Aaron cried. "He's got a gun."

Reflexively Matt swung his arm in a wide arc, knocking the gun from Cutler's hand. "What's the matter?" he taunted. "Afraid to fight like a man? Or are you only brave when you're bullying helpless women and animals?"

"Why, you…" Cutler charged again, but this time Matt was ready for him.

He feinted to one side, and Cutler sailed past, tumbling in the dirt. When he managed to scramble to his feet, Matt caught him with a blow that had Cutler wheezing and Matt's knuckles bleeding.

As Cutler fell, Matt caught him by the front of the shirt and hauled him up. "You're not getting off this easily."

"Neither are you." Cutler's hand reached inside his shirt and came away holding a knife. "Your wife isn't the only one who knows how to use one of these things."

With one quick movement he lunged. Only Matt's quick thinking saved him from taking a fatal thrust to the heart. Instead, as he deflected the blow, the blade sliced into his shoulder, sending blood streaming down his arm.

The pain was so intense he felt his vision begin to fade. He staggered, and Cutler's hands closed around his throat. "Never had no use for traitors and Rebs," he muttered as he began to squeeze.

Matt could hear his children shouting, and someone weeping. But the sounds seemed to ebb and flow, and he knew if he didn't break Cutler's grip, he would soon be lost.

Matt brought his head up, hard and fast, under Cutler's jaw, and had the satisfaction of hearing bone grind against bone. "And I've never had any use for bullies," he managed, when he'd caught his breath.

With a snarl of pain and rage Cutler reared back. Matt's fist landed squarely in his face, breaking his nose.

With blood streaming down his face, he came at Matt like a raging bull, driving him into the corral with such force the rails toppled.

"This is for your wife, Reb, who was always too good for the men in our town." He brought a fist into Matt's stomach, doubling him over.

At his taunt, something in Matt seemed to snap. He hit Cutler so hard he could feel the jolt all the way up his arm. When the sergeant staggered, Matt hit him again, driving him up against the railing. Then he unleashed a series of blows that brought Cutler to his knees. Matt hauled him to his feet and hit him again, sending him sprawling face first in the dirt. Again Matt hauled him up, unleashing another blow to his face.

"Matthew." Izzy was at his side, clutching his arm. "Stop. Please, you have to stop before you kill him."

But Matt was beyond hearing. He shook off her arm and hauled the limp form of Cutler by the front of his bloody shirt. "Come on," he snarled. "Don't quit on me now. I'm just getting started."

"Matthew." Izzy was weeping now, though she wasn't aware of her tears. "Your children are watching. Please, you must stop now. I beg you."

Somehow her words managed to penetrate the red haze of fury that had Matt in its grip. He released his hold on Cutler, allowing the limp form to fall into the dirt.

It took all of his willpower to remain on his feet, but he was determined to see this thing through. He turned to the lieutenant. Though his left arm hung, bloody and useless, and his face was a mass of blood, welts and bruises, his voice was strong.

"You owe me five hundred and thirty dollars."

"I thought it was five hundred and forty," the young officer said.

"The stallion is no longer part of the bargain." Matt glanced to where the horse stood, at the far side of the corral, nostrils flaring, eyes wide and frightened.

The young lieutenant nodded. "It's a shame to lose such a fine piece of horseflesh. But I understand." He handed Matt the leather pouch before turning to his soldier. "Private Davis," he called. "Load Sergeant Cutler into the wagon. And let's get these horses back to the post."

"Yes, sir."

He turned to Matt and offered a handshake.

Matt winced as a thunderbolt of pain snaked up his arm.

"It was a pleasure doing business with you, Mr. Prescott."

"Anytime, Lieutenant. Just see that Cutler never sets foot on my property again."

The young officer nodded. "I understand. It's men like him who give the army a bad name." He started to turn away, then paused, took a deep breath and said, "Forgive me for not recognizing your name sooner, Captain Prescott. My uncle often spoke of you. He said the army would have been proud to have an officer of your calibre, educated at West Point, who served his country so honorably, remain in the service."

"Thank you, Lieutenant." He saw his children forming a protective ring around him and was determined to remain standing for their sake. "But army life wasn't for me."

Within minutes the wagon, with Cutler dumped unceremoniously into the back, and the herd of mustangs tied to a lead rope behind, rolled across the meadow.

Matt winced as his children hugged him. He studied Izzy, standing all alone, twisting her apron between her hands.

"Isabella made you a special supper to celebrate," Del said.

"I'll be along in a little while. I've got something to attend to here first."

The children saw him flick a glance at the stallion.

And then, suddenly, Aaron understood. "You're going to set him free, aren't you, Pa?"

Matt nodded. "After what Cutler did to him, he'll never trust man again. And I can't say I blame him. He's earned the right to be free."

As he made his way slowly, painfully across the corral, the mustang reared up, then began backing away. With soft words and easy, unhurried movements, Matt was able to remove the saddle and bridle.

"Come on," Matt called to the others. "Let's give him some time to adjust."

Following his lead, they walked a distance away, leaving the horse alone in the open corral.

For long minutes the stallion sniffed the air, as though searching for a scent. Finally, after circling the enclosure several times, he walked through the open gate and stared at the people who were watching him.

When they made no move to stop him, he started at a trot across the meadow.

He turned once, as if to make certain he wasn't being followed. Then, with a toss of his head, he began to race across the meadow until he was swallowed up in the distant woods.

Del glanced at Izzy. "Are you crying, Isabella?"

Izzy had to blink hard to keep the tears from flowing. "Maybe just a little. I'm so glad he's free." She turned in time to see Matt stagger. All the color had drained from his face.

She quickly took charge. "Aaron, Benjamin, Clement, help your father into the cabin."

"I can do it mysel—" He started to turn away, then blanched at the pain and snagged Aaron's shoulder to keep from falling.

"There's no time to argue. Del," Izzy called, "you come with me."

They hurried ahead, with Matt and his sons trailing slowly behind.

"That was really something the way you smashed your fist into Cutler's stomach, Pa." Benjamin pounded a fist against his hand, relishing the moment.

"I was afraid," Clement admitted, "when I saw Cutler pull his gun on you, Pa."

"Yes, but did you see the way Pa knocked Cutler's gun away?" Aaron proudly bore the weight of his father, who was leaning heavily on his arm as they stepped into the cabin.

"And that knife." Clement glanced at Izzy. "Cutler said you…"

She spilled some of the hot water she'd been pouring into a basin. For a moment everyone went very still.

She cleared her throat. "Children, help your father into bed."

From the cupboard she removed the bottle of whiskey, then she picked up the supplies and followed the others into the bedroom. As they gathered around the bed, still reliving every moment of the fight, she called for silence.

"What your father needs now is for all of you to leave him alone."

"But what about his wounds?"

"I'll help him. And when they're washed and bound, what he'll need most is rest and quiet. So I suggest you eat your supper and then take yourselves up to bed. We've all put in a very long day."

Before they could argue Matt lifted a hand. "Isabella's right. Good night, children."

"Good night," they called in unison.

As she closed the bedroom door she could hear the children's voices, hushed but still excited, drifting about the cabin. Could hear the dogs fighting over the scraps. Could hear the call of a coyote on a distant hill.

She shivered.

She would mend Matthew's wounds as best she could. Then it would be time to face some very hard truths.

The wounds her lies had inflicted would be much harder to mend.

Chapter Twelve

It was quiet in the bedroom, except for the sound of Matt's labored breathing. In the circle of light given off by the lantern, his features were pale and drawn.

"I hope you don't feel as terrible as you look."

His tone was sharp. "Go away. I'm not fit company just now."

She shook her head. "It isn't pleasant company I'm here for. Just lie still and I'll tend to your wounds."

When he started to protest, she knelt in front of him and touched a finger to his lips. "First I'll have to take off your clothes, Matthew, and see what I have to deal with."

Too weak to argue, he lay back as she stripped away the tattered, blood-soaked remnants.

She couldn't hide her shock at the sight of the bloody mess. Then, steeling herself, she dipped a cloth in the hot water and began to wash his wounds with lye soap.

He sucked in a breath at the pain. "Are you sure you aren't here to finish what Cutler started?"

"I'm sorry to add to your pain, Matthew." She

worked quickly, efficiently, finishing with the painful area around the wounded shoulder, then the wound itself.

"Is this really necessary?"

She nodded. "Unless you'd like to take a chance on only one good arm in the future."

He gave a sigh of resignation. "All right. Do what you have to."

"Here." She passed him the bottle of whiskey and waited until he'd taken a generous swig. Then she took the bottle from his hand and poured a liberal amount on the wound.

He set his teeth against the pain. "Damned waste of good whiskey," he managed to say between clenched teeth, and took the bottle from her. This time he drank several long, deep gulps.

"I'd know all about whiskey and its uses." She corked the bottle, then applied a fresh linen dressing.

At that he held his silence. But he could still hear in his mind Cutler's taunts about the tavern wench. It made his blood boil all over again, thinking about the pained expression on her face at Cutler's revelations.

"Now that eye, *Captain* Prescott."

He tried to chuckle, but it came out as a strangled hiss of pain. "That was…long time ago. I don't have…any fancy titles now." His words were beginning to slur as the whiskey and exhaustion had the desired effect.

"Mm-hmm." Holding the lantern close, she examined the swelling that had one eye almost closed. "You're going to have a lovely bruise all the way to your cheek. I think I know something that will help."

She dipped a square of linen into cold water, then pressed it to the swollen eye.

"Now lie back," she commanded.

"Why?"

"I'll see if you broke any ribs." She began gently probing.

Matt winced. "Easy."

Her fingertips skimmed his torso. "Is this better?"

"Yes." He closed his eyes. "You have a much lighter touch than the army surgeons."

"I suppose you speak from experience?" She caught sight of several faded scars. Two were obvious bullet wounds. One, long and thin, appeared to have been caused by a knife or rapier.

He nodded, then opened his eyes to find her leaning over him, their faces nearly touching. "I took... couple of bullets. A stab or two. But I was one of...the lucky ones."

"Was it Chancellorsville that convinced you not to follow your father's dream?"

He shook his head and sucked in another breath when she began to bind his ribs. "I think I always knew...I wanted to be a farmer. But the bloody massacre at Chancellorsville made me realize the futility of guns and fighting."

"You must have had a momentary lapse today."

He almost smiled. "I have to admit. It felt good. I was in a mood to kick something. And...kicking Cutler's hide...gave me real pleasure." His words became even more slurred with each passing moment.

"Then I'll admit, it gave me some pleasure, too.

But only for a moment. When I saw the pain you were forced to endure…'' She looked away.

Moved, he touched a hand to her face. ''Sorry, Isabella. I don't usually…indulge in such things. We have…so little time in this life. From the day I came home from the war, I was obsessed…with peace. All I've ever wanted was to be left alone…to follow my heart.''

''And your heart led you here.''

''Yes.'' His eyes closed.

''It wasn't my heart that led me here, Matthew. It was…'' She glanced down. The pain, which only moments ago had pinched his features, had now slipped away, leaving him relaxed and almost smiling.

''Matthew?'' She slipped her hand in his. The big, work-roughened fingers didn't return her grasp.

''Good. You've moved beyond the pain.'' And she would be spared admitting the truth for a while longer.

''Sleep now,'' she murmured.

On a sigh, he did.

It was pain that woke him. Pain that exploded through his head, radiated from his shoulder and seeped into every part of his body. It hurt to move. It hurt more to lie still.

He turned slightly, to ease his stiff shoulder, and had to bite down hard on a bitter oath.

Then, in a sliver of moonbeams, he saw her. Sitting on a hard kitchen chair, which she'd pulled alongside the bed. The blanket she'd tucked around her had slipped to the floor. She was still wearing her gown, which bore the traces of blood and dirt from his wounds. Her hair had slipped from its ribbon and streamed across her face, dipping over one eye in a most beguiling way.

He touched a hand to the clean dressings at his shoulder, then gingerly pressed a finger to the swelling beneath his eye. Bits and pieces of memory began to slip into place. He could recall the touch of her hands, as soft, as gentle as spring rain on his flesh. And the sound of her voice, low, soothing. She had calmly, efficiently handled everything. The children and their needs. Supper. Bedtime. As well as his needs. She had cleaned and dressed his wounds. Had given him whiskey to ease the pain. A soft bed to cushion his aches.

But what about her needs? Who saw to that?

He saw her eyes flicker, then open. At once she was on her knees beside the bed, touching a hand to his forehead.

"Matthew." Her voice was a whisper in the moonlight. "How long have you been awake?"

"Just a few minutes."

"How do you feel?"

"Ever been through a battle?"

She shook her head.

He chuckled, though it ended on a wheeze of pain. "That's how I feel. Only worse."

"Can I get you something?"

"Water would be nice."

She stood, crossed the room, then returned with a cup. Sitting on the edge of the bed, she cradled his head on one arm while holding the cup to his lips.

He took a long drink, then lifted a hand to the swirl of hair that curtained her cheek. "The army never had such beautiful nurses."

"I'm not beautiful." She moved away, placing the cup on the night table.

"Are you calling me a liar?"

"You're just...being kind, Matthew. I know what I am."

"And what are you, Isabella?"

She took a deep breath, keeping her gaze averted. This was so painful. But it had to be done. "I'm a liar. Everything I've ever told you is a lie."

"Everything?"

He saw the flush that stole over her cheeks. "Almost everything. It truly was Aaron's letter that brought me here. I guess that's just about the only truth I've told. But I didn't read it in church. In fact, I was never inside the church in my town. Women like me weren't welcome. So I used to peek through the windows."

"Why?"

"I liked the singing. And the sound of the preacher's voice. Oh," she added with a start. "There's another lie. The preacher wasn't my father."

"I know. At least, I'd guessed as much."

He said it so simply she had to stop and turn. "You knew?"

"You may call yourself a liar, Isabella, but you're not a very good one."

"I see." The flush on her cheeks deepened. She turned away. "I didn't have a father. Or a mother. I was an orphan. I spent the first ten years of my life in the Philadelphia Home for Foundlings.''

Ten years. She would have been Clement's age. The thought brought as much pain as his wounds. ''Then what happened?''

''I was considered old enough to earn my keep. So I was sent to work in the home of Mrs. Eudora Hastings. She said I had a sweet nature, and so she kept me around for the next two years as a companion for her children.''

Izzy wasn't aware of the look that came into her eyes at the memory. She clasped her hands together. ''Oh, those were lovely times. I used to pretend that Mrs. Hastings was my mother. She was a stern woman, very demanding, but fair and very wise. She was a follower of Reverend Halfyard, who ran the foundling home. She decided to teach me to read and write after she found me looking through a picture book one day. You can't imagine what that meant to me. But then...'' Her smile underwent a transformation as she struggled to keep it from fading.

''Mr. Hastings died, and Mrs. Hastings was forced to take her children to her brother's home in New York. She couldn't afford to take me along. But before she left, she sat me down and said she wanted to talk to me like a daughter. She explained that a girl all alone in the world had special problems. She warned me that men would try to hurt me. And that I must resist them in any way I could. Because once I allowed one of them to hurt me, it would be never ending. And good people would have nothing more to do with me. She asked me to promise that I would always fight such men and lead the life of a good, God-fearing woman. And though I didn't quite understand what it was she wanted from me, I gave her my solemn vow. So I allowed her to cut off all my hair, because she said it would be a source of temptation to men. And I agreed to heed her warning to dress only in simple clothes that would not draw attention to myself.''

"Isabella, I think…"

"No. Let me get through this." Her smile faltered, but she bravely bit her lip, determined to confess everything while he was a captive audience.

"Since I had already left the foundling home, I was not permitted to return. In order to survive, I was forced to accept employment at the local tavern. At first I was only expected to help in the kitchen." She twisted her hands together in her lap. "That's where I learned to cook and clean, or take a beating at the hands of the owner, Mrs. Purdy. But it was her husband I really feared. One night Mr. Purdy got drunk and tried to…"

Matt's eyes narrowed. With each word from her lips his anger and outrage were growing fiercer.

Seeing it, she was quick to soothe. "Oh, Mr. Purdy didn't manage anything. He was too drunk. But his son found me crying and gave me his knife, and warned me to seek shelter in a loft in the stables, where I'd be able to see anyone who came in. And that's where I slept from then on."

"In the stables." Fury darkened Matt's eyes.

"It wasn't so bad. Oh, there were times it grew bitterly cold in winter, and stifling in summer. And sometimes I smelled as bad as the animals. But that loft in the stables became my haven. Even when I had to begin working in the tavern, filling tankards and serving the tables, I preferred the safety of the loft to the room in the attic that the Purdys offered me.''

''I take it you didn't like working in the tavern.''

She shook her head. ''I detested it. The men, especially after they'd had too much ale and whiskey, were often cruel.''

Matt recalled Cutler's comments about prodding her with a stick to watch her limp. In an instant the fury was back, burning like bile in his throat.

''There is something else.'' Izzy's voice lowered.

Her look was so grave he found himself wondering what could be more serious than what she had already told him.

''I lied about Aaron's letter. But you must never let him know.''

''What about the letter?''

''It did arrive, as I'd said, at the First Pennsylvania Congregation. But after it was passed from family to family for several weeks, someone brought it to the tavern and nailed it to the wall, where it became the object of ridicule.''

Though Matt felt a flash of anger for the sake of his innocent son, he had to admit that he wasn't surprised. ''It sounds like the sort of thing that would be snickered over by the tavern crowd. I doubt there are many in this world who would be willing to leave the comfort of family to make a home in the wilderness for four motherless children.''

''But, you see, Aaron's letter spoke to a need in

me. All I've ever wanted was to be part of a family. What was the risk, if it meant I could finally have my heart's desire?''

Her eyes gleamed with the memory. ''I tore down his letter and read it night after night until, finally, I found the courage to answer it. And, oh, the fine stories I began to spin in my mind. I would start a new life, with a fine new name, Isabella McCree. And Izzy the Gimp would be forever forgotten, except by the drunks at the Purdy tavern.''

''Is the tavern where you first met Cutler?'' Matt could scarcely speak his name without gritting his teeth.

She looked away. ''Cutler. And others. There were a lot of men who tried to follow me outside and have their way, but after I carved up Otis Blandin one hot summer night, they pretty much left me alone. The word got around that I was a bit touched in the head.''

''Is that why you never married?'' Matt asked softly. ''Because you...carved up Otis Blandin?''

''Oh, no. I've always known I wouldn't be wed. That's why I had no way of preparing how to be a wife, how to give a husband his rights. It was explained to me in the foundling home that no man would ever marry a cripple.''

At his arched brow she screwed up her courage and removed her shoes. ''This was a lie, too, Matthew.'' Though this was the hardest of all to admit, she let out a small sigh of relief now that it was over. It was painful to reveal all her secrets, but it also gave her a sense of freedom.

She wiggled her toes. ''These shoes hide my deformity, but they're quite painful to wear after many hours each day. My one leg is shorter than the other. Reverend Halfyard explained that my mother probably committed some sin with her legs, and that was why I was born like this.''

"Sinned with her legs?'' Matt couldn't keep the bitter sarcasm from his tone. ''Did the good reverend explain how that could be possible?''

"He said my mother was probably a thief who could outrun the authorities. And so, as retribution, I would never be able to run and play like other children.''

"What nonsense. And you believed him?''

Izzy shrugged. ''It seems as good a reason as any.''

"Did no one ever suggest to you that nature simply erred?''

"Reverend Halfyard said there is a reason for everything under heaven. And the sin of my parents was visited upon me.''

"Isabella.'' Matt's teeth were clenched as tightly as his fists. ''I have no patience with such nonsense. Nor should you. These things simply happen, for no good reason.''

"That's easy for you to say, Matthew, since nature was very generous to you and your children. But once I've displayed my deformity, you'll see for yourself.''

She got to her feet and began to limp around the room.

As she passed the bed Matt grabbed her hand, stopping her in midstride. He drew her close, then said, ''Show me your foot, Isabella.''

She hung her head. "Don't ask this of me, Matthew."

He pressed her hand between both of his. "Show me."

Her movements were stiff and awkward as she lifted her skirts.

"Up here." His tone was gruff as he patted the edge of the bed.

She lifted her foot to the mattress.

In the moonlight he studied it. "The only deformity I see are the marks of the tight laces and the red, swollen toes from the confining shoes. Otherwise, I see only a small, dainty, perfect foot."

"It is not the foot that is deformed, Matthew. It is my leg. And the shoes add just enough height so that I don't limp when I walk."

"You aren't listening to me, Isabella. Maybe this will convince you." He shocked her by pressing his lips to her foot. "Your foot is not deformed. And neither are you."

She felt a jumble of sensations rocketing through her, leaving all her defenses shattered.

He kissed her toes, her instep, her arch, her ankle. She felt so weak she feared for a moment she might fall.

"Matthew, I..."

"You're cold." His warm fingers traced her calf, sending prickles of pleasure along her spine. "Come to bed, Isabella."

"I...can't." She lowered her foot to the floor and started to step back.

He caught her hand, holding her when she would have run.

"There's no need to worry about my...husbandly rights. In my condition, all I can do is hold you." He lifted aside the blankets and drew her down until she was lying beside him. "And even that might prove to be too much." He rolled to his side and caught his breath on a pain.

"Here. Lie still." She eased the pillows around him, cushioning his painful shoulder. Then she curled up beside him, feeling the warmth of his body.

"Warm enough?" He linked his fingers with hers.

"Yes."

"Good. Now go to sleep. And I'll do the same."

The last thing she saw was the glimmer of moonlight in his eyes and the curve of his lips as he smiled at her. Tears of gratitude, of relief welled up, blurring her vision as they spilled over, coursing down her cheeks. With his thumbs he wiped away her tears and pressed her cheek to his chest.

Against her will, her eyes closed. Feeling safe and warm, she slept.

Chapter Thirteen

Matt lay listening to the soft, steady sound of breathing beside him. The moonlight had faded, with only the faint glimmer of starlight through the darkened windows.

His body ached in places he hadn't even known were there. But the knowledge that Isabella was sharing his bed made the pain tolerable.

He thought about all the things she'd told him. Painful, secret things that had caused her shame for a lifetime. Yet she'd taken that first tentative step out of the darkness.

He shifted so that he could watch her as she slept. Her hair spilled across the pillow. Starlight uncovered even more hidden glints of gold among the brown strands. Her brow was smooth and unlined, reflecting a sweetness, an innocence that were a joy to behold. Her lashes cast long, spiky shadows on her cheeks. Her nose, small and upturned, and her full, pouty lips begged to be kissed.

He couldn't resist the temptation and brushed a kiss as light as a snowflake across her nose and mouth.

She came instantly awake.

"Matthew." She leaned up on one elbow, shoved hair from her eyes. "I thought for a moment you had..." She swallowed back what she'd been about to say. What fanciful dreams had she been spinning? Dreams of a lover's kisses as delicate as a raindrop. "Did you sleep?"

"A little."

She touched a hand to his forehead. "You have no fever. How do you feel?"

"Sore. But I'll live."

"You must be hungry. You never ate a thing yesterday. I'll go fix you something."

"Wait, Isabella. Relax a minute." She was always scurrying off to work, so eager to please.

He closed his hand around her wrist, then placed her fingers on his, measuring. "So small and slender. How can such small hands do so much work?"

"All my life I've had to work or starve. I guess hard work is just a habit."

"You're becoming a habit with me, Isabella. A very pleasant habit."

She sat back, warm and languid. Maybe she hadn't only dreamed that kiss. "I...am?"

"Mmm-hmm." He pressed her palm to his lips, starting a series of delicious tingles along her spine.

"You don't mind that I can't...that we haven't..." Her voice trailed off with embarrassment.

He wanted to laugh. But she was so earnest. "I won't press you, Isabella."

"You won't?"

He shook his head. "When you're ready, we'll simply let it happen."

"But how will I know?"

"You'll know."

"But how?"

"Trust me, Isabella. When the time comes, you'll know."

"I hope you're right. But—" she swallowed "—what if it never happens?"

He gave an exaggerated groan. "Then I'll just have to go around the countryside fighting tough army sergeants. Or even grizzly bears. After all, a man has to find some outlet for his frustrations."

That had her giggling.

Matt thought it the most delightful sound he'd ever heard. "You have a wonderful laugh. You ought to do it more often, Isabella."

"My heart just feels so light. Now that you know the truth about me, I feel free. Free to be myself."

"If you could be anything in the world, what would you be?" he asked.

She stretched out beside him and closed her eyes, lifting her arms over her head. "Part of a big, loving family. It's all I've ever wanted."

He leaned up, staring down at her. "You don't want much, do you?"

Her eyes snapped open. "Not much? Matthew, it's everything."

"Then your wish is my command." He brushed his lips over hers. "Will you settle for a husband and four children?"

She could see herself reflected in his eyes. Could

feel the thrill of his kiss all the way to her toes. For a moment her heart seemed to stop. Then it began thundering in her chest. "Would you mind...doing that again, Matthew?"

"This?" He touched his mouth to hers, all the while watching her eyes. They widened, then fluttered closed.

On a moan she lowered her arms and clung to his waist. Her fingers encountered bare flesh, and she experienced another thrill.

It felt so good to touch him. To feel his strong, solid flesh beneath her hand. And the feel of his mouth on hers, that strong, clever mouth that made her pulse pound and her breath back up in her throat.

Was this wrong? But how could that be? They were husband and wife. Surely this was not what Mrs. Hastings had meant when she'd demanded a vow of virtue.

Matt came up for air and heard her sigh of frustration. "More?"

She smiled. "Yes. Oh, yes."

It was just a simple kiss. Mouth to mouth. And yet, it was so achingly sweet it changed everything. There could have been thunder and lightning. An earth tremor. And all she would care about was this. This rush of heat. This roar of two heartbeats. And her world tilting dangerously out of control.

He kissed her with a skill that left her breathless. There was such patience in him. Laced with a hint of danger. The combination was potent. Like a drug. Weakening her.

The innocence in her, the fear warred with a woman's awakening desire.

"Kiss me back, Isabella." Sweet heaven, he needed her to.

His words spurred a boldness in her that neither of them expected. Suddenly she was clinging to him, her mouth hot and hungry, her body straining toward his.

Stunned, he dragged her closer and plundered her mouth. The scent of cinnamon and sugar and the clean, fresh fragrance of cooking were all around her. He breathed them in, needing to fill himself with her.

He knew every sound in this cabin. The hiss and snap of the fire. The creak of logs in the cold night air. The sighing of the wind along the chimney. But for now he was deaf to all but the sound of her loving. She whimpered as her hands roamed his flesh and her mouth moved on his, wanting more, taking more. Her breath was coming faster now as she lost herself in the pleasure.

His fingers found the buttons of her gown. This time there was no frantic tearing of fabric, no haste. Instead he unbuttoned slowly, lazily, slipping it further and further off her shoulders. His lips followed, burning a trail of fire down her throat, across each bared shoulder.

"Oh, Matthew. That feels so good. Can you do it again?"

Her simple request staggered him. He had to rest his forehead on hers a moment, to summon the gentleness she required. A need was building in him. A force that would require all his control to tame.

And so he kissed her neck, her shoulders, and drew

her gown away before reaching for the ribbons of her chemise. She gasped in surprise when he tossed it aside, freeing her breasts. But before she could protest, he covered one firm peak with his mouth, and her body arched instinctively.

"Isabella, you're so beautiful."

In answer she moaned, low and deep. With each brush of his tongue, each tug of his lips, there was an answering tug deep inside that had the heat building, and a mixture of pleasure and pain that left her gasping.

She made no protest when his hands moved lower, to remove her petticoat and heavy cotton stockings. He knew, by the way she quivered at the touch of his fingers and mouth, that she was becoming lost in the passion.

This was how he'd dreamed of her all those long, empty nights. Naked. Willing. Eager.

"I want to look at you, Isabella. And touch you. All of you."

She expected a wave of shame, but none came. There was no embarrassment. No feeling of wickedness. Only this need. Building. Growing. Was this how it was between husbands and wives? Was this how it ought to be?

"You're so soft. So lovely. Even lovelier than I'd dreamed." With hands and mouth he touched and tasted until her breath hitched and her body arched with need.

"Sweet salvation, Matthew." The words were torn from her lips. "I don't know what to do."

"There's nothing to do. Just let it happen."

"I don't... I can't..." Her breath backed up in her throat. She felt as if she were standing on the highest mountain peak. One step and she'd soar. But fear, the fear of falling, held her back. And so she clung, afraid to relax, afraid to let go.

And then he touched her as no man ever had before. And he found her hot and wet and ready. His hands, those clever, greedy hands, took her over the first peak.

She was out of control. There were so many sensations colliding, convulsing through her that she couldn't seem to get her bearings. She flew. She soared higher than she'd ever dreamed. And when she struggled to catch her breath, he gave her no chance to recover before he took her on an even faster, more dizzying spin.

He knew if he didn't find release for his own need soon, he'd go mad. Covering her mouth with his, he murmured, "Hold on to me, love."

Love. The word was like a beacon in a storm. A bright, blinding light that swept away all the darkness from her heart.

Love. For that simple word she would follow him through the unknown. Would walk through fire. Endure any hardship. She gritted her teeth, anticipating pain.

He entered her then, as slowly, as gently as he could manage. Instead of the expected shock and pain, she knew only more and more pleasure, exploding through her in shock wave after shock wave.

She felt more alive than at any time in her life. Energized, she clutched him, her strength matching his as she wrapped herself around him, her body moving with his in perfect rhythm.

They felt themselves drowning in a deep, dark river of passion. They rode it, swept along in the current, until, spent, cleansed, they lay, struggling for breath.

They lay, still joined. Tremors continued to rock them as they floated gently back to earth.

Neither of them was willing to break this fragile bond they had forged. But as Matt nuzzled her face, he tasted the salt of her tears.

Tears? God in heaven, he felt his heart jolt, then stop. "Isabella, I've hurt you. How could I…what was I thinking?" He cursed himself for being a brute. A barbarian. "I was too rough. I forgot how innocent you are." With a muffled oath he rolled aside, hating himself for having been the cause of her pain.

At once she knelt up, framing his face with her hands. "You didn't hurt me, Matthew. I'm crying because…because I'm so happy."

"You're sure?" He covered her hands with his own, gripping them tightly. "You aren't just saying that?"

She shook her head, and the smile she gave him melted the ice around his heart and had it beating once more. "Is it always as wondrous as this?"

"It can be. When it's right."

"And what makes it right?"

He drew her down until she was lying on top of him, her forehead pressed to his. His breath came out in a long, shuddering sigh. "When it's between two people who care about each other."

She felt fresh tears cloud her vision. With her eyes closed tightly, she clung to him, reluctant to let go. "I do...care about you, Matthew."

"And I care about you, Isabella." He wrapped his arms around her, molding her to the length of him. She fit so perfectly. As though made for him alone.

Incredibly, he could feel himself becoming aroused again. "I'm not sure how it happened. Or when. Maybe it was seeing you with my children." He smiled, and the warmth of it was in his voice. "Or maybe it was the first time I tasted your biscuits."

She lifted her head. An impish smile touched her lips. "So that's it. It's really my cooking you've grown fond of."

"You really are a remarkable cook. If I didn't know better, I'd think some clever woman taught you the secret to every man's heart."

"Oh, perhaps." She caught his finger between her teeth and drew it into her mouth.

The rush of heat caught him by surprise. "I know one thing, Isabella. It isn't your cooking I'm thinking about right now."

"It isn't?" Though her smile was as innocent as ever, he had the impression that it masked a glimmer of newfound knowledge.

"If you're not careful, I may keep you awake all night." When her smile grew, he whispered, "You don't seem too upset by my suggestion."

She gave a gentle shake of her head. "I wouldn't mind at all. In fact—" she timidly brushed her lips over his and thrilled at the groan that escaped him "—I have so much I'd like to learn." Emboldened by his reaction, she lowered her mouth for another kiss. "That is, if you're not hurting too much to teach me more...."

His moan turned into a growl of pleasure. In one quick motion he rolled her over and covered her mouth in a hot, hungry kiss. "Where would you like to begin?"

"At the beginning, please." At his astonished look she added, "I wouldn't want to miss anything."

In the darkness Matt winced at the twinge of pain in his shoulder. All night, there'd been no time to think about the pain. It had been completely obliterated by the loving. And what loving.

Once Isabella had overcome her fear, she had become a most delightful surprise. Her lovemaking had been by turns shy and bold, simple and exotic. He had never known such a night of pleasure.

He reached for her and was disappointed to find her gone. But before he could get up and go in search of her, he saw the flickering of lantern light as she made her way to the bed.

"What's all this?"

She set a tray on the pillow and knelt beside him. "Food. I'm worried about you. You didn't eat a thing yesterday."

"And you're afraid all the exertion you put me through will be the death of me?"

She blushed and reached for a steaming cup of coffee. "Here. This will warm you."

He accepted it and drank, then handed it back to her. "I know a better way to keep warm."

She couldn't help laughing. "Indeed you do. But now you must eat something." She handed him a plate on which she'd piled several slices of roast venison and biscuits spread with honey.

He ate in silence, occasionally sighing over the tenderness of the meat and the sweetness of the biscuits.

"Here." He offered her the last bite of biscuit, then drew her close and licked the honey from her lips. "As wonderful as your cooking is, you taste even better."

"Then I don't know why I bothered to feed you," she said with a little pout.

"I was wondering the same thing." He set aside the plate and lifted a hand to stroke her hair. "But then I realized how clever you've become."

"Clever?"

He caught a strand of her hair and drew her fractionally closer, all the while loving the emotions he could read in her eyes. "You planned all this so that you could build up my strength for more loving."

She pressed her hands to his chest. "Matthew. It's almost dawn. The children will be waking up soon and wanting their breakfast."

"Really? I hadn't noticed." He dragged her close, pinning her beneath the weight of his body. "I guess we'd better hurry then."

"Matth—"

He swallowed her protest and muttered against her lips, "I have so much loving to share, Isabella. Let's not waste a minute."

With soft sighs and whispered words they slipped once more into that secret, passionate world that only lovers can share.

Chapter Fourteen

"Pa." Aaron, just entering the cabin, nearly dropped the pail of milk when he saw his father walking out of the bedroom. "You're up and about already?"

"Of course, boy." Matt shot his son a radiant smile.

"How're you feeling, Pa?" Del climbed down from the loft and paused at the foot of the ladder.

"Fine. Never better."

Benjamin and Clement glanced at each other in surprise, before visibly relaxing. After the vicious fight they'd witnessed between their father and the sergeant, they'd fretted that their father would be laid up for days, or possibly weeks.

"Come and eat," Izzy called. "You children must be starving." She turned from the stove and handed Del a platter of scrambled eggs.

As the others passed the food around the table, Aaron fell silent and studied Izzy. She was barefoot, and limping slightly. Not so much that anyone would notice, but the more he watched, the more he realized she moved with an awkward, uneven gait. He experienced a wave of bitter anger, recalling Cutler's crude remarks. Though the younger ones might think otherwise, he was convinced that it hadn't been Cutler's treatment of the stallion that had triggered his father's rage; it had been his cruel taunts about Isabella.

The boy had spied her gown, freshly washed, flapping on the clothesline outside. In its place she was wearing one of Matt's shirts and a pair of Clement's britches and had tied an apron over them. Her hair was wild, flying in all directions, even though she'd tried to tame it by tying it back with a ribbon.

She appeared flustered, but that was understandable, considering the circumstances. After all, she'd practically had to pry their father off Sergeant Cutler. For a few tense moments, they'd all thought their pa would kill him.

"There wasn't time to bake fresh biscuits this morning, so I toasted yesterday's bread and sprinkled a little sugar and cinnamon on top." Izzy set a plate on the table and handed Benjamin a platter of sliced venison.

"Coffee, Matthew?" She paused beside his chair and filled his cup.

"Thank you." He looked up and gave her a smile that would have melted a winter's worth of snow atop the Sierras.

She blushed furiously and glanced away.

Aaron gaped at the two of them. Despite the dressings bulging beneath the collar of his father's shirt, and the ugly purple bruise spreading around his eye and cheek, he looked as frisky as that old roan stallion surrounded by a herd of mares. On Isabella's cheeks were two bright spots of color. And when she returned Matt's smile, her own was dazzling.

The truth hit Aaron with all the force of a raging blizzard. His jaw dropped. His eyes widened.

"Aaron?"

He blinked. And realized everyone was looking at him.

"I said, would you like some milk, Aaron?" Izzy was standing beside him, holding aloft a pitcher.

"Yes'm. Thank you." His hand shook as he accepted the glass of milk.

To hide his embarrassment, he downed it in one long swallow.

"I spotted some tracks across the south meadow yesterday, Pa." Clement wiped his mouth with the back of his hand. "Looked like a pretty big herd of mustangs. Want to have a look after breakfast?"

Matt shook his head. "Not today, son."

At his unexpected refusal, everyone looked up at him.

"I've never known you to pass up a chance to track a herd of mustangs, Pa. What's wrong?" Benjamin asked in alarm.

"Nothing. It's just that I've got plans for today." Matt casually drained his cup.

"Plans?" Izzy turned from the fire.

"I thought we'd all take it slow and easy today. Maybe take the wagon down to the meadow and have ourselves a picnic."

"A...picnic?" Izzy spilled the coffee and had to

stoop to wipe it up. She looked up from the floor. "We're going to ride all the way down to the meadow just to have a picnic?"

"Unless you can think of something you'd rather do."

Izzy shook her head. "I can't think of a thing, Matthew."

The children glanced at one another, wondering what to make of this.

"Well, then." Matt helped himself to another piece of cinnamon toast. "How soon can everybody be ready?"

Caught up in the excitement, the children began gulping their milk and swallowing the last of their breakfast.

"Soon's I can get on my boots," Benjamin shouted, struggling to sort through the pile of boots beside the door.

"Soon's I can hitch the team." Clement was already headed outside.

"Soon's I can lock up my chickens." Del raced to the door, with the hounds bounding after her.

"I'll get my dress from the line." Izzy hurried away, untying her apron as she walked. "But I'll need some time to prepare the food."

"Take all the time you need." Matt poured himself another cup of coffee and turned from the fire, pleased with himself. When he spotted Aaron still seated at the table, he took the seat across from him.

"Something on your mind, son?"

"No, sir. Yes, sir. I mean…" The boy ducked his

head, then slowly lifted his gaze to his father. "You're different this morning."

"I am?" Matt set down his cup and crossed his arms on the table. Then he slowly nodded his head. "I guess I am. Marriage to the right woman does that. Softens some of the hard edges. Makes you want to do nice things for the people you love. You don't mind?"

"No, sir. I'm glad. And I'm glad you stopped Sergeant Cutler from hurting Isabella."

"I'm not proud of fighting, but it had to be done." Matt stood and rounded the table, dropping a hand on Aaron's shoulder. "I have you to thank for all this. For making us a family again."

"I didn't do that, Pa. Isabella did."

Slowly Matt absorbed the jolt of knowledge and nodded his head. "I guess you're right, son. It is Isabella who's made us a family again."

"And I sure am glad that you and Isabella finally found that...sweetening you told me about, Pa." With a grin, the boy pushed away from the table and hurried out the door.

Matt waited until the door closed behind him. Then he threw back his head and roared with laughter. They'd found the sweetening, all right. And by God, it was finer than old wine.

"Do you know any good songs, Isabella?" As the wagon rolled across the meadow, the children's voices rang with dozens of questions.

Izzy turned on the hard wooden seat and faced the children, who were lounging in the back of the wagon, along with the eager hounds, who were clearly enjoying this rare treat. "Most of the songs I learned in the tavern aren't fit for children's ears. But I do remember one I used to hear the people singing in church."

"I thought your pa was the pastor," Del said innocently.

Izzy braced herself, prepared to answer truthfully. The boys would have absorbed some of the facts from what Sergeant Cutler had said. But most would have been lost on this innocent little girl. "That was a lie, Del. I made that up, because I wished I had folks like the reverend and his wife. The truth is, I grew up in a foundling home."

"You mean you were an orphan?"

"That's right."

"If you never knew your folks, how'd you get to be such a good ma?" Clement asked.

Did he have any idea what a compliment he'd just paid her? Izzy had to swallow twice before she could find her voice. "I guess…I just try to be the kind of mother I'd always wished for."

She felt a squeeze of her hand and looked down to find that Matt had linked his fingers with hers.

"I know a song," he said. To lighten the mood he led them in a spirited rendition of "Amazing Grace." Through it all, Izzy watched and listened in wonder. His voice was a rich, clear baritone.

"You sing it better than our town's minister did."

He made a slight bow. "Thank you, ma'am."

"Where did you learn the words, Pa?" Aaron asked.

"When I was a boy, my folks and I sang it every Sunday, with the rest of the people in our congregation."

"Then how come you told us you didn't know how to pray?" Benjamin asked accusingly.

Matt winced. "I guess I'm guilty of lying, too."

"But why?" his son demanded.

"Maybe there's just been too much anger in me to allow any room for good things, like laughter, or songs, or prayers."

Del touched a hand to his shoulder. "Is the anger all gone, Pa?"

Matt nodded. "I certainly hope so."

"Is it gone 'cause you beat up on Sergeant Cutler?" Clement asked.

"Maybe. But I think the real reason might be Isabella." Again he squeezed her hand and saw the flush that stole over her cheeks. His tone warmed. "She just makes it easy to forget everything except the good things."

"Wait till you see the good things she packed in the picnic basket," Del said with a grin.

"Sh." Izzy put a finger to her mouth. "That's our secret, remember, Del?"

"Oh. Yes'm. I almost forgot."

The two shared a conspiratorial smile.

Benjamin pointed to the dusty toes of her boots, poking out from beneath the hem of her skirt. "How come you're not wearing your shiny shoes today, Isabella?"

Aaron gave him a swift punch in the arm to silence him. "Don't you know anything?"

Surprised, Benjamin punched him back. "Now, what's that supposed to mean?"

"It means if you had any sense at all you wouldn't ask such a question. You're as dumb as those boys in town."

"Am not." The younger boy looked wounded and baffled.

"Are, too." Aaron doubled up his fist, prepared to land another blow.

"Wait." Izzy touched a hand to his arm. "Thank you for defending me, Aaron. But Benjamin didn't mean anything by his question. And he deserves an answer." She turned to the others. "I was born with one leg shorter than the other. My shoes add just enough height so that my limp isn't noticeable. But they're very heavy, because of the added weight, and must be laced very tightly. So I thought I'd give my feet a rest today. Especially since your father assured me he doesn't mind that I limp."

"I don't mind, either, Isabella," Benjamin said softly.

"Neither do I," Clement chimed in.

Following her brothers' lead, Del echoed their words. "Me, neither. You're still pretty. And you cook better'n anybody in the world."

Izzy leaned over the seat and gave each of them a hug, reserving the biggest hug for Aaron, who had jumped to her defense. She leaned back, enjoying the wind in her hair, the sun on her face. And enjoying most of all the realization that the girl who had spent a lifetime alone was suddenly surrounded by fierce protectors.

Matt glanced over and saw the tears she was trying to blink away. "How about another song?"

Minutes later the air was filled with laughter as he led them through a chorus of silly rhyming words he'd learned as a boy. Hearing the laughter of Matt and his children, Izzy dried her tears and found herself laughing along with them.

Her heart had never felt so light. Or so filled with love.

"This looks like a good spot." Matt reined in the team and climbed down from the wagon, then lifted his arms to assist Izzy. But instead of setting her down, he swung her around and around before pressing a kiss to her temple.

"Matthew." She blushed and glanced at the children and dogs scrambling from the back of the wagon. "What will they think?"

"That I've completely lost my senses." He kissed her again, then set her on her feet and retrieved the food basket. As he handed it to her, he leaned close. "Maybe we could send them to play in the fields for an hour. Then I could do more than just kiss you."

"Matthew Jamison Prescott." She shot him a horrified look. "I believe you have lost your senses."

"Maybe I've just found them." He touched a hand to her cheek. "Thanks to you, Isabella."

With the hounds leaping about in a frenzy of activity, Matt went off with the boys in search of wood for a fire, leaving Izzy and Del to lay out the food.

"Pa's acting funny." Del helped Izzy spread a

blanket beside a stream. "He never even mentioned our chores."

"Maybe he needs a day to recover from his wounds."

The little girl shrugged. "He doesn't act like he's hurting. He just isn't acting like Pa."

Izzy set a crock of lemonade in the stream to cool, then brushed her damp hands down her skirt. "Is that good or bad?"

Del brightened. "It's really good, Isabella. There were a lot of times that I thought Pa had forgotten how to smile."

Izzy felt an ache around her heart. For the man who had lost his reason to smile. For the children who had been forced to watch helplessly while he worked his way through his grief. But at least, she thought, they'd had each other. And now they had her, as well. She whispered a solemn vow to do everything in her power to see that they always had a reason to smile.

"Come on." She dropped an arm around the little girl's shoulders and led her toward the picnic basket. "Let's turn this meal into a feast."

It was indeed a feast. Rabbit, cooked over the fire until the meat fell from the bones. Venison steaks, brushed with honey and sizzling over the flames. Biscuits so light they melted in the mouth. Potatoes, carrots and turnips simmered in broth and mashed together with butter. And to top it all off, little tarts filled with apples and cinnamon.

The children had climbed trees, turned cartwheels and chased after the hounds, working up fierce appetites. Matt and Aaron had chopped down a dead tree and loaded the logs into the back of the wagon.

Now, replete, refreshed, Matt rolled a cigarette, then lifted a burning twig from the fire and held it to the tip. "I don't believe I've ever eaten anything so fine." He drew smoke into his lungs and leaned back against the trunk of a tree.

"There's still one tart left." Izzy glanced around, but the children had wandered off and were engaged in a game of tag.

"Not even one more bite. Sit here with me."

"I should clean up a few things first."

"We came here to relax, Isabella. Not to make more work for you." He patted the grass beside him. "Come here."

With a sigh, she sank down beside him and stretched her feet toward the fire. They sat in companionable silence, listening to the laughter of the children drifting on the breeze.

Matt drew up one leg, resting his arms on his knee. "It's good to hear them laugh again."

"Losing their mother…" Izzy touched a hand to his sleeve. "I can only imagine how terrible it must have been for them. For you."

He shook his head. "I only made things worse for them. I had all this anger. And no one to direct it at except them. I'm lucky they don't hate me."

"Matthew. How could they hate you?" Her fingers tightened on his arm. "You're their father."

"Do you think that's enough?" His tone was rougher than he'd intended. "Do you really believe that just being a parent will make us good? That our children should forgive our every fault?''

"I think—" seeing the mixture of pain and anger in his eyes, she chose her words carefully "—that children are capable of forgiving almost anything, as long as they know that their parents are sorry.''

"Ah. Repentance.'' He took a deep drag on the cigarette, filling his lungs. "I've known enough of that to last a lifetime.''

He tossed aside the stub, watching as the flames devoured it. When he looked up, the anger had seeped away. He glanced across the meadow, where the children were tossing sticks to the dogs and chasing furiously after them when they failed to bring them back.

"I think this might be the perfect time to see if I can steal more than a kiss.''

She pretended to be shocked. But when he gathered her close, her arms wrapped around his neck and her lips parted in anticipation. He kissed her long and slow and deep. At her eager response, he felt a wave of heat that started at his toes and shot straight to his loins.

Just then Del ran up, chasing one of the hounds, and nearly tripped over them.

"Come on, Pa,'' she called. "You've got to help me catch Shilo. He's got one of my boots in his mouth.''

"Matthew, those are the only boots she owns,'' Izzy whispered.

He groaned and pressed his forehead to hers. Then, banking his inner fire, he gave her a quick, hard kiss before getting to his feet. As he helped her up he whispered, ''I'll chase the fool dog now. But when we get back to the cabin tonight, don't forget where we left off.''

She laughed as he raced off beside his daughter. But as she began clearing up the remains of their picnic, she had to stop and touch her hands to her hot cheeks. Just thinking about the pleasures that awaited her had her heart fluttering like a caged bird.

She wouldn't forget. Nor would she ever have enough of Matthew's loving.

Chapter Fifteen

Izzy lay in the big bed, feeling oddly comforted by the steady rise and fall of Matt's chest. She'd never known such peace.

Last night, driving home from the meadow, she had experienced such a torrent of emotions. Bittersweet longing at the press of his hip against hers on the hard wooden seat as they jolted along in the wagon. A rush of tenderness at the sight of Matt carrying his sleeping daughter to her bed in the loft. And then, when he'd come to her with that dark look and kissed her until she was breathless, she'd experienced a wild rush of need, so hot, so swift it left her shaken to the core.

This man, so angry, so wounded, touched her in a way no other man ever could.

He had overcome all her fears, beaten down all her defenses. She felt safe with him. No harm could possibly touch her here. Best of all, she felt free to be herself. No more pretenses. No more lies. She had finally found…home. The realization brought a mist of tears to her eyes.

"I know I look pretty rough. But am I so repulsive I make you cry?"

"Matthew." She sat up, hair tumbling. "I didn't want to wake you."

"You didn't. I woke myself. Now, what's so terrible it has you shedding tears?"

"They're happy tears. I was thinking how much I love you. And your children. And this cabin."

He didn't know what had him more shaken. Her simple honesty. Or the fact that he'd never expected to hear those words again in his lifetime. His heart seemed to swell until it was too big for his chest.

"Come here." He gathered her into his arms and pressed his lips to her temple. His hands began a slow, rhythmic exploration. "Looks like we've both caught it," he muttered against a tangle of hair.

"Caught what?"

"The fever. There's no cure. But there is a treatment I highly recommend."

"Really? What is it?"

He began unbuttoning her night shift. His lips followed the trail of his fingers. "This. And this. Hmm. And this."

With exquisite tenderness he showed her, more than any words ever could, the depth of his love.

"Pa. You in there? Isabella? Anybody?"

At the sound of Aaron's voice, Izzy stirred in Matt's arms, then, as the realization dawned that she and Matt had fallen back asleep, she sat up.

"Matthew. Sweet salvation. It's late morning. The children…"

"Will be just fine." He drew her down for a long, leisurely kiss. "It won't hurt them to wait a few minutes for their breakfast."

"But they'll think we're..." She pushed against him, struggling to sit up. Her cheeks were crimson. "They'll know that we..."

"That we slept together? That we loved?" He chuckled. "Isabella, how long will it take you to accept the fact that we're married? That we have the right to enjoy a little private time together?"

"I guess—" she looked away "—old habits are hard to change."

"It's all right." He sat up and drew her back against him, trailing his lips along the back of her neck. "I'm grateful for all those years you were overly modest. Now I don't ever have to imagine another man's hands touching you."

As she sighed and angled her head, giving him easier access, he murmured, "But I'm even more grateful that you're such a quick study."

"I have learned a lot. Thanks to your patient instructions."

"Not nearly as patient as you think." He bit back a smile, thinking about all the passion, the frustration he'd had to deal with.

Izzy sighed. She could go on like this forever, just being held in Matthew's arms and kissed so sweetly. She turned and brushed her lips over his before sliding out of bed. "Now let's get dressed, before Aaron decides to fix breakfast himself."

That had Matt slipping into his trousers and tugging on his boots. "This could be dangerous. I don't think

I could stand to go back to those days of half-cooked meat and biscuits as hard as bullets.''

The two of them were still chuckling when they stepped out of the bedroom.

Aaron was at the door, lugging a pail of milk. Del had just entered with a basket filled with eggs. Benjamin and Clement were washing up in the basin by the door. The hounds were milling about, eager to be fed.

Izzy was a model of efficiency as she set a pan of biscuit dough on the fire, scrambled a bowl of eggs and sliced meat. Handing the scraps to Clement, she said, ''Take the dogs outside, please, Clement. I think this should satisfy them.''

''Yes'm.'' He held the door and the hounds raced ahead of him.

Without a word, Del and Benjamin began to set the table, while Aaron filled their glasses with milk.

Matt stirred the coals in the fireplace and added a log. As the flames licked along the bark he glanced around at the tranquil scene. It amazed him that only weeks ago they had faced each day with dread. Their days had consisted of a meal of hard biscuits and half-cooked meat, endless hours of backbreaking work and an even drearier evening meal, before falling into bed, too exhausted to even dream.

''Breakfast is ready,'' Izzy announced.

Matt and the children took their places at the table, and she began passing the platters of food.

As she took her place at the table, Matt shocked her by saying, ''Why don't you teach us one of your blessings, Isabella?''

For the space of a heartbeat she could only stare at him. Then, bowing her head, she murmured, "Bless this food. And those who share it."

"Amen," Matt said.

The children, who had watched and listened in wide-eyed silence, followed his lead and repeated, "Amen."

"Was that praying?" Del asked innocently.

Color flooded Izzy's cheeks. "I don't know any real prayers. These are just some things I made up, so I'd feel like those folks who went to Sunday prayer meetings."

"The words don't matter," Matt said softly. "It's the thought that counts."

Izzy sipped her coffee and hoped it would melt the lump in her throat.

"I'm going to need my hair cut again soon, Pa." Aaron ran a hand through his hair, brushing the bangs from his eyes.

"Me, too." Benjamin lifted his long dark hair away from his collar.

Matt winked at Izzy. "Tell me, wife. Do your talents run to haircutting, too?"

She shrugged. Right now, her heart was so light she'd try anything. "You can find out right after breakfast." As an afterthought she added, "I wonder how you'll look bald, Matthew. That is, if we discover I don't have any talent for haircutting."

The children howled, and Matt gave a look of mock pain before joining their laughter.

When the dishes were done, Matt located a pair of scissors and joined the others, who were waiting outside. Aaron had carried a kitchen chair into the sun-light.

"Who's willing to be my first victim?" Izzy snipped the air with her scissors.

"I guess I am." Aaron, always the responsible one, removed his shirt and draped a towel around his shoulders.

Izzy combed and cut, while the others watched and offered comments.

"You're cutting too much, Isabella." Benjamin caught a wisp of fine blond hair that drifted past him on the breeze.

"You keep that up, he'll look like old Mr. Sutton," Clement said with a giggle.

Del hung upside down from a branch of a tree and studied her oldest brother. "I think you look just fine, Aaron."

"Are you almost through, Isabella?" he demanded.

"Just a few minutes more." She combed his hair, clipping as she did, then took a step back to admire her work. "What do you think, Matthew?"

He nodded. "That's a much better haircut than I ever gave. Go along inside, son, and see what you think."

Aaron raced to the cabin to study himself in the cracked mirror of his father's bedroom. Minutes later he emerged with a wide smile on his face. "I look like a man, Pa."

"That you do." Matt turned to Benjamin. "Your turn, boy."

Izzy cut his hair, then Clement's, earning praise from both boys.

"Now me." Del straddled the chair as her brothers had done.

"I thought…" Izzy paused, proceeding with caution. "That is, you have such pretty hair, Del, you might want to consider letting it grow."

"What for? It'll just get in my eyes when I'm doing my chores."

"I could braid it. Or curl it. Or tie it back with ribbons and combs. In fact, wait right here." Looking just a bit mysterious, Izzy raced inside, then returned carrying the pink gown she'd been making out of scraps of fabric. In her other hand was a matching pink ribbon.

"Is that mine?" the girl asked in disbelief.

Izzy nodded. "Do you like it?"

"It's too fine for me to wear. I'd get it all dirty the first time I did any chores."

"You wouldn't wear it for chores. This is for special times."

"Like when? We don't have any special times."

Izzy shrugged. "You can wear it when we go t town. And no one will ever again need to ask if you're a girl."

"I don't care what they think." Del's lips curled into a pout.

"Of course you don't. But there's no sense trying to look like your brothers, either. Don't hide yourself away, or pretend to be something you're not. That's what I did, Del. It was dishonest. Be proud of who you are."

The little girl was about to refuse, when Aaron said, "I think you should give it a try, Little Bit. And I think you should do as Isabella suggested and let your hair grow, too.''

"You do?''

He nodded. "You'd look awfully pretty in that pink dress and long yellow curls.''

"You wouldn't laugh?'' she challenged.

He shook his head. "I won't laugh. Promise.''

Since her hero had suggested it, Del didn't have the heart to refuse. "All right, Isabella. We won't cut my hair…yet. And I'll try the dress later.''

"You won't be sorry.'' Izzy tied the girl's hair back with the ribbon, then turned to Matt with a dazzling smile. "Your turn, Matthew.''

He knew why his wife had fought so hard to persuade Del to let her hair grow. He could still recall his outrage at the thought of a well-meaning woman cutting off all of a child's beautiful hair so that she wouldn't entice a man. He pushed the thought aside, determined to put it out of his mind.

He unbuttoned his shirt and wrapped the towel around his shoulders. But as she lifted the comb and scissors, he caught her hand. "Just a friendly warning. When you're finished, I'd better not see any scalp.''

"Can I help it if the scissors slip?'' she asked innocently.

Getting into the spirit of her teasing, the children giggled and called, "Better watch out, Pa. Isabella's hands are mighty slippery.''

Despite the laughter and teasing, she managed to finish cutting his hair. When he looked in the chipped mirror, he was forced to admit it was the best haircut he'd ever had.

"Very handsome," she said, coming up behind him.

"Me? Or the hair?"

"The hair, of course. Your face is barely tolerable."

He dragged her close. "Careful. You wouldn't want to rile me."

She was laughing, but there was a devilish glint in her eyes. "Maybe I would."

"Woman." He kissed her full on the lips, while the children stood in the doorway of the bedroom, laughing and clapping. "You're just full of surprises. Now I have one of my own."

"What is it?" She was as eager as the children.

"I thought we'd drive down to Sutton's Station today. See if we can spend some of our money."

"On what?" Izzy was still reeling from his kiss and sought to steady her spinning brain.

"Oh. Seed. And nails for the addition. And maybe even a new pair of britches for Clement."

"What's wrong with the britches I'm wearing?" the boy asked.

"Nothing. Except that Isabella likes wearing them, too. And I can't say I object to her wearing your britches once in a while. Actually, I like the way she looks in them." He winked, and Izzy blushed clear to her toes, while the children giggled. This was a side to their father they'd rarely seen. And one they were beginning to warm to.

"Seriously," he added, "you'll be needing some supplies before the snow closes the trail to town. After that, we're going to be pretty isolated."

"Will we stay here and do your chores, Pa?" Del asked.

Matt shook his head. "I thought I'd made that clear. We're all going." He glanced at Izzy and held her gaze until her cheeks were flushed. "We're a family. And we're going to town as a family. Del, why don't you take along some of your eggs?"

"You mean it, Pa?" The little girl's eyes lit with pleasure.

"I do. And, Benjamin, you might want to bring along some of your honeycombs. And, Clement, how about bringing some of your pelts? Like Isabella said, I think Webster Sutton would be willing to buy them from you."

The children were all staring at him as if they couldn't believe what they'd just heard.

"Now," he said with a grin, "how soon can everyone be ready?"

Izzy and the children were already scattering, too excited to even reply.

"Will you look at that." Aaron, seated on the wagon beside his father, whistled through his teeth as his little sister walked from the cabin, followed by Izzy.

Del was wearing the gown Izzy had pieced together from scraps of pink fabric. To hide the many seams, she had threaded pretty pink ribbon across the bodice and around several tiers of the skirt, turning it into a frothy pink confection.

"Well, don't you look pretty." Matt climbed down

and gave his daughter an admiring look before lifting her into the back of the wagon.

"Do I really, Pa?"

"As pretty as a little wildflower," he said, tousling her hair.

"Paaa." She smoothed the tangles and blew the bangs from her eyes. "Isabella says I'll have enough hair to curl in a couple of weeks. What do you think?"

"I think," he said diplomatically, "Isabella knows more about such things than I do." He turned and caught his wife's hand, leading her to the wagon. He lifted her up to the seat as easily as he'd lifted his daughter, then climbed up beside her and flicked the reins.

As the wagon rolled across the meadow, the hounds set up a chorus of barking and followed along until Matt gave them a stern command. At once they fell silent and returned to the cabin.

"I wish they could come with us, Pa," Del said wistfully.

"They won't mind," he said.

"Especially when they see the surprise I left for them," Izzy added.

"What surprise?" Del asked.

"A pan of meat scraps. They'll be so full, they'll probably sleep until we return. They won't even have time to miss us."

Soothed, the little girl stopped fretting and picked up one of Clement's pelts, pressing the softness to her cheek.

As they neared Sutton's Station and heard the

sound of voices and laughter, Izzy saw the children
begin to tense. She studied the boys in their carefully
mended clothes, their neatly combed hair, and Del,
who was already clutching Aaron's hand for comfort.
Hoping to put them at ease, she said, ''Remember.
Strangers won't judge us by the clothes we wear, but
by the smiles we wear. So put on your best smile and
see if you can't make a new friend today.''

Though the children looked doubtful, they climbed
down from the wagon and trailed behind Matt and
Izzy, their arms laden with the goods they were hoping to sell.

As they entered the general store they saw a group
of children clustered around Gertrude Sutton, who
was holding an armload of baskets and giving instructions in a loud voice. Benjamin, Clement and Del
deposited their goods on the counter, then turned to
listen to what she was saying.

''We'll allow you to keep any apples you find. We
ask only that you return the baskets to us after you've
emptied them into other containers at home.''

She glanced over at the newcomers. ''We're clearing the orchard before the winter snows come. Would
you children like to join us?''

''You mean we get to keep all the apples we find?''
Benjamin asked.

''That's right.'' Gertrude Sutton held out several
baskets.

After seeing their father's nod of approval, the children accepted.

''What about our eggs and honeycombs and
pelts?'' Del asked.

"I'll talk to Webster about them," Matt promised.

The children followed the others from the store. As they walked away, Gertrude was overheard remarking to Del, "What a beautiful dress. I don't believe I've ever seen you looking so fine, Delphinium."

"Thank you, ma'am." Del's voice was high-pitched with pride. "My new ma made it for me."

"Well. You're a very lucky little girl."

"Yes'm."

It took Izzy several attempts before she managed to swallow the lump in her throat. Did Del have any idea what she had just said? New ma. Oh, the sound of it was so sweet, Izzy thought her heart might explode with happiness.

Seeing the way she had to struggle with her emotions, Matt squeezed Izzy's hand as they turned away.

Webster Sutton looked down from his perch on a ladder where he was arranging a display of ladies' hats.

"How do, Matt. Mrs. Prescott."

Matt nodded. "Web. My family and I thought we'd better stock up on supplies before the snow comes. And we brought some goods for trading."

"I'll take a look at them in a minute." The older man pointed toward a young woman standing behind the counter. "My niece, Sara Jane, just came in from St. Louis to help out. If you can't find something, just ask her. Sara Jane, this is Mr. and Mrs. Prescott."

The girl wore a crisp white apron over a gown of pale blue. Her hair was the color of honey, her pretty little face dusted with freckles. When she smiled,

Aaron, trailing behind his father, stopped dead in his tracks.

Seeing his reaction, Izzy said, "Hello, Sara Jane. I'd like you to meet Aaron."

"Hello, Aaron." Her voice was as soft and pretty as her face.

When Aaron finally found his voice, all he could manage was a feeble, "Hello." Then he blushed clear to his toes.

"Where's your ranch?" she asked.

He took a step closer, until only the counter separated them. "Up in the Sierras."

"That's why I haven't seen you in town before." Her cheeks became a most beguiling shade of pink. "I would have remembered you."

"How long will you be staying?" Aaron leaned casually on the counter, hoping she wouldn't notice the way his legs were shaking.

"As long as Uncle Webster will have me. My parents died in a carriage accident, and he and Aunt Gert are all the family I have left."

"I'm glad. I mean...I'm sorry, about your folks and all." He felt the warmth creep up his neck. "But I'm glad you had someone here to take you in."

"So am I." She smiled then, and he felt a tightness in his throat that made it hard to swallow. "Can I help you find something?"

His mind raced. There must be something he could look at. Something that would keep her near him.

"You might want to look at some good boots for winter, Aaron," Izzy prompted. "You've outgrown the ones you're wearing."

He shot her a grateful look. "Yes'm. Could you help me, Sara Jane?"

The girl led the way between the aisles, with Aaron following. He could be heard saying, "I suppose I'll have to settle for practical boots. But if I ever got enough money saved, I'd buy those fancy boots over there, and that big black hat next to them."

"Oh. Wouldn't you look fine in them?" Sara Jane's voice was tinged with awe.

"Poor Aaron." Matt leaned close and whispered in Izzy's ear. "The young fool's lovestruck and doesn't know what hit him. Before you know it, he'll be like one of those dumb calves, going willingly to the branding."

Izzy touched a hand to his cheek. "Sounds like someone I know."

They were still chuckling minutes later as Matt began hauling sacks of flour and sugar to the wagon, while Izzy studied bolts of fabric and patterns for warm winter shirts.

"I'll need some nails, Web," Matt called.

"What're you building now?" Webster put away his ladder and came around the counter, where he examined the goods for bartering.

"Going to add on to the cabin. Maybe build a bigger barn."

"Must have had a good year," the older man said as he hauled down a barrel of nails.

Matt nodded. "Crops were only fair. But that last herd of mustangs made me enough to see us through the winter."

"That's all a man can ask for." Webster began

measuring nails into a small cask. "You already cut the timber?"

"Some. Been cutting trees whenever I had time. Letting the wood age. There's enough for the cabin. Should be more than enough for a barn by spring." Matt nodded toward the children's goods. "Everything meet your approval?"

"They're fine. Tell Del I'll buy all the eggs she can get me. And there's always a market for honey around these parts. Just can't get enough sweet things. As for the pelts, they'll do nicely, with winter coming on and all." He looked up. "I think there's enough here to exchange for the nails and maybe something extra thrown in for good measure."

Matt shook his head. "These belong to the children. I'll let them decide what they want in exchange. As for the nails, I'll pay for them."

"Suit yourself." Webster Sutton counted the money and handed Matt back his change.

By the time the children returned from the orchard, their baskets were bulging with apples. Benjamin and Clement were laughing with a group of boys their own age. Del and a little girl were giggling as they balanced a heavy basket between them.

"Look, Pa. Emily and I picked all these. There must be a hundred or more." Del's eyes were sparkling. "We took one basket to her house. And her ma gave us each a cookie. And then she helped me carry this basket here."

"That's nice. Looks like you worked awfully hard. Did you manage to eat any while you picked?"

"Uh-huh." The two girls nodded and, giggling, scampered away.

Matt emptied the apples into the back of the wagon, then returned the empty basket to Gertrude.

"I'm much obliged for the apples," he said.

"And I'm grateful to have the orchard cleared before the snow." She glanced away, then cleared her throat. "Your children are turning out real nice, Matt. I'd say you and your new bride can be proud."

"Thank you, Gertrude. Much of the credit goes to Isabella."

"Hmm." She pursed her lips and studied him a moment, then turned away. "I'll expect you folks to stay for supper before you head back up that mountain."

"That's generous of you. We're much obliged. But I'm afraid we'll have to get started now if we're going to make it home by dark."

"I'm sorry to hear that. I'd like to get to know your bride better. Next time. Promise?"

"You bet." He watched as she hurried inside the store. He took his time securing the sacks and barrels, savoring the rare sound of laughter he could hear drifting through the open door.

When he entered the store he found the children balancing a mysterious assortment of parcels and packages. "Well, I see you've figured out how to spend your profits. Is everybody ready to go home?"

Izzy and the children nodded and began making their way to the wagon. Only Aaron hung back, reluctant to say goodbye to the pretty little girl who was hanging on his every word.

"When I get enough money saved," he told her, "I'll be back for that hat and those fancy boots."

Matt reached into his pocket and withdrew a handful of bills. When he handed them to Aaron he saw the boy's jaw drop. "You did the work of a man, son. You deserve to share the profits. I only wish it could be more."

He walked away before Aaron could protest. But minutes later, as he climbed up into the wagon and took his place beside Izzy, he was rewarded by the sight of his son stepping into the afternoon sunshine wearing a black cowboy hat and shiny black boots.

The boy who had entered the store was transformed before their eyes into a man. One who stood tall, walked proud and squeezed the hand of the girl standing beside him.

"I'll be back in the spring, Sara Jane," he called as he sprinted to the wagon and pulled himself up to the seat beside Izzy.

"I'll be here waiting, Aaron."

Matt flicked the reins and the team leaned into the harness. As the wagon pulled ahead, Aaron turned to wave. His sister and brothers did the same, until the town and its occupants were out of sight.

Then, for a brief time, they all fell silent, replaying in their minds the excitement of the day, hugging tightly to the memories. For the first time that any of them could recall, they had touched, and been touched warmly by, strangers. And had parted friends.

Chapter Sixteen

The sky was awash with stars. An occasional cloud scudded across the moon, obliterating its light. The night breeze had died, leaving the land hushed and silent, except for the call of a wolf.

Izzy had long ago given in to sleep, her head resting on Matt's shoulder. In the back of the wagon, the children had curled up beneath the blankets and were dreaming.

Smoke from Matt's cigar spiraled upward and dissipated into the night air. He glanced over his wife's head to where his oldest son sat staring into the darkness.

"Can't sleep?"

"No, sir."

"Something on your mind, son?"

"No, sir." Aaron cleared his throat. "Yes, sir. How does a man know...? That is, how can you tell when you meet the right woman?"

"I guess—" Matt blew out a stream of smoke "—there's no sure way of knowing. Some of us make some mighty big mistakes before we get it right."

"But what makes it right?"

Matt shook his head. "It's surely not the way a woman looks, though that's most often what we notice first. And it's not the way she dresses, or the color of her eyes or hair. I guess it's something your heart sees. A goodness in her heart that reaches out to yours."

The boy was silent for a long time before he said softly, "Sara Jane sure is sweet."

Matt drew on his cigar. "She seems to be. But looks can be deceiving. You didn't get to spend much time with her."

"An hour. Maybe two. I guess it'll be a while before I get to see her again."

"And when you do, you might be different. Or it might be Sara Jane who's different."

"In what way?"

Matt shrugged. "One of you might grow up more than the other. Or want something more out of life. You've both got a heap of growing to do yet."

"Yes, sir. But what if we both still feel the same way?"

Matt tossed his cigar into a stream and wrapped a steadying arm around his sleeping wife before the team stepped into the icy water. "You're thinking about love and marriage and forever after?"

Aaron ducked his head. "I didn't think I'd ever want that. Not after you and Ma..." He cleared his throat again. "But now...I guess that's what I'm thinking. But how will I know when I'm ready? When she's ready?"

Matt guided the team up the opposite bank, pleased

that his wife continued to sleep. "I don't know that I'm the right one to ask. I'm much better at understanding mustangs than I am people. But I'd say that with each season you'll have a clearer idea of what you want out of life. And who you want to share that life with." He turned and gave his son an encouraging smile. "Now, that ought to give you plenty to chew on over the long winter, son."

"Isabella."

She felt the gentle shake and looked up, confused for a moment, until she saw the darkened outline of their cabin and heard the baying of the hounds.

"Are we home already?"

He wondered if she knew how easily the word *home* had come to her lips. "Yes. Here, I'll lift you down."

She touched her hands to his shoulders and felt his strong arms around her. As he slowly lowered her to the ground, he brushed his lips over hers. The flare of heat was instantaneous.

"Would you like a late supper before we go to bed?" she asked.

"What I'd like," he muttered against her mouth, "is to take you to bed right now. But I think the children will be hungry after their journey."

"I'll see to it." She turned away and let herself into the cabin, with the dogs close on her heels.

One by one the children followed, clutching their parcels. Without a word of direction each of them took up a chore until, in no time, the cabin was warmed by the blazing log on the hearth and made cheery by the fragrance of meat sizzling in a pan and coffee boiling over the fire.

"It's nice not to have to shoo the chickens out, isn't it, Pa?" Del was happily setting the table.

"I'd say so." He set a second log on the fire and got to his feet.

"And it smells a whole lot better in here, too, since they have their own coop." Aaron carefully hung his new hat on a peg by the door, then slipped out of his boots and began to rub the dust from them with his sleeve.

"Everything's a whole lot better since Isabella came to live with us." Benjamin held a match to the lantern and set it on a corner table, where it cast a golden glow over everything.

He and Clement exchanged knowing smiles. "Would you like to see what we bought, Pa?"

"Wouldn't you like to eat first?"

Both boys shook their heads.

"All right." Matt poured himself a steaming cup of coffee and turned from the fire. "Let's see how you spent your hard-earned money."

"Isabella, you have to look," Benjamin called.

She carried a platter of cold meat and bread to the table. "I can see from here."

"No." With an air of mystery the two boys led her toward a chair and forced her to sit.

"You open it, Isabella." Clement placed a large parcel wrapped in brown paper onto her lap.

"But why?"

"You'll see."

She was aware of everyone watching her as she

carefully untied the string. The paper fell away, revealing a jaunty white bonnet trimmed with pink, yellow and white ribbons.

"Oh, my." She brought her hands to her cheeks, staring at it as though it might rear up and bite her.

"Isn't it pretty?" Benjamin was grinning from ear to ear.

"What is it?" Del demanded.

"It's a bonnet, silly." Clement's smile was beginning to fade. "Mrs. Sutton said all the ladies are wearing them. Do you like it, Isabella? We thought you could wear it to town. And to—" he shrugged and his voice wavered "—anyplace you want."

She couldn't stop the tears that sprang to her eyes.

"Now look what you did." Aaron, always the protector, jumped to her defense. "You made Isabella cry with that stupid gift."

"Oh, no, Aaron." She stood and touched a hand to his shoulder, before blinking away the tears. She turned to the two boys and gave them a tremulous smile. "It's the most beautiful hat I've ever seen."

"Then why are you crying?" Del demanded.

"Because it's so beautiful. And because I've never received a gift before." She opened her arms and drew Clement and Benjamin close. "I can't believe you'd spend all your money on me."

"What else would we spend it on?" Benjamin looked slightly embarrassed. "We've already got everything we want."

"So do I," she whispered as she brushed her lips over their heads.

Reaching up, she pinned the bonnet to her hair, then stood back. "What do you think?"

The boys beamed.

"You look like a real fancy lady," Benjamin said.

Clement nodded in agreement.

She turned to Matt, who had watched the entire scene in silence. "What about you, Matthew? Do you approve?"

Something flickered in his eyes. A look of pain mingled with pleasure. Then it was gone, and he was smiling. "I think you'll be the envy of every woman in Sutton's Station."

Del picked up her parcel, which she'd dropped on a chair. "I guess I may as well show you what I bought." Unwrapping the paper, she held aloft a bottle of murky liquid.

"What's that?" Aaron leaned down to read the label.

"It's Dr. Goody's Liniment and Elixir. I bought it for you and Pa, to put on your bruises."

"Well, that's real nice, Little Bit." Aaron took the bottle from her hand and read the back of the bottle. "Effective for bruises, burns, contusions, cuts, scratches and horse bites. Can also be used on livestock."

Matt and Aaron exchanged quick grins.

"Do you like it, Pa?"

Her father swung her up into his arms and kissed her soundly. "I like it very much. Thank you."

"There's something else." She unfolded the paper further and lifted out something that caught and reflected the firelight. "It's for you, Isabella."

"Another gift?" Izzy stared at the little girl's outstretched hand. "What is this?"

"A comb for your hair."

Izzy knelt down and drew Del into her arms. "I don't know what to make of this. Two gifts in one day." She kissed the little girl's cheek, then examined the comb. It was a simple little thing, made of tortoiseshell. "It's almost too pretty to wear. I'll tell you what. I'll wear it now, and when your hair is long enough, it will be yours."

Del's eyes were shining. "You mean we'll share?"

Izzy nodded, then hugged her again.

Matt opened the cabin door and stepped outside, then returned carrying a parcel. "I was going to save this for later. But since you're opening presents, you may as well open mine, too."

Izzy's eyes widened. "I don't think I can take any more surprises, Matthew. Why don't you open it for me?"

He shook his head and thrust it into her hands. With the children urging her on, she tore the paper and let out a gasp as layers of pale lemon-yellow fabric began to spill through her hands.

"It's a dress," Del cried.

Izzy was holding the gown a little away from her, trying to take it all in at once. The row of matching white buttons that ran from neckline to hem. The neat little collar trimmed with delicate lace. The wide yellow sash. The long flouncing skirt, caught here and there with bows and displaying more of the lace. And to go with it, a matching yellow shawl, with an intricate pattern of squares and circles, trimmed with a lush fringe.

"I hope it fits." He was watching her reaction, worried about the way her eyes were filling and her lips trembling. "If you don't like the color…"

"Don't like…?"

They watched in horror as she burst into tears.

Feeling tense and awkward, Matt laid a hand on her shoulder. "I'm sorry. I'm not very good at this. I had to guess at your size. But Gertrude Sutton said you could exchange it for another if you wanted."

"Another? How could I ever want another dress?"

He was feeling more confused by the minute.

"But if you don't like it…"

"Oh, Matthew." Her voice was choked with tears. "I've never in my life had a store-bought dress before. Don't you see? My first gifts, my first gown, my first shawl…" Her lips quivered and the tears coursed down her cheeks. "It's all too much. I think my heart is too full." With a sob she ran into the bedroom.

For the space of several minutes Matt and his children stood staring at the closed door. Then, gathering his wits, he said, "I think we'd better eat the meal Isabella fixed for us."

"What about Isabella?" Aaron asked. "Don't you think you should go to her, Pa?"

"I think maybe she needs some time alone." Matt led the way to the table and began to pass the platter of meat. His own appetite, he realized, had fled.

"Do women always cry when they're happy?" Benjamin glanced at his father.

Matt shrugged. "I guess sometimes they cry. But sometimes they laugh, too."

Over a mouthful of bread and honey the boy asked, "How are we supposed to know what to expect?"

"We don't, son. That's what makes life with them so interesting."

A short time later they all looked up as the door to the bedroom opened. Izzy stepped out, wearing the new gown, and over it, draped around her shoulders, the matching shawl. Her hair had been pulled to one side and fastened with the comb.

Matt wasn't even aware that he'd pushed away from the table and was standing, a look of pure pleasure lighting all his features, his right hand reaching out to her.

"Isabella. You look..." Like a goddess, he thought. A vision too perfect to be real. But he wasn't a man of words. And so he said simply, "You look pretty."

"Thank you." She took his outstretched hand and reached up with her other hand to touch his cheek in a gesture of tenderness. "I feel pretty. Thanks to you, Matthew." She turned and her smile encompassed all of them. "And you, children. You've made me feel very special. I only wish I'd had some way of buying you something, as well."

"We don't need things, Isabella." Aaron spoke for all of them. "You've already given us the one thing we thought we'd never have. A ma who enjoys being with us. Doing for us. Being part of our family. That's all we've ever wanted."

Izzy took a deep breath, struggling against fresh tears that threatened. "Well, let's have our supper."

She sat, still holding Matt's hand. With her other hand she reached out to Aaron. The others around the table did the same.

"Bless this food," she said. "And those of us who share it."

"Amen," the others intoned.

As she filled her cup, Matt picked up his fork and began to eat. Suddenly he was ravenous.

Izzy removed the new gown, hanging it carefully on a peg. As she sat on the edge of the bed and removed her stockings and petticoat, she couldn't help staring at it. It wouldn't be easy for her to wear something so fine while she did her daily chores. Especially since she still had her old gown. But she would wear it proudly. Because she had seen her reflection in Matthew's eyes. A reflection of love and beauty.

She heard his footsteps as he returned from the barn. Heard the cabin door open and close. Her heartbeat quickened. She was just starting to rise when he came to her. He stepped quickly inside, then leaned against the door, watching her.

She felt the familiar skitter of nerves when those dark, hooded eyes were trained on her.

She picked up the simple white gown. "I was just going to put on my night shift."

He took it from her hands. "No. I want to see you like this."

Her first inclination was to cross her arms in front of herself. But he took her hands, holding them in his, and studied her with such intensity she felt the heat rise to her cheeks.

"I'll blow out the lantern."

"Leave it. I want to watch you. I want you to see me as I love you, Isabella."

He reached up and removed the comb from her hair, watching through narrowed eyes as honey waves drifted around her face. Turning her toward the cracked mirror, he picked up the brush and began to run it through her hair.

"Soft," he murmured. "Everything about you is so soft. Your voice. Your manner. Even the way you love."

She watched his reflection, stunned by the intimacy of his touch. She felt a tingling that soon spread through her body.

"Why don't you ever look in the mirror, Isabella?"

"I've never liked looking at myself. I'm not pretty."

"Not pretty? Isabella, you're beautiful. How can you not see?"

He lifted his gaze and met hers in the glass. Desire, hot, piercing, flared when she saw the need kindled in his eyes.

His hand stilled. The brush clattered to the floor. Neither of them took notice.

"Do you know how much I want you?"

She leaned back against him, weak with need. "No more than I want you, Matthew."

As soon as the words were spoken, she let out a gasp. It was true. There was no longer any fear or shame or hesitancy. She wanted him. Loved him. It was as simple as that.

But when she started to turn toward him, he held her still and reached for the ribbons of her chemise. As the sheer fabric parted, she was shocked by the image in the mirror. Of her bared breasts, seeming to fill his palms as they stroked. Of his mouth pressing hot, wet kisses along her neck and shoulder.

Her breath came out in a long, slow shudder. Her knees weakened and she was forced to lean against him.

His hands, those strong, clever hands, continued their ministrations until her skin was heated, her heart racing.

"Matthew. Please."

"Not yet." The words were an effort. His voice was rough with passion. But he wanted to take her to the very edge.

He pressed his lips to a tangle of hair at her temple, breathing in the scent of her. Then he lowered his mouth to the curve of her neck, loving the texture of her skin, the taste of it.

His work-roughened fingers on her breasts were unbearably arousing. His hot breath tickling her ear had her writhing and moaning. And still he gave her no release.

Tentatively he moved his hand down her stomach and felt her quivering response. It excited him not only to feel her reaction, but to watch it in the mirror. To see her eyes widen, then grow slumberous as his touch became more intimate.

Never before had he wanted so desperately to give, to touch, to taste. To take. To share.

He couldn't hold on much longer. He knew his control was about to snap. Still he fought it back, banked it, wanting to give her more.

His fingers found her hot and wet. It took no more than a simple stroke to take her over the first peak.

"Matthew." His name was a strangled cry on her lips.

But he gave her no time to speak as he took her up and over again before lowering her to the bed. And then they were tangled together. Moving in an ageless rhythm that gave him, at long last, his release.

Izzy lay in the darkness and brushed away her tears. She wasn't a woman given to crying. Yet she'd wept more in the past few days than she had in all the years that had gone before.

Her life had always been hard. But she had toughened herself, refusing to give in to difficulties or defeat. And always there had been the dream. Of a man who would love her. Of home and children. And now, in this rough cabin in the wilderness, she had found her heart's desire.

Her heart was so filled with love, with happiness, she could hardly take it all in. She was almost afraid to sleep, for fear of waking and finding it was all a dream.

"Something wrong?" Matt's voice beside her in the darkness had her turning toward him.

"There's nothing wrong, Matthew." She laid a

hand on his chest. "Everything is so right. So perfect."

He drew her hand to his lips and kissed each finger. "You're cold. Come here." He lifted the blanket and she snuggled against him.

"I didn't mean to wake you," she whispered against his lips. "I was just counting my blessings."

"Then add this to the count. I love you, Isabella." He ran soft wet kisses along her throat, then unbuttoned her night shift and moved his mouth lower, burning a trail of fire along her flesh. "More than I thought it possible to love any woman."

"And I love…"

He cut off her words with a lingering kiss.

And then there was no need for words.

Chapter Seventeen

"There's a bite to the air." Matt entered the cabin with an armload of logs and deposited them beside the fireplace. "Snow's not far behind."

Izzy looked up from the fire, where she was stirring a skillet of eggs and potatoes. "I don't understand all this talk of snow. We had snow in Pennsylvania. But we never made such endless preparations." She shook her head. "Logs piled to the roof. Enough flour and sugar to last a year or more. Is all this really necessary?"

"You might have had snow." Matt reached over her shoulder and helped himself to a hot potato slice. "But I'll bet you've never seen snow like we have in the Sierras."

"Snow is snow." She filled several platters and carried them to the table. After a blessing, they began to eat.

Matt studied the way she looked in her yellow gown, with the tortoise shell comb in her hair. "Isabella, you look as pretty as those buttercups that grow up in the hills in summer." He glanced at her bare feet poking out from beneath the hem of her skirt. "And I'm glad you've given up those tight, fancy shoes."

Warmed by the compliment, she touched a hand to the apron she'd added for good measure. "I just hope I can do my chores without ruining my new dress."

"You'll do just fine." He turned to his children. "I thought I'd go across the meadow to that stand of old trees and start hauling the timber for our addition. I'd like to get it started before—" he glanced at Izzy and grinned "—the snow comes."

She returned his smile. "You see? You spend an awful lot of time making plans around that snow."

The others chuckled.

"Do I have to go, Pa?" Del was busy stuffing her mouth with eggs and biscuits.

He sipped his coffee. "Is there something you'd rather do?"

"Isabella said she'd teach me how to make apple cobbler."

He tried not to show his astonishment. It was the first time he could ever recall his daughter not wanting to share her brothers' chores. "Well then, I guess you'd better stay here and have a cooking lesson." He set down his cup and winked. "Just see that you save some for me."

"We'll make a whole batch of it. Won't we, Isabella?"

Izzy nodded. "Enough to satisfy four hungry men."

"We ought to be starving by the time we haul those timbers home." Matt drained his cup, then pushed away from the table and reached for his cowhide jacket. His sons followed suit.

Outside Matt hitched the team and the boys climbed into the back of the wagon. With a flick of the reins they took off, headed across the distant meadow. Running alongside were the hounds, setting up an eager chorus of barking. Izzy and Del stood in the doorway waving until they were out of sight. Then they closed the door, shutting out the bitter wind.

"Can we start the apple cobbler now?" Del was dancing with excitement.

"Not just yet." Izzy couldn't help grinning at Del's impatience. "First I'll have to go down in the fruit cellar and bring up a basket of apples. Then we'll have to peel them."

"I'll go." The little girl grabbed a parka from a hook by the door and tossed it over her pink gown. "You don't want to get your new dress all dirty."

"Why, thank you, Del. But what about your new dress?"

"I'll be careful."

Izzy was touched by her thoughtfulness. "All right. While you're doing that, I'll get out the flour and sugar."

The door closed behind Del, and Izzy began humming a little tune as she measured the ingredients into a bowl. That done, she crossed the room and struggled under the weight of a heavy log.

She heard the cabin door open, felt the cold rush of air that caused the sparks to leap and flare. Wiping her hands on her apron, she straightened and paused to watch as the log caught fire. "Close the door quickly, Del. This must be the price I'm to pay for chiding your father. It really does feel like..." She turned. The words she'd been about to speak died on her lips.

Sergeant Harlan Cutler stood in the doorway clutching Del in his arms. He had one arm wrapped tightly around the girl's waist. In his other hand was a pistol, which was pressed to her temple.

"Well, now." He kicked the door shut and turned with a grin, revealing tobacco-stained teeth. "Ain't this cozy? Just me and Izzy the Gimp. And one of Prescott's little bastards."

At that Del began to kick and scream. Cutler cocked the pistol. The sound, though little more than a click, seemed to reverberate in the room.

"Del. Don't." Izzy's voice was barely a whisper. "Don't move. Don't give him any reason to hurt you."

"Oh, I intend to hurt her. Though it won't hurt me a bit." His laughter scraped across Izzy's nerves. "Ain't never had me a young one before. This ought to prove real interesting."

At his meaning Izzy had to fight a wave of revulsion.

"And you, Miss High-and-Mighty." His smile grew, giving him a dangerous, feral look. "I've got special plans for you. You always thought you were too good for the likes of me. But I'll show you what a real man can do. By the time I'm through with you, that husband of yours will wish he'd never heard of Harlan Cutler."

Izzy struggled with a show of bravado. "My husband will be coming in from the barn any minute now. You'd better get, if you know what's good for you.''

''Is that so?'' He spat a wad of tobacco on the floor and threw back his head in shrill laughter. ''Funny. I'd have sworn that man in the wagon, heading down the trail, looked just like Matt Prescott. And those little bastards in the back of the wagon looked like his, too.''

Icy fingers of fear slithered along Izzy's spine. He'd been watching them. Watching and waiting for a chance to find her alone. To have his revenge for the beating he'd taken at Matt's hands.

His smile disappeared as quickly as it had come. He tossed Del to the floor with such force she lay in a heap, struggling for breath.

Izzy let out a cry and rushed to the little girl's side. ''Are you all right, Del?'' She touched a hand to the child's forehead, which had begun to bleed. ''Here,'' she whispered, pressing an edge of her apron to stem the flow.

Then she gathered her into her arms and hugged her fiercely. Over Del's head she watched the play of emotions on Cutler's face. There was an edge of madness in his movements. Wild laughter one moment, raw fury the next.

He aimed the pistol. ''Move aside. I intend to start with the girl.''

''No.'' Izzy wrapped her arms around Del, turning her body so that the child was shielded. ''You'll have to kill us both.''

''Oh, I intend to.'' His voice had become icy calm.

"But I have plans for you first. Before you die, I'm going to have me a whole lot of fun. Now, move away."

Izzy's mind raced. There was no fear for herself now. All her thoughts were centered on Del. She could fight this monster. She could kick, claw, bite. But one shot from his pistol would end any chance she had to keep him from brutalizing this innocent child. Sweet salvation. There had to be a way to save Del.

She had a sudden thought. Maybe she could barter for Del's safety.

"Let the child live and I'll...I'll go away with you. You can do to me what you please, for as long as you please."

His evil smile grew. "Oh, I intend to do just that. Right here. Right now."

"But Matthew could return at any time." She could see that her words struck a nerve. Cutler's gaze swung toward the door of the cabin. "And when he does...."

His eyes narrowed. "You're playing me for a fool."

"You're a fool if you stay here. My husband will kill you." Her arms tightened around Del, and for a moment she closed her eyes against the fear that pulsed through her. "But if you don't harm the child, if you leave her as you found her, untouched, I'll go without a fight. And I'll stay with you for as long as you choose. Then you can do—" she shuddered "—whatever you want to me."

She could see him weighing the wisdom of her offer.

"It'd hurt Prescott real good if I hurt his little bastard. And I want to hurt him for what he did to me. But from what I've heard, it'll kill him if I take away his pretty new bride." His lips peeled back into a vicious snarl. "Come on, then. I'll need time to cover our trail."

He stepped closer and hauled Izzy to her feet. For a moment her heart stopped when he turned toward Del, still curled up on the floor. She saw his finger tremble on the trigger of his pistol and the knot of terror that rose up in her throat nearly choked her.

"If you hurt her my offer is withdrawn. I'll claw and scratch and fight you until I'm dead. And you might manage to take some pleasure in it. Or—" she spoke each word slowly, in order to make her point "—my husband might return in time to kill you. And he will surely kill you if he finds you."

She could see that Cutler's fear of Matt was stronger than his desire for the child.

"Go on, then." He waved his pistol toward the door.

"I'll...need a shawl." She wanted—needed—to draw his attention away from Del.

"Get it. And be quick about it."

"It's in the bedroom."

As soon as she turned away he followed her, while still keeping the little girl in his line of vision. "You try anything funny, I'll start with the kid." He grinned. "Wonder how she'd look with that pretty little dress wrapped around her throat."

Izzy stumbled blindly into the bedroom. In a mindless daze she pulled on her worn traveling boots, then reached to the top of the dresser for her shawl.

"Hurry up. What's taking you so long?"

"I'm coming." The drawer was partly open. Inside she could see the glint of her knife. The thought of it was too tantalizing to resist. Using the shawl for cover, she reached inside. Her fingers closed around the cold edge of her knife. Her hands were trembling so violently, she almost dropped it. In one quick motion she pretended to let the shawl slip from her fingers. As it fluttered to the floor, she bent and managed to slide the knife into her boot. A moment later she straightened and strode from the room.

"Don't go with him, Isabella." Del's voice rang with fear.

"You shut your mouth." Cutler crossed the distance between them and pulled her little arms roughly behind her back, securing her wrists and ankles with rawhide. "He's going to hurt you, Isabella. Please don't go."

"This'll shut you up." While Izzy watched helplessly, Cutler tied a rag around the child's mouth, cutting off her words.

"I'll be all right, Del." Izzy knelt and pressed a kiss to her cheek, tasting the salt of her tears. "You're safe now, honey," she whispered. "That's all that matters."

"Come on." With a vicious tug Cutler hauled Izzy to her feet. "Before I change my mind and take the kid, too."

At the door he shoved her ahead of him, then

turned and aimed the pistol. When Del cringed, he gave a cruel sneer. "I'll let you live, you little bastard. But only so you can tell your pa I got his woman. Tell him Harlan Cutler hasn't forgotten how it felt to be humiliated in front of his captain. Tell your pa when Harlan Cutler's done with his high-and-mighty new bride, there won't be anything left for him. Or for any man."

"Cold?" Cutler's big rough hand pawed the goose-flesh on Izzy's arms. "Hell, I'll make you all nice and warm when we stop for the night." He nuzzled his face against her hair and she was forced to endure the stench of his breath. "Wish I could be around that cabin to see your man's face when he finds his little brat hog-tied and his wife missing." He nudged his mount up a steep incline. "I'm glad now I didn't kill the kid. I want Prescott to know who took his wife. And why. That'll be the best torture of all."

Despite the pounding of her heart, keeping time to the pounding of the horse's hooves, Izzy struggled to hold her nerves at bay. She knew what lay ahead for her. But at least Del had been spared the same fate. That was the only thing that mattered. She would have willingly died rather than see Del suffer such brutality at the hands of this madman.

Still, she wasn't entirely without hope. She had her knife. Though it was little defense against Cutler's gun, it gave her some measure of comfort. And if there was the smallest moment of opportunity, she would use it. That knowledge would sustain her through this ordeal.

The rush of wind bit into her face as Cutler urged his horse up the wooded slope.

She had hoped that he would head for the valley, where someone might spot them. But she realized that he was heading high into the mountains, away from civilization. She stared around, trying to mark their trail. But it was impossible in this heavily forested area, where each cluster of trees, each rushing stream blended together into an impossible maze.

She shivered, plotting a way to escape. But even if she should succeed, how would she ever be able to find her way back to Matthew's cabin?

She wouldn't think of that now. She would concentrate on conserving her strength, so that if Cutler displayed any sign of weakness, she would use it to her advantage.

She closed her eyes and wished she knew a prayer. But her mind had gone blank. And her body had begun trembling uncontrollably in the biting cold.

She nervously drew her shawl close and plucked at the yarn that formed the fringe. When the thread unraveled, she stared at it a moment. Then, as a plan began forming in her mind, she opened her fingers and allowed the bit of yarn to flutter to the ground.

It seemed impossible that anyone would notice bits of yellow yarn against the snow. Still, it was the only thing she could do.

Please. The word rang over and over in her mind like a litany. *Please. If there is any way possible, let these tiny threads mark the way.*

"Mmm-mmm. I can almost taste Isabella's apple cobbler, Pa." In the early dusk of evening, Aaron sat beside his father on the hard front seat of the wagon.

"Me too, son." Matt flicked the reins, urging the team across the meadow. "I hope Del left us some."

In the back, Benjamin and Clement sat atop a pile of timbers, taking every bump and jolt like seasoned rodeo riders.

The hounds, trotting alongside, spotted the cabin and took off at a run, setting up a chorus of barking. When they reached the closed door they leapt and scratched, trying to force their way inside.

"I guess they're looking for apple cobbler, too," Aaron said with a grin.

"I don't blame them." Matt's smile suddenly faded when he glanced toward the cabin. No smoke drifted from the chimney. No lantern light filtered through the windows.

He reined in the team and grabbed hold of his rifle. Slipping to the ground, he called, "Something's wrong. You boys stay here until I give a sign that it's safe to come closer. You hear?"

Before they could respond he was racing across the meadow. At the door he signaled the hounds and their barking ceased as they dropped to the ground. Matt pressed his ear to the door. Hearing no sound within, he kicked it in and strode inside. For a moment all he could see was the emptiness. Then, as his eyes adjusted to the gloom, he made out a figure on the floor. His heart stopped as he crossed the room. Kneeling, he saw Del's wide-eyed stare, pleading silently for release. Within moments he cut the rawhide bindings and tore away the gag.

"Oh, Pa." For a few seconds all she could do was cling to him, weeping as though her heart would break.

He gathered her close and closed his eyes as relief poured through him. "Are you hurt, Del?"

"No, Pa. Just scared." She stared over his shoulder at her brothers, who, ignoring their father's command, had followed.

With a cry, she flew across the room and fell weeping into Aaron's arms. The boy picked her up and cuddled her.

"I couldn't work through the rawhide, Aaron. I tried." She held up her wrists. They were raw and bloody. "But no matter how hard I tried, I couldn't break free."

At the sight of her pain, Aaron hugged her fiercely and pressed his mouth to her hair. "You're all right now, Little Bit. But you cut yourself up really good. You must be hurting."

"It doesn't matter. I don't care about anything except getting Isabella back."

Matt felt his heart stop, his blood run cold. "Getting her back? Where is she?"

"She's gone, Pa."

"Gone?" For a moment his face went completely blank. This couldn't be happening again.

Then, as if from a great distance, his daughter's words broke through his thoughts. "Sergeant Cutler caught me coming out of the root cellar. He said he was going to hurt me and Isabella. So she made a bargain with him. She said she'd go with him, if he'd promise not to hurt me."

Matt's face twisted into a mask of rage. "Go with him? Where? Where was he taking her, Del?"

The little girl was crying again, sobbing against her big brother's shoulder. Her words were barely coherent. "I don't know, Pa. He just said to tell you he'd come for his revenge. And that when he was through with Isabella, there'd be nothing left. Oh, Pa." Between choking hiccups she managed to say, "He's going to kill her, isn't he?"

"No, Del. He isn't." Matt touched a hand to her hair, then strode into the bedroom. When he returned he had strapped on a pistol and holster and was carrying a rifle and a pouch filled with bullets. In his eyes was a steely look that was all too familiar to his children.

He turned to Aaron. "You'll see to the others, son."

"Yes, sir."

"Bring her back, Pa," Del cried.

He stalked to the door. "You can count on it."

Chapter Eighteen

The horse climbed steadily, passing through snow-covered forests, fording icy streams.

Izzy's gown and thin shawl offered no protection from the bitter cold. She had long ago lost all feeling in her hands and feet.

Cutler, huddled inside his army-issue winter parka, seemed to take no notice. He guided his mount with a steady hand.

It occurred to Izzy that he rode like a man with a destination in mind. This was no random race to put as much distance as possible between himself and Matt's cabin.

"Where are we going?" She found even those few words difficult through chattering teeth.

"Impatient for me, huh?" His shrill laughter scraped her already raw nerves. "Not far now. Up there." He pointed and she peered through a curtain of snow to a stand of trees in the distance.

It wasn't until they had passed beyond the trees that she caught sight of a small, primitive lean-to built into the side of the mountain. One wall leaned at a precarious angle. The roof appeared to be caving in. Evergreens had grown up around it, making it almost invisible until they were nearly upon it.

"Cozy little place, don't you think? I found it a few days ago, while I was out scouting around." Cutler halted his horse and slid from the saddle, dragging her from the back of the animal like a sack of flour. Her shawl drifted to the ground, where it lay forgotten.

After so many hours in the saddle her legs refused to support her. She dropped to her knees in the snow. With a curse he hauled her to her feet and shoved her, tripping and stumbling, ahead of him through the doorway.

She felt the brush of cobwebs across her cheeks. Heard the rustle of creatures fleeing in the dark. And then Cutler struck a match and held it to a lantern, dispelling the gloom.

The dank earthen floor was littered with animal bones carried by predators. Snow had blown in through chinks in the walls.

"It's not much shelter, but nobody will be able to find us up here. And it'll give me a chance to—" he grinned "—take care of a little business."

The tremors started again, and this time she couldn't stop them.

"Sit down," he commanded.

She stared around. When she didn't move quickly enough he gave her a rough shove that sent her sprawling. Straddling her, he yanked her arms behind her back and secured her wrists with a strip of rawhide, before binding her ankles, as well. Then for good measure, he threaded a length of rawhide between the two sets of bindings and drew it so tightly her knees were bent and her body arched like a bow. She had to bite her lip to keep from crying out in pain.

"We call this hog-tied, city girl. You're trussed up just like a hog for butchering." He leaned close and gave a vicious tug on her hair. His fetid breath made her wince. "Think you're brave, don't you? This is nothing compared to what I'm going to do to you later. Then we'll see how brave you are."

He saw the color drain from her face. Pleased, he sat back on his heels.

"That's better. You just keep remembering where you are now, Miss High-and-Mighty. There's no law in this godforsaken wilderness except the law of the gun. And right now, I'm the one holding the gun."

With a peal of high-pitched laughter, he sauntered away and stepped out into the snow. Minutes later he returned carrying several logs. In no time he had a fire started.

Izzy lay in a heap, grateful for what little warmth she could absorb. The sleeves and bodice of her gown were soaked, the hem crusted with snow.

She watched Cutler's every move. When he stepped outside she began struggling to maneuver her bound arms toward her boot. If she could reach her knife, she could cut the rawhide and at least have a chance to fight him. Like a contortionist she twisted, turned, wiggled, writhed. But no matter how hard she tried, she couldn't reach the knife, which remained tantalizingly just out of reach.

With a hiss of pain she gave it one last try. A shadow fell over her, and she stilled her movements.

"What's this?" With the butt of his rifle he lifted her skirt and drew it up to her thighs. Seeing her flinch, he caressed her flesh with the rifle. "I guess you just can't wait to get out of those clothes."

He was looking at her in a way that made her skin crawl.

"Well, don't you worry. I'll have you out of your things in no time." He dropped the saddlebag he'd been carrying. After rummaging through it, he lifted out a jug of whiskey and took a long, slow pull. Then he wiped his mouth with the back of his hand and continued staring at her.

"I'd share my food and drink." He removed some dried meat and a biscuit from the saddlebag and began to eat as he hunkered down in front of the fire. "But there's no sense feeding someone who won't be around to see the light of morning."

"I thought—" her throat was so dry she could scarcely form the words "—you'd be taking me with you."

"Did you, now?" He speared her a grin, then polished off the rest of the hardtack. That done, he lifted the jug for another long drink. "When I leave here, I'll be traveling alone. See, I figure this business between us will be over tonight. After that, I'd be a fool to take you along. You'd only slow me down. And I want to stay far ahead of that avenging husband of yours. Though I surely would like to see his face when he finds you. Or what's left of you."

He removed his parka and tossed it aside, then began nudging off his boots. He paused long enough for another long drink of whiskey, then slipped his suspenders from his shoulders and reached to the buttons of his shirt.

With each movement, Izzy's throat tightened, and the hard knot of fear grew.

Matt knelt by an icy stream and studied the remains of a hoofprint. He knew, by the slight irregularity, that this was Cutler's mount. The sergeant had been clever, crossing and recrossing as many as half a dozen times to confuse anyone tracking him. There were a dozen different trails he could have taken from here. And a fresh snowfall was already obliterating any tracks.

Matt swore in frustration. Every delay would cost Isabella dearly. He got to his feet and studied the surrounding woods, trying to think like the sergeant. Where was Cutler heading? Which way had he gone?

A tiny flutter of yellow caught his eye. Walking closer, he saw that it was a bit of yarn, snagged to the branch of a tree. He caught it and rolled it between his fingers. Could it possibly be...?

Pulling himself into the saddle, Matt urged his horse up the steep wooded trail. Before he'd gone very far he caught sight of another length of yellow yarn. And then, up ahead, yet another.

He plucked the thread from the snow and held it to his face, needing to smell Isabella. But there was no trace of her scent. All he could smell was fear. It wasn't fear for his own life. What clutched at his heart was fear for Isabella.

Would he be in time to save this brave, clever woman who had bartered her own life to save his daughter? Would she be forced to revisit all her childhood nightmares? Would she have to endure at Cutler's hands those things she had most feared?

Would the cost be even greater? Would she be forced to pay the ultimate price, as well?

He couldn't allow himself to think about that now. His eyes narrowed as he followed the trail. All his thoughts, all his energies were focused on the task that lay before him.

He'd thought, after the war, that he'd put the killing behind him. Now, suddenly, it had become necessary to do it again. He was very good at it. His jaw firmed. Too good. He had no doubt that he would kill Sergeant Harlan Cutler without a twinge of regret. But would he be in time to save the woman he loved?

"Wonder what ole...Otis would say if...see me now."

Cutler's words were badly slurred as he lounged in front of the fire and took another long drink of whiskey. It sloshed down the front of his shirt and he absently wiped at it, then tipped the jug again, nearly missing his mouth.

"Me and Izzy the Gimp." He snorted with laughter, followed by a loud belch. "Only this time you don't have that knife." He shook his head. "You really carved him up good. Bled like a stuck pig." That had him laughing harder. "Stuck pig. Just like you. Hog-tied." He laughed so hard at his own joke, he had to wipe his eyes with his sleeve.

"This'll be even better than my revenge against that...sniveling lieutenant." He looked up, eyes glazed. "Did I tell you he ordered me out of the army? After all the years I've given, just ordered me off the post. Called me a drunk. Said I brought dishonor to his troops." The laughter was gone. Wiped instantly from his face. In its place was a dark scowl. "But I got him for that. Turned all the damned mustangs loose. Opened every corral before I left, so's that snot-nosed Trowbridge won't even have enough horses to send out a search party."

Izzy's arms and legs had gone numb. At first the rawhide biting into her flesh had caused nearly unbearable pain. But now, thankfully, she had moved beyond it.

Her voice seemed almost detached from her body, but she had to keep him talking. Talking and drinking. "Aren't you afraid of a court-martial?"

Cutler laughed. "They have to catch me first. And by the time they round up enough horses to chase me, I'll be panning for gold in California. Or maybe Alaska. Hell, I could be halfway across the country and Trowbridge will still be trying to figure out how to act like a soldier. The only reason he's an officer is because of his name. His uncle was some big general. Lieutenant Trowbridge is always quoting him. Said, when he was dismissing me in front of the entire company, that your husband, Captain Prescott, was the kind of man the army needed. Distinguished himself at Chancellorsville. Risked his life for his men. And even after taking a couple of bullets, wouldn't leave the field of battle until all his men were accounted for.'' His agitated tone became suddenly icy calm. "Well, we'll see how much of a hero he is when he finds out what old Harlan Cutler did to his woman.''

He stretched out on the dirt floor and pressed a hand to his eyes. ''Too damned warm in here.'' He tried to drink, but this time he missed his mouth completely and the whiskey trickled across his cheek, down his jaw, circling around his neck before pooling on the floor.

Izzy remained very still, watching. Was he really asleep? Or was he testing her?

Every instinct told her to move cautiously. Cutler was like a sleeping bear. If anything should trigger his rage, she would be helpless against him.

Still, if she didn't act quickly, she might miss her only chance for freedom.

He had decided not to take her along. That meant he would kill her here. And soon.

For the past hour she had been testing the strength of the rawhide that bound her. It was impossible to break free. Her wrists and ankles were raw and bloody from the effort. But there was a way. The only way she could think of.

She glanced nervously at the fire. If she could crawl close enough, she could burn the rawhide bindings. Of course, there was a good chance that she would burn herself, as well. And if the flame should catch her hair or gown, she could face a very painful death. But she was going to die anyway. And death at Cutler's hands would be more painful than anything else she could imagine.

In order to pull this off, she mustn't allow herself to cry out, no matter what.

This was not a time for weakness, she told herself. With a madman like Cutler, there would be no second chance.

Matt pulled his hat low over his forehead and urged his mount into the driving snow. The trail had been climbing steadily for the past hour. A trail covered with drifts that reached nearly to his horse's belly.

He'd rarely been to this part of the mountain. There had been no need, since the mustang herds stuck to the lower meadows. But he recalled, on his rare sojourns, steep cliffs, narrow trails and deep, dangerous ravines.

Cutler had chosen well. A woman like Isabella wouldn't stand a chance in such primitive countryside, should she manage to escape. But at least, Matt consoled himself, they were still moving. That meant that Cutler couldn't do too much harm. But if they were to stop…

Matt pushed aside the disturbing thought. Up ahead he spotted the tiny strip of yellow yarn fluttering from the branch of an evergreen and whispered a prayer of thanks for Isabella's resourcefulness. Without it, he'd have never been able to track her this quickly.

He lifted his head, then reined in his mount and drew in a sharp breath. There was just a whiff of wood smoke. It had to be some distance away. But it started his heart racing, his blood heating. Cutler had taken shelter.

That meant that Isabella was now in grave peril.

He urged his horse into the drifts. There was no time now for caution. He had to find them. Before it was too late.

Izzy inched her way along the dirt floor. Because of the way she was bound, every movement was sheer torture. Never before had she used so much energy to make so little progress. But at least she was closer to her goal.

She could feel the heat of the fire now. Could see the flames licking along the log.

Cutler's snoring stopped, and he muttered something in his sleep.

Izzy froze, her heart pounding.

When the snoring resumed, she rocked and swayed, inching closer to the heat.

It was her intention to back up to the fire in the hope that the flames would find the strip of rawhide that connected her wrists to her ankles. Once that was burned away, she would be able to retrieve her knife from her boot and cut away the rest of her bonds.

Sweat now beaded her forehead as she wriggled closer to the flames. Heat seared her flesh and for a moment she lost her nerve. What had she been thinking of? Did she really think she could expose herself to such pain without a whimper?

Cutler rolled to his side, muttering a string of oaths.

Without giving herself time to consider, Izzy arched her back to the flame and squeezed her eyes tightly shut. The heat was so intense she had to clench her teeth to keep from crying out. The air was filled with the pungent odor of burning leather. In an instant the leather strip fell away and her body straightened.

On a hiss of pain she rolled aside and reached for the knife in her boot. In one quick motion she cut through the rawhide at her wrists and ankles.

"What are you…?" Cutler, still groggy from whiskey and sleep, rubbed a hand over his eyes. Then, seeing her getting to her feet, he sprang at her.

The force of his body knocked the knife from her hands and all the breath from her lungs. Dazed, she lay beneath him, struggling for air.

"Why, you little…" He swung his arm and brought it against her jaw with such force it had her head spinning. "You thought you'd sneak away from Harlan Cutler? Now I'll show you what happens to people who think they're so smart."

Pinning her with his body, he had no trouble imprisoning both her hands in one of his. Then he reached over her head and retrieved the fallen knife.

His eyes, which only seconds earlier had been dulled by sleep, now glittered with madness. "As I recall, you always kept this blade honed sharper than a man's razor."

To prove the point, he pressed it to her throat. She sucked in a breath, afraid to move, afraid to breathe.

A trickle of blood oozed, forming a ribbon of red.

"This should prove to be real handy." He held the knife aloft so that the blade reflected the glow of firelight. Then, watching her eyes, he lowered the knife and in one smooth motion slit her gown from throat to waist. The remnants fell away, revealing a delicate chemise.

"All these fancy clothes." His eyes narrowed. "Let's see what you're hiding under them. Must be pretty fancy, too, since you'd never let any of us have a look."

Before he could raise the knife again there was a rush of wind that sent the flames leaping, the sparks flying. The door was kicked in with such force it tore from its hinges and sagged against the wall.

Standing in the doorway was Matt. His voice was colder than the storm raging just beyond their range of vision. "Step away from my wife, Cutler."

Despite his bulk, Cutler was on his feet and dragging Izzy along with him.

In one quick stroke he held her in front of him and pressed the knife to her throat.

"We're not playing by your gentleman's code of honor now, Prescott. If you want her to live, toss down your gun."

"Don't, Matthew." Izzy was close to hysteria. "If you do as he says, he'll kill us both."

"Shut up, woman." To get his point across, Cutler increased the pressure against her throat and smiled when she cried out in pain.

Enjoying himself, he ran a finger across the trickle of blood, then lifted it to his lips. "Tastes real sweet, doesn't she?" In the blink of an eye his smile was gone. His eyes darkened with rage. "If you want her to live, Prescott, you'll do as I say. Now."

Izzy watched in horror as Matt tossed aside his gun. And was left to face the madman with nothing but his bare fists. And the anger that simmered inside him.

Chapter Nineteen

Matt studied the woman in Cutler's arms, taking in the torn gown, the pain-glazed eyes, the blood oozing at her throat. It tore at his heart to see her like this. But at least, he consoled himself, she was alive. For now.

He should have had a plan. But when he'd seen her shawl buried in the snow and had heard the sounds of a struggle going on inside the lean-to, there'd been no time. He'd been half-mad with pain and rage and fear.

He cursed and called himself every kind of fool. When fighting a madman, there are no rules but one. Survival.

"All right, Cutler. I'm unarmed. Since your fight is with me, let the woman go."

"Oh, that's real good, Captain." Cutler threw back his head and laughed. "You and I already had our fight. Now it's time for fun. Only I'm going to have all the fun. And all you get to do is watch."

He pointed with the tip of the knife. "Sit down over there. Where I can see you." He tossed Matt a strip of rawhide. "Tie your ankles with this." He watched Matt's movements, then said, "Do you take me for a fool? Tighter."

Satisfied, he handed Izzy another length of rawhide and removed his own pistol from the holster. "Tie his hands behind his back. And don't try anything funny or I'll have to shoot him. And you can have the pleasure of watching him die."

As she crossed to Matt, Cutler added, "'Course, I'd rather he'd live, so he can see what I'm going to do to you."

Matt brought his hands behind his back. "Are you all right, Isabella?"

She knelt behind him and struggled to keep her voice from trembling. "I'm fine, Matthew. Especially now." It was true, she realized. The moment she touched her hand to Matt's she experienced a strange sense of peace. "Is Del all right?"

"Just scared. Not for herself. For you."

Cutler waved his pistol. "Shut your mouths and get done with it. Tie his hands. Now."

Izzy wrapped the rawhide loosely around Matt's wrists, then got to her feet.

"Get back over here. And be quick about it."

Izzy returned to Cutler.

Seeing the look on her face, he scowled. "You look too smug. You think you've fooled me, don't you?"

She shot him a sly smile. "I don't know what you're talking about."

"Prescott's bonds." He swore fiercely. "You didn't tighten them, did you?"

She shrugged. "I guess you'll just have to see for yourself."

"Oh, I will, Miss High-and-Mighty." He gave her a rough shove. "And then I'll deal with you."

With the knife in one hand, his pistol in the other, he stalked to Matt's side and bent down. "Let me have a look at those wrists."

Before Cutler knew what hit him, Matt landed a fist squarely in his nose, snapping his head back. Blood spurted, spilling down the front of his shirt. For a moment Cutler was too stunned to react. Then, instinctively, he tossed the knife to the dirt and his fist shot out, catching Matt a glancing blow to the temple.

Matt was ready for him. Though his ankles were still bound, he kept his feet planted firmly while he aimed a blow to Cutler's midsection that had him grunting in pain. Then another to Cutler's jaw that sent his gun dropping from his grasp before he toppled backward.

Matt dropped to his knees to retrieve the pistol. But as his fingers closed around it, Cutler brought his knee to Matt's groin and he doubled over in pain.

Cutler scrambled around in the dirt until he located the gun. With blood spilling down his face, he stood over Matt and took aim. "Say goodbye to your bride, Prescott. This is the last time you'll see her. And just so you understand, before I'm through with her, she'll be begging me to kill her, too."

Before he could squeeze the trigger, his body gave a sudden convulsive jerk. There was a look of stunned surprise on his face. Then, as realization dawned, it slowly dissolved into a look of pain mingled with fury.

He turned, aiming the gun at Izzy. Before he could fire, his legs folded and he dropped, as if in slow motion, to the floor. The hilt of Izzy's knife protruded from his back. Blood spilled down his shirt in ever-widening circles.

Across the room, Izzy watched with a mixture of horror and revulsion as he gave up his life. Then, as if in a daze, she crossed to Matt's side and sliced through the rawhide binding his ankles.

"I've never...killed before." Tears of shock, of relief flowed down her cheeks to form dirty little streaks.

"I know." Matt leaned against the wall, cradling her in his arms.

"He was going to kill you, Matthew. I couldn't let him do that."

"It's all right." He brushed his lips over her temple, rocking her the way he'd often rocked his children.

"I'm sorry I brought you so much trouble. But I didn't know what else to do. He was going to hurt Del. I had to find a way to stop him. He was an evil man." She looked up at him, her eyes a little too bright. "Why, Matthew? Why are some people so evil?"

"I don't know. The whiskey, maybe. Or maybe something that went wrong when they were young. But there's no excuse for it. We all have choices to make in this world, Isabella.'' His eyes were bleak. "And some people make the wrong ones.''

"He always enjoyed hurting me. Even when I was very young. He knew the names hurt.''

Matt clenched his teeth, feeling a new rush of anger and protectiveness that blazed like fire in his gut.

"But I could take the names. Izzy the Gimp. Miss High-and-Mighty. Those are only words, after all. But what he really liked was firing up the other men and trying to get them to hurt me, too. He was the one who dared Otis Blandin to follow me into the stable. Poor Otis never would have thought of it himself. I think…''

He waited. When she didn't go on, he said, "What do you think, Isabella?''

"I think Harlan Cutler wasn't enough of a man. And so he tried to hide it by acting like he was more of a man.'' She glanced up. "Does that make any sense?''

"It makes perfect sense.''

"But I never wanted to take his life.'' The tears started afresh. "I never wanted to take anyone's life.''

"I know. Some have a taste for killing. And some of us are just thrust into it. And the memory of it lingers for a long time.''

"Is that what happened to you, Matthew? Were you thrust into killing?''

He thought of the war, the sounds of gunfire and bayonets clashing, the cries of the wounded, the smell of death. There were times he'd feared he would never be able to put it behind him. But with time, and the love of his children, he'd forged a new life. New memories to be savored.

"It wasn't for me, Isabella. But I did what I had to. And so did you."

"Will I ever forget?"

"I hope so. I'll help you all I can." Matt wrapped his arms around her and held her, stroking her hair, murmuring words meant to soothe and comfort.

Then he caught sight of her hands. They were charred and blackened, covered with raw, ugly blisters, some puckered, others oozing fluid. "Dear God, Isabella. What did he do to you?"

She lifted her palms, staring at them in surprise. With all that had happened, she hadn't even been aware of how badly burned they were. "I had to break free of the rawhide. It was the only way I knew."

He kissed her forehead, her cheek, her lips. "Oh, my sweet, brave Isabella."

He went outside to retrieve something from his saddlebags. Then he returned and bathed her hands in snow before pouring a liberal amount of liniment on them. "I hope," he murmured, "that Dr. Goody's Liniment and Elixir proves to be worth whatever Del spent for it."

She gave him a brave smile.

He gathered her once more into his arms and held her.

Outside the wind howled and the storm finally blew itself out. And as the hours passed, the storm brewing within Matthew faded, as well. He hoped, he prayed the cruelty and the killing were finished. As for him, he would be content to spend the rest of his life like this. Holding his wife. Knowing she was safe.

The hounds set up a chorus of barking that had the children racing to the door of their cabin. When they caught sight of their father in the saddle, holding Izzy in his arms, they raced outside and circled his horse.

"I knew you'd find her, Pa." Del was crying and tugging on the reins.

"Are you all right, Isabella?" Benjamin and Clement were reaching up to take her as their father dismounted.

Aaron stood to one side, staring not at his father and Izzy but at the horse behind them, which carried a blanket-draped figure. "Is that Sergeant Cutler?"

"Yes, son."

"Did you kill him?"

Matt glanced at his wife, then at his son. "It's a long story. Let's get Isabella inside first. She needs a little tending."

"Yes, sir."

The children hurried ahead to hold the door while Matt carried her inside and settled her in a chair by the fire. Then he led the horses to the barn and placed Cutler's frozen body in the back of the wagon. As long as the air remained this cold there was no rush to haul the body to Sutton's Station and file a report for the territorial marshal.

Inside the cabin Aaron pulled up a bench for Izzy's feet. Benjamin hurried to the bedroom and returned with pillows for her back. Clement poured her a cup of coffee. Del climbed up in her lap and hugged her fiercely.

"I was so afraid, Isabella."

"So was I, Del."

"You were?" The little girl pulled back to see her face. "You didn't act like it. I thought you were so brave."

"I didn't feel very brave. I just did what I had to."

Aaron knelt down beside her chair. "Pa said you saved Del's life."

Izzy clutched the child tightly. "I would have done whatever I had to for Del. Or for any of you."

Benjamin studied her hands. "How'd you do that, Isabella?"

"Sergeant Cutler tied my wrists with rawhide. The only way I could get free was to stick them in the fire."

The thought of such a desperate act had them sucking in their breath.

"Does it hurt?"

"Only a little."

The children looked at her with quiet respect.

Matt, who had been watching and listening in the doorway, cleared his throat. "Why don't you let Isabella rest now, and give me a hand rustling up some food."

"Yes, sir." The boys got to their feet.

Del didn't move, except to draw her arms even tighter around Izzy's neck. And from the looks of it, she was prepared to hold on all day. In fact, she looked as though she might never let Isabella out of her sight again.

* * *

"The snow held off." Matt entered with an armload of logs and nudged the door shut behind him. "But judging from that sky, it's not far behind."

"Much snow up in the mountains?" Aaron turned from the fire, where he'd cooked venison just the way Izzy showed him.

"More than usual. Once it gets here, we'll be spending a whole lot of time inside." Matt winked at Izzy, loving the flush that rose to her cheeks. "Can't say as how I'll mind it this year, though."

"How are these biscuits, Isabella?" Clement held the plate out to her, forcing her to taste.

"Mmm." She nibbled, smiled. "Perfect, Clement."

"Are those eggs ready yet, Del?" Matt watched as Benjamin finished setting the table.

"Just about ready, Pa."

The little cabin had taken on a festive air. The previous evening Matt and Izzy had answered all the children's questions and, at Izzy's insistence, had sat with them until they'd fallen asleep. Then, exhausted, they had tumbled into their own bed.

Sometime before dawn they had awakened and had come together with a love, a tenderness that had surprised them both.

Now, feeling that they had crossed yet another barrier, they began to relax and enjoy their reunion. This special breakfast felt like a celebration.

Aaron placed a platter of venison on the table. "How are your hands this morning, Isabella?"

She held them up. "Healing nicely. Thanks to Dr.

Goody's Liniment and Elixir. And to your father's quick treatment.''

"Pa knows how to fix anything," Benjamin said proudly. "One time I fell out of the wagon and broke my leg. Pa fixed it good as new. See." He paraded around the table to prove there was no lingering limp.

"Goodness." Izzy put a hand over her heart. "How in the world did you fall out of the wagon?"

"It was late. Ma was coming back from town and she was…" He stopped, appalled at what he'd almost said. He cast a stricken look in his father's direction.

Matt was scowling.

No one said a word.

"I almost forgot to wash up." Benjamin rolled his sleeves and made a production of washing before returning to the table. Without looking at the others, he bowed his head and said, "Well, aren't we going to ask a blessing?"

"Yes. Of course." Izzy glanced around, then spoke the words that had become their special blessing.

As they passed the food and began to eat, she found herself wondering, not about the words Benjamin had said, but about what he hadn't said. It had to do with their mother. Whatever it was, they all knew.

When it came to their past, and especially their mother, there was definitely a conspiracy of silence.

"Wind's picking up. Just a matter of time before the first storm of the season hits." Matt came in from the barn and slapped his hat against his thigh before hanging it on a peg. "I thought maybe I'd head down to Sutton's Station."

"Alone?" Izzy looked up from the table, where she was painstakingly braiding Del's hair. She had removed the dressings from her hands, but her fingers were still stiff and awkward.

Matt nodded. "That way the boys can be here with you and Del."

"Matthew." She laid down the brush and crossed to him, placing a hand on his sleeve. "The danger's passed. You can't spend the rest of your life worrying about our safety."

"And why can't I?" He kissed her, hard and quick. "I took a vow that said I had that right."

"Oh, Matthew." She felt a sudden flutter around her heart. When he said things like that, it nearly took her breath away.

"What's this?" He tipped up her chin. "Tears?"

"Just—" she swallowed "—I've been all blubbery since I got back here. I guess it was coming home and having the children fussing over me and all. I've never had anyone care about me before. It's a little..."

"Overwhelming?"

"Yes." She sniffed.

"Good." He kissed her again. "I hope twenty years from now you're still feeling overwhelmed by all of us."

"I will."

"Promise?"

From across the room Del called, "Isabella. When are you going to finish my hair?"

Izzy laughed and took a step back. "No more distractions."

He caught her shoulder. "Until tonight. Then I plan plenty of distractions."

She was still blushing when she returned to Del's side.

They all looked up at the sound of approaching hoofbeats.

Matt picked up his rifle, then opened the door to peer outside. "Well, I'll be. It's the stage."

As Izzy and the children crowded around the doorway, he shot Izzy an embarrassed frown. "Sorry. I forgot to send word to Webster Sutton that we wouldn't be needing it after all." It seemed like a hundred years ago since he had considered sending his new bride back to her home in Pennsylvania. Now it was the furthest thing from his mind.

He strode forward. "I'll just tell old Boone it was all a mistake. He'll understand."

"Maybe he's got mail for us, Pa," Aaron called to his retreating back.

"Maybe. I'll ask." While Izzy and the children continued to watch from the doorway, Matt called out a greeting and stood talking for several moments to the grizzled old driver.

Suddenly the door of the stage opened. A woman stepped out and called Matt's name.

He turned and stared at her without saying a word.

Izzy had never seen such a dazzling creature. Her gown was red, with a flounced skirt, long, slender sleeves and a low neckline that revealed a great deal of flesh. Her figure was stunning, with a tiny waist, softly rounded hips and high, firm breasts, most of which were exposed. Her yellow hair was arranged in flirtatious sausage curls that had been pulled to one side and tied with a red ribbon.

Izzy was aware of a sudden tension among the children. Though they were all watching the woman, they hadn't spoken a word.

"Shouldn't we invite her in?" Izzy turned to Aaron. "I could make coffee."

"She won't want coffee." Aaron's tone was flat.

"And how would you know that? Who is this pretty lady, Aaron? Don't tell me you all know her."

He lifted his gaze to hers. His eyes, she noticed, were as dull, as lifeless as his words. "She's our ma."

Chapter Twenty

Izzy stood riveted to the spot. Too shocked to speak. Too numb to weep. All she could do was foolishly stare at this ravishing creature who was standing in a pool of sunlight, exchanging words with the driver, who, despite his advanced age, was looking at her as though she were the object of his every fantasy.

Izzy swayed and had to steady herself against the door. "Your…mother?"

"Yes'm." Aaron thrust his hands deep into his pockets and stared at the toe of his shiny boot.

"But I thought…" She swallowed and tried again. "I thought your mother was dead."

"I wish she was." Del's lower lip quivered.

"Delphinium." Izzy rounded on her, eyes hot with passion. "What a wicked, wicked thing to say. We must never wish ill on anyone. Especially the woman who gave you life."

"She said I was an…accident."

Izzy had to catch her breath from the shock. What kind of woman would ever say such a thing to an innocent child? Del had probably misunderstood.

"So...so was I, I suppose. But that doesn't change the fact that she is your mother. I would have given anything to have known my mother."

"Not if she was like ours." Benjamin and Clement, so different in looks and temperament, stood close together, shoulders brushing, fists clenched. A wall, Izzy thought. Or a fortress under siege.

The woman turned and started toward the cabin, leaving Matthew standing beside the stage, talking to the driver.

At the door she flicked a glance over the children. "Is this any way to greet me?"

The children stared at her in sullen silence.

"All right. If that's the way you want it." She brushed past them and turned to Izzy, taking in the torn gown, the scarred hands. "I see Matt's still opening his door to strays. Could you fetch me a drink? I'd love whiskey, but I'll settle for tea. It's been a long, difficult journey."

Like a queen she swept into the cabin and stared around in disdain. Though she noted the changes, she appeared unimpressed as she wrinkled her nose and sniffed the air.

Izzy moved like a woman in a trance. Her limp seemed even more pronounced as she crossed to the fireplace. Wrapping a towel around her hand, she lifted the blackened kettle from the fire. Matt entered the cabin just as she was pouring.

Grace gave a sound that could have been a laugh or a jeer. "I see you're still using those old dishes. You should have seen the ones I had in San Francisco. Real china and crystal from England. And the hotel room was bigger than this old cabin and barn put together. By comparison, this place is even more of a hovel. But then, I suppose it suits the people willing to live this way.''

When Matt and the children didn't offer a word in their own defense, Izzy handed her the tea and fled into the bedroom, unable to bear any more. As she swept past Matt, she caught the hard, brittle look in his eyes. A look she hadn't seen since her first weeks here. Somehow she'd managed to forget the dark, dangerous man he had been when she'd first met him. Then he had seemed to her to be a man capable of violence. A man filled with bitterness and hatred.

How could she have forgotten?

She closed the door and leaned against it, closing her eyes against the pain.

How could he have lied to her about something as important as this? He'd led her to believe his wife was dead. That he needed a wife. That his children needed a mother. And all this time, it was a lie. He'd been covering up the fact that his wife, the mother of his children, was very much alive. What was worse, he'd encouraged his children to lie, as well.

Tears burned her eyes and she blinked furiously to stem the flow. She wouldn't cry over a liar, a cheat. If there were any tears to waste, they would be for the fool who had actually believed in fairy tales and happy endings. But now, thanks to this latest surprise, that fool was dead. As dead as she'd believed Matthew's wife to be.

Whipping herself into a furious rage, she found her old worn tapestry valise and started stuffing in the few items she had brought with her when this odyssey had begun so long ago. She stripped off the yellow gown, which only days ago she'd worn with such pride. The charred cuffs, the bloodstained bodice now had her gritting her teeth in humiliation. How pathetic she must have seemed to Matthew and his children, in comparison to the woman in the other room.

She pulled on the shabby gown she'd brought from Pennsylvania. Then she removed the tortoiseshell comb and placed it, along with the fancy bonnet, on the dresser top.

Into the valise she tossed a threadbare apron and the hated shoes. She would never wear them again. Not for any man. She sat on the edge of the bed and pulled on her old boots.

She felt the sag of the mattress and an ache as painful as any dagger thrust pierced her heart. She ran a hand over the carefully mended coverlet. How she had loved this bed. And the man who had slept in it beside her.

Then the anger flared once more. How could he have made her feel so loved, so cherished, when he already had a wife? How could he have been so deceitful?

She picked up the valise and opened the door. At once the voices were stilled.

Reading her intentions, Matt crossed the room, barring the door. ''Where do you think you're going, Isabella?''

''I don't know. Somewhere. Anywhere.'' She bit her lip to stop the quivering. She wouldn't cry. Not here. Not now. Not in front of Grace.

Slipping the plain gold band from her finger, she handed it to him. Her words came rushing out in a firestorm of rage. "You lied to me. You let me think your wife was dead. But here she is. So beautiful. Such a lady."

He started to speak but she cut him off. "How could I possibly think I could take her place? It must have been quite amusing to you to watch Izzy the Gimp, the object of an entire town's ridicule, coming to you hat in hand."

The rush of fury caught Matt by surprise. His voice was thick with it. "Don't do this, Isabella. Don't ever say such words."

"And why not? They're the truth. Just this once, you owe me that. You do know what truth is, don't you, Matthew?"

He looked away. The muscle in his jaw was working furiously.

"Did you marry me because I was merely a convenience?"

He nodded, determined now to give her all the honesty she deserved. "I suppose so. In the beginning. As I was a convenience for you. But once I got to know you, I realized that you were all the things I'd ever wanted in a wife."

When she began to shake her head, he caught her by the shoulder. "Do you know what it does to me to see you washing our clothes, mending them, baking bread and biscuits, soothing hurts? Making a home for us? And doing it all with such joy? Because of you we've become a family again. Because of you our hearts are mending. We've begun to hope again.

And to love. That's what you gave us, Isabella. Hope. Love. In our eyes you are, and always will be, the most beautiful creature in the world.''

Tears sprang to her eyes and she blinked furiously. "In my whole life, I was afraid I would never hear such words from a man who loved me. And now—" she shook her head "—I'm afraid to believe you, Matthew. Afraid, because the lies come so easily to your lips.''

"I wouldn't lie to you, Isabella. Not about something as important as this.''

Her tone deepened with emotion. "You let me believe Grace was dead. That's the same as a lie. And what is worse, you encouraged your children to lie about it, as well. I can't stay here, Matthew. Don't you see? I have to go.''

She brushed past him and hurried to the waiting stage. Old Boone scratched his head, then, at her command, flicked the reins, and the team took off in a cloud of dust.

The children came tumbling out the door of the cabin, shouting unintelligible words that were lost in the din of creaking harness and pounding hoofbeats. Izzy refused to look back, knowing if she did, her heart would shatter into a million pieces.

"It's not much of a room, dear." Gertrude Sutton led Izzy to a tiny attic room containing a cot, a wooden chest and a rocking chair.

A cold wind whistled through the rafters, ruffling the blanket at the foot of the bed.

"We recently took in our niece, Sara Jane, and gave her the big bedroom downstairs. Otherwise…"

"It's fine. Really." Izzy sank down on the edge of the cot, still clutching tightly to the valise.

The older woman studied this pale young woman who seemed unaware of who or where she was. She'd seen that same look on her husband's face when he'd returned from the war without his hand. Shock. That's what it was. She'd suffered some sort of terrible blow.

"You just sit here awhile, dear. I'll be back shortly with some tea."

"Please don't fuss. I don't want to be any trouble."

"It's no trouble at all." Gertrude took her leave and hurried down the stairs. Then she went in search of the stage driver, who was out back talking with her husband.

A short time later she carried a tray to the attic room. Izzy was still sitting on the edge of the bed, still clutching tightly to her valise.

Gertrude set the tray down atop the chest and poured two cups of tea.

"Here, dear. Drink this. It'll warm you."

Izzy seemed surprised to see her. With an effort she released her hold on the bag and accepted the tea.

Gertrude settled herself in the rocking chair and sipped. "I spoke with Boone. He tells me he drove Grace Prescott up to Matt's place."

Izzy nodded her head.

"Did she say something to rile you?"

Izzy shook her head.

"Boone says you left in quite a hurry. Came flying

out of the cabin and ordered him to bring you to town. Something must have happened to set you off.''

Izzy took her time lifting the cup to her lips, tasting the tea. In her whole life she'd never had anyone to confide in. But this woman, with her quiet manner and gentle questions, inspired her trust. And she needed desperately to trust someone. ''I thought... that is, Matthew led me to believe...that his wife was dead.''

''I see.''

''And what was worse, he encouraged the children to do the same. I don't understand how he could turn his own children against their mother. They never spoke of her. I thought they were grieving for the dead. And all along they were lying to me.''

At last, Gertrude was beginning to understand. ''So. You didn't know about Grace. Quite a looker, isn't she?'' The older woman watched her guest's face for some flicker of emotion.

''She's beautiful. Like a queen in one of those fancy picture books.''

Gertrude sniffed. ''I guess there are some who look at Grace and see a beauty. Those of us who know her see only a shallow, empty statue.''

Izzy's head came up. She couldn't seem to believe the hateful words this kindly old woman was saying.

''Grace's beauty has always been her curse. She thinks that face, that body give her the right to trample other people's hearts. People who should have mattered to her. But she's too busy loving herself. She tossed everyone aside. Her husband. Her children.''

''*Her* children? Don't you mean Matt's, as well?''

The older woman took a deep breath. "It's not for me to say. But if I had to hazard a guess, I'd have some doubt about that. The oldest boy bears some resemblance to Matt. As for the others..." She shrugged. "There were so many men in Grace's life."

Izzy's jaw dropped. Before she could protest, Gertrude held up a hand.

"Knowing Matt, it doesn't matter one whit to him whether those children are his by birth or by heart. They're his. His responsibility. His reason for living. And he loves them all equally."

Izzy was struck speechless by what she'd just heard. When she could finally gather her wits, she set aside her tea. "How painful must it have been for a proud man like Matthew to accept such deceit."

Gertrude nodded. "Indeed. Painful and humiliating. Matt's a good man. The best. But he and the children were aware that tongues were wagging. And gossip, especially such as that, can be cruel. Everybody knew about his wife, of course. Grace used to come into town while he was working in the fields. She'd drag those little ones along and leave them sitting in the wagon for hours while she was in the saloon. She'd go off with any cowboy who flattered her. I tell you, that woman is crippled."

At that, Izzy's eyes widened. "Mrs. Sutton, I must warn you that you are speaking to a cripple."

The older woman flicked a glance at Izzy's feet. "I noticed a bit of a limp. To me, that's not being crippled. But Grace Prescott. Now, there's a woman who is. She has no heart. No soul. The real beauty, the beauty that counts, was never in her.'' She took a deep breath. "You said you couldn't understand how Matt could turn his children against their own mother. He didn't do that, my dear. Grace did. With her cruelty. Her neglect. Her drinking."

Izzy blanched and thought again about what Benjamin had almost revealed. He had been thrown from a wagon at night with his mother driving. Had she been returning from the saloon in town? Had she recklessly ignored her children's safety for her own selfish pleasures? Was that what he'd almost said?

Gertrude could read the turmoil in Izzy's eyes. "I can see why a proud man like Matt Prescott might not want to talk about his past. But that doesn't excuse him. He should have told you about Grace."

She stood, smoothing down her skirts. "I'd better get downstairs and start cooking. You rest now, dear. I'll call you when supper's ready."

As soon as the older woman had taken her leave, Izzy began to pace.

Her heart was aching for the pain Matthew and his children had been forced to suffer. But that didn't alter the fact that he had married her when he'd already had a wife.

"Oh, Matthew." She paced to the window, seeing in the distance the towering, snow-covered peaks of the Sierras. "What have we done? Whatever have we done?"

Weary beyond belief, she dropped down on the cot and cried herself to sleep.

"Isabella."

Izzy squeezed her eyes tightly shut, trying to blot

out the sound of Matthew's voice ringing in her head. But it wouldn't go away. There it was again. That deep, soulful sound of his voice calling her name. Tearing new holes in her heart.

"Isabella."

The hand at her shoulder gave a gentle shake.

She awoke with a start. Shoving the tangled hair from her eyes, she looked up to see Matt standing over her. It took her a moment to realize she was in the attic room above the Suttons' mercantile.

"What are you doing here? Why did Mrs. Sutton allow you up here?"

"She couldn't stop me. And I came to set things right between us."

"It's too late for that, Matthew." She got to her feet and crossed to the window to put some distance between them. She couldn't think when he was near. And right now she needed a clear head. "You lied to me. You let me believe that Grace was dead."

"Grace is dead to me. And to the children, as well."

"Mrs. Sutton told me how Grace mistreated you and the children. Don't you see, Matthew? You're just saying that to hurt her the way she hurt you."

"I'll admit there was a time when she could hurt me. Hurt all of us. But that's been over for a long time." His voice was quieter now than it had been back at the cabin, but just as angry. "On the day that you arrived here, there was a letter from Grace, telling me she had obtained a divorce in St. Louis, so that she could marry one of her cowboys."

"A divorce?"

He nodded. "Her latest cowboy promised her money, a trip to San Francisco and a lifetime of pleasures."

Izzy remembered the packet of letters, which Boone had left with her when she'd first arrived. It hadn't occurred to her to wonder where they'd come from.

"It wasn't the first time Grace left me, but it was—for me, for the children—the final time."

"Then why did she come back?"

"Apparently her cowboy used her, then left town without her. He never had marriage on his mind in the first place. So she's here now, not because she has a need to see any of us, but because she needs money."

"What if she asked to come back for good?"

"It will never happen. A woman like Grace could never stay in one place. Especially a place like this, with no one around to dance to her tune." He shook his head. "But if she should ask, we'd have to refuse. The divorce was her final break."

Seeing the hesitation in her eyes, he held out his hand. "Will you trust me, Isabella? I'd like you to come downstairs with me."

Though she didn't know where this would lead, she accepted his hand and hesitantly walked beside him.

He stepped outside and led her toward the stage. Old Boone was already in the driver's seat, whip in hand. Seated inside was Grace. At the rear of the stage a crude wooden casket had been secured, bound for the territorial marshal.

The children were gathered around, kicking dirt with the toes of their boots, staring hard at the ground. When they saw Izzy they looked away, embarrassed.

Matt reached into his pocket and withdrew a wad of bills. They were, Izzy knew, all that was left of the money he'd earned from the sale of the mustangs. The money he'd hoped to use for seed and for a bull to enlarge his herd.

"I don't know how far this will get you, Grace. But when you get there, find yourself a job or a cowboy with a future. Because there's nothing more here for you. Do you understand?"

Cool blue eyes studied the woman beside him, before coming to rest on his. Grace's smile was as cold as her eyes. "I won't be back. You have nothing here I want. You never did."

Izzy caught her breath at the venom in the woman's tone. Before she could stop herself the words were torn from her. "But the children…"

"Are all his now." Grace gave a contemptuous laugh. "And yours, from the looks of things. You're welcome to them all."

She flicked a final glance over them, then called to the driver, "Let's get out of here. This place makes me weary."

Old Boone cracked the whip and the team leaned into the harness, leaving a cloud of dust in its wake.

Until they were out of sight, no one moved. No one spoke. And then, as if a dark cloud had suddenly lifted, revealing a beautiful rainbow, the children turned to their father and Izzy.

"You still planning on spending the night in Sutton's Station, Pa?" Aaron had his arm around Del.

The sight of them brought a lump to Izzy's throat. Until this moment she hadn't understood just how beautiful their love was. But if she'd had a big brother, she would have wanted one just like Aaron. And if she could have had a little sister, she couldn't have dreamed up one sweeter than Del. These children might not be born of her flesh, but, like Matthew, they owned her heart.

"If I have to." He clamped his jaw and turned toward Izzy. "It all depends on Isabella."

"I don't know what you're talking about." She glanced from him to his children. "What depends on me?"

"My life. My future. My happiness. They all depend on you, Isabella. I..." He turned to include the children. "*We* came here to ask your forgiveness. And to beg you to come home with us."

"But I..."

He touched a finger to her lips to still her protest. "Before you say a word, I have something important to say. You shared all your private pain with me. You bared your soul. And I refused to do the same. I know now that was wrong. It was just foolish pride that kept me from telling you about Grace. But I'll never do this again. From now on, if you'll give me another chance, I promise to share everything with you. There will never again be any secrets between us."

"I..."

"Pa." Aaron reached up to the wagon seat and

thrust a bunch of wildflowers into his father's hand. "You forgot about...you know."

"Oh, yes." Matt handed her the flowers. "We picked these along the way down the mountain. I thought...we thought it was time I started courting you."

"Courting?" She couldn't help chuckling. "Isn't it a little late for courtship, Matthew? After all, we're already husband and wife."

"Are we?" He tipped up her chin, staring into her eyes. "Are you still willing to be my wife, Isabella?"

She glanced at the children, who were watching her with such intensity it made her heart ache. When she glanced back at him he was holding up the plain gold band he had retrieved from his pocket.

With a solemn look he got down on one knee. "Isabella, I didn't do any of this right the first time, but I'd like to do it right now. This ring first belonged to my grandmother, then to my mother. And it once was worn by Grace, until she threw it back in my face. I'd be honored if you would wear it. That is, if you're still willing to be my wife."

"Oh, Matthew, I've never wanted anything more in my whole life than to be your wife." She held out her hand and he slipped the ring on her finger. She stared at it for long moments, then caught his hands and helped him to his feet.

He framed her face with his hands and gave her a long, lingering kiss.

The children sent up a rousing cheer that had heads poking out of doorways in the mercantile and saloon. Del leapt into her arms and nuzzled her cheek. The boys formed a circle around her, hugging her fiercely. And all the while she stared over their heads at the man who couldn't seem to stop grinning.

Gertrude Sutton stepped out on the porch. "Sounds like a mighty happy group. Will you folks be staying for supper?"

Matt glanced at Izzy, then at his children, before turning to her. "Thanks for the offer, Gertrude. But we'd like to get back to our cabin before dark."

"And you, dear?" She smiled at Izzy and was relieved to see the smile returned. "I take it you won't be spending the night here?"

"No, Mrs. Sutton. But I do thank you for your hospitality. You were very kind to me."

"Think nothing of it, my dear. I hope one of these days we'll get better acquainted."

"Thank you. I'd like that."

Izzy allowed herself to be helped up to the wagon seat, while Aaron accepted her valise from Mrs. Sutton's hands.

As Matt turned the team toward home, the first big wet flakes of snow began drifting down.

"Look, Pa," Del shouted. "It's snowing."

Matt grinned. "Looks like it's going to be a norther."

"Is that bad?" Izzy shot him an anxious look.

"Depends. It could mean we'll be snowbound for a few weeks."

"You mean we can't leave the cabin at all?"

"Oh, we'll make it to the barn and back. But that's about as far as we'll risk it until there's a break in the weather."

"Whatever will we do?"

He touched a tentative hand to her shoulder. When she didn't flinch, he wrapped his arm around her and whispered against her temple, "I guess that depends, too." He smiled. "You did say you always wanted to be part of a big family, didn't you?"

"Yes."

"Then how about...enlarging our family?"

"You mean—" she caught her breath at his meaning "—we might think about having a baby, too?"

His smile grew. "Well, let's see now. We've already got an Aaron, a Benjamin, a Clement and a Del. I've been thinking that it's time for either an Edward or an Esther."

As his meaning dawned, she giggled. "You mean you named them for the letters in the alphabet?"

"Can you think of a better way to pick names?"

She thought a moment. "I guess not. But what will we do for money, Matthew? You gave all ours away."

"I guess I'll just have to hunt up another herd of mustangs. Aaron spotted some tracks this morning. The biggest herd so far." He kissed the tip of her nose. "I'm told, thanks to Cutler's vengeance, the army is eager to buy all we can sell them."

Suddenly her enthusiasm was boundless. "Does that mean next year, if you sell another herd, we might even try for a Frank or a Fanny?"

He threw back his head and roared. "Mrs. Prescott, are you going to go and get greedy on me?"

"I do think it might be fun to see how many letters of the alphabet we could get through."

He drew her closer and touched his lips to the snowflakes that dusted her lashes. "Let's just take one letter at a time."

"I'm willing, Matthew." She brushed her mouth over his. "As long as we can begin tonight."

He glanced at the darkening sky. "Night comes a lot earlier in the winter up here in the Sierras."

She touched a hand to his chest, loving the strong, steady feel of his heartbeat. "I knew there was a reason why I loved this place so much." She smiled. "And the people in it."

"I'm so glad, Isabella—" his tone was as gentle as his touch "—that you've come back to your family."

Family. It was a word that had always made her ache with desire. And now it was hers. This wounded man and his wonderful children belonged to her. And she to them.

This once frightening wilderness had become her haven.

Home, her heart whispered as she thought about the cozy cabin waiting for them. *Home,* her heart whispered as she glanced at the children, snuggled beneath their blankets in the back of the wagon. *Home,* her heart whispered as she felt the warmth of her husband's hand enveloping hers.

Izzy the Gimp had died in that lean-to in the mountains. But Isabella Prescott, wife, mother, teacher, lover, had just been born into the most wonderful family. And her love, her patience and most of all her courage had changed her life, and the lives of this new family of hers, for all time.

* * * * *

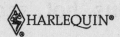 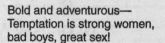

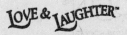

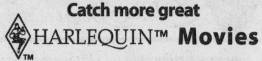

Happy Birthday, Harlequin Historicals!

Now, after a decade of giving you the best in historical romance,
LET US TAKE YOU BACK...

to a time when damsels gave their warriors something to fight for...ladies wooed dashing dukes from behind their fans...and cowgirls lassoed the hearts of rugged ranchers!

With novels from such talented authors as

Suzanne Barclay	**Margaret Moore**
Cheryl Reavis	**Ruth Langan**
Deborah Simmons	**Cheryl St.John**
Susan Spencer Paul	**Theresa Michaels**
Merline Lovelace	**Gayle Wilson**

Available at your favorite retail outlet.

HARLEQUIN®
Makes any time special™

Look us up on-line at: http://www.romance.net   HH10ANN

COMING NEXT MONTH FROM

HARLEQUIN
HISTORICALS